Unclaimed Baggage

JEN DOLL

FARRAR STRAUS GIROUX
NEW YORK

For the friends lost but never forgotten,
and the friends we have yet to meet

Farrar Straus Giroux Books for Young Readers
An imprint of Macmillan Publishing Group, LLC
175 Fifth Avenue, New York, NY 10010

1   3   5   7   9   10   8   6   4   2

fiercereads.com

Library of Congress Cataloging-in-Publication Data

Names: Doll, Jen, author.
Title: Unclaimed baggage / Jen Doll.
Description: First edition. | New York : Farrar Straus Giroux, 2018. |
    Summary: Told from three viewpoints, teens Doris, Nell, and
    Grant find friendship and the possibility of love while working in
    Unclaimed Baggage, a store that sells items that went missing
    during airline travel.
Identifiers: LCCN 2018001430 | ISBN 978-0-374-30606-9 (hardcover) |
    ISBN 978-0-374-30607-6 (ebook) | ISBN 978-0-374-31220-6
    (international edition)
Subjects: | CYAC: Friendship—Fiction. | Stores, Retail—Fiction. |
    Luggage—Fiction. | Lost and found possessions—Fiction.
Classification: LCC PZ7.1.D638 Un 2018 | DDC [Fic]—dc23
LC record available at https://lccn.loc.gov/2018001430

Our books may be purchased in bulk for promotional, educational, or business use. Please
contact your local bookseller or the Macmillan Corporate and Premium Sales Department
at (800) 221-7945 ext. 5442 or by email at MacmillanSpecialMarkets@macmillan.com.

"If you don't get lost, there's a chance you may never be found."
—UNKNOWN

Unclaimed Baggage

PROLOGUE

A clang rang out through baggage claim as the carousel groaned into action. Arriving passengers jockeyed for positions around the metal edges of the machine, craning their necks and tapping their feet, as desperate for a glimpse of their luggage as they would be to see friends or family members.

Some bags had been wrapped in plastic by nervous people; others had bright ribbons tied around the handles to distinguish them from one another. There was a bossy sign warning everyone to make sure the luggage was indeed their own before leaving the terminal, but hardly anybody took the time to do that. In haste, mistakes had occurred.

A little boy frolicked along the raised metal edge of the

carousel, shouting, "Look at me!" until his weary mother collected him. *"Excuse me"* was the law of the land, though it was generally uttered in a way that was less polite and more "Outta my way. Can't you see I'm standing here?!" There were elbow nudges and rude remarks and "Hey, watch it, buddy!"s. Slowly but surely, the passengers filed out into the world, taking with them their precious belongings, compactly contained in suitcases that most of the rest of the time were confined to the undersides of beds or the backs of closets.

With a low squeal, the carousel halted. A new flight would be in soon, and the same thing would happen, and then again.

For now, no one paid any attention to the suitcase that remained. It was small and purple and leopard-printed. It was a bag intended for adventures, intended for life. But its owner had failed to retrieve it, so it sat alone in the middle of the quiet baggage carousel, in the very place it was not supposed to be.

PART I

June

1

Doris

HELLO. I speak to you from where I stand amid hundreds, maybe thousands, of boxes, bags, trunks, containers, and suitcases. I'm in the stockroom of the store where I work, Unclaimed Baggage, which is a place that, yes, sells baggage that was never claimed from airports and other transit hubs to lucky new owners. Think of us as an animal shelter for goods. Does anything here look like you could give it a forever home?

As usual, I'm alone in the back. I pick up the microphone I just found in the suitcase I've been unpacking. It doesn't have batteries, so humor me. *Is this thing on?*

Please allow me to share my Number One top talent, the thing that will make me famous if ever I go on a reality TV show or participate in a Miss America pageant (two things I will surely never do). Are you ready?

Wait. I should probably manage expectations. If you're like most people, you're not going to be that impressed by what I'm about to reveal. You're going to say, *Anyone can do that. All you have to do is pay attention.* Or, maybe you'd be harsher: *That's a dumb talent. That's not even a talent! Ugh, show me your baton, girl—get out there and twirl!* To which I would say, stop being so sexist and give me a chance to speak, please. Even if I am just talking into a dead microphone in a stockroom full of used items.

My name is Doris. I am sixteen, and—along with slightly ragged fingernails (I've promised myself this will be the year I finally stop biting them); long, so-dark-everyone-says-it's-black-but-it's-really-dark-brown hair; and two chocolate-colored irises that give looks described as both "penetrating" and "pugnacious"—I come complete with a love of lists (especially those that include parentheticals!), a passion for drawing, and the "gift of gab," which is how my aunt Stella used to tease me about how much I talk.

I also bear the distinction of being pretty much the Number One weirdo liberal agnostic in my minuscule Alabama town, which gives all kinds of grief to my parents. When I decided to petition against the school-sanctioned prayer at each football game, Mom and Dad retaliated by praying louder than anyone. You'd think adults would be over that kind of stuff, but nope: The desire to fit in appears to be a lifelong human condition. Unless you're like me, I guess.

But back to that talent.

Imagine me leaning in close to the mic, gesturing a little, dropping my voice to a sultry whisper: *I can find things.* Your lost keys. The neighbor's missing cat, awkwardly named Pussy. Maya Bloom's retainer, let us never speak of that dark day again—the smell of the dumpster in which it was located is lodged permanently in my left nostril. Billy Pickens's trombone, which didn't really go missing so much as it was purposely tossed into my backyard on the last day of school because, top secret intel: Billy Pickens *despises* trombone. Or my mom's sunglasses: Nine times out of ten, they're right on top of her head.

It's not a superpower—that would be fairly lame, as superpowers go. Who'd pick finding things over flying or shooting fire from their eyes or being able to turn water into Diet Coke? But it's been helpful, I have to say. Not just personally, but professionally: I find things for my job.

Or, more accurately, *things find me.*

Think about all the flights around the world happening at the same time, and how if even one percent of that luggage doesn't make it back to its owner, pretty soon you'll have a massive pile on your hands. What happens to all that stuff? Airlines try to reunite people with their belongings, but they don't always succeed. After a certain amount of time, those orphaned items are sold to stores like Unclaimed Baggage and auction houses where people show up to bid for suitcases they aren't even allowed to look inside. You might hit it big, or you might end up with a pile of soiled shirts. Game of chance, meet laundromat.

Most days I work in the stockroom, going through shipments. What I find ranges from the spectacular (a vintage Oscar de la Renta gown with only a tiny spot at the hem; I could have worn it to prom, if I had any interest in such things) to the abysmal (old boxer shorts that require me to disinfect myself with an entire bottle of hand sanitizer). Even better, I find those items— well, not the boxer shorts—homes. For example:

1. The doll that made my old piano teacher, Mrs. McClintock, cry because it was a replica of the one her grandpa had given her when she was a tiny girl.
2. The skateboard that class stoner Bruno Havens yanked out of my hands with the only scream of joy anyone's ever heard Bruno Havens emit because it was signed by some famous skater named Tony. Then Bruno actually hugged me, which is *unprecedented*.
3. The designer purse sold out everywhere that Ms. Lee, our extremely stylish vice principal, simply had to have. I kept it hidden in the back until she could pick it up, ensuring my path to a really good college rec letter, even if I am a godless heathen.

I've been working at Unclaimed for two summers now, so I've seen plenty of stuff come and go. It's a lot like life that way. Everyone's always looking for something. And we're all carrying around the memories of what we've lost. Which, by the way, is far more than just possessions.

For example, my closest friend, Maya Bloom, who's not only the one Jewish teenager in our town, but also the only lesbian who's actually out (a lot of people around here seem to think that's worse than not being so sure about the existence of God), got a job as a camp counselor in Mentone this summer, so I'm here, left behind, my life the same but also different. I miss her, but at least I know she'll be back.

Then there are more permanent rifts: Friendships that go awry and can't ever be fixed. You can lose your mind, your heart, your dreams, your community, your job. You can lose someone you love. Or, to a less tragic extent, your virginity. (My parents would be relieved to know I still have my own.) Even age disappears, year after year. In two more years, high school will be gone. I'll head off to college, and all of this life I've had here will be, well, if not lost, closed. A chapter behind me.

Earlier today I was heading back to the stockroom after my lunch break when I found a kid. This kid was alone and loitering near the toy section, but he wasn't paying attention to any of the toys. That set off the alarm bells. He was five or six years old, a chubby boy with spiked-up hair and cargo shorts and a frown on his face. He looked at me, and I knew.

"You're lost," I said, and his big, round eyes, they got hopeful.

"My mom is here somewhere," he said, and I said, "Of course she is." I took his hand, which was slightly sticky. He squeezed mine back in a way that felt like he was preparing to hold on for dear life.

"Don't worry; we'll find her," I told him, and walked him over to Customer Service, where my nemesis, Chassie Dunkirk, was waiting to return a pair of sparkly high-heeled shoes. Her boyfriend, Mr. Football Player Champion of the World (or at least Our Small Town), Grant Collins was holding her name-brand purse. Chassie had her arm in a sling, the result of what even out-of-the-loop me knew was a cheerleading injury from earlier in the year. More worrisome than that was the fact that their lips were pressed against each other's so hard I was afraid they might pass out on the floor in front of me.

"Ahem," I said, causing them to turn around. That's when I saw that Chassie wasn't with Grant Collins at all. She was making out with a senior who graduated in May, which is pretty shocking information, because in the history of our town, it's never not been Chassie and Grant.

"Oh. *Excuse us*," said Chassie.

The guy looked at me and then at the floor, and I remembered his name. Mac Ebling. He'd been on the football team with Grant.

Chassie noticed the kid clutching my fingers. "Blake Jarvis," she said, "you've got chocolate on your shirt." She rolled her eyes and turned back to Mac: "Let's get out of here. I'll just keep the shoes. My arm hurts, and this place smells like mothballs and death."

"I'm lost!" Blake Jarvis announced forlornly, but Chassie was already out the door, Mac Ebling's hand tucked snugly into the back pocket of her denim shorts. I gently tugged my charge toward my boss and the owner of Unclaimed Baggage, Red Finster.

"Found a new friend, Doris?" he asked. "Blake Jarvis, where's your momma? I really liked that duet you sang together at the church concert last week. That was real pretty."

Suddenly I understood why everyone seemed to know Blake Jarvis except me—they all go to church together. Church is big in my town. Church and football, which I don't care much about, either. A bunch of jocks hurting one another and themselves as people stand around and cheer? No, thanks.

Blake Jarvis tried to smile, but his lip quivered. "I. Don't. Knowwwwww," he answered, his face crinkling into a pool of almost-cry.

"Wanna make an announcement for her?" offered Red, and Blake Jarvis shook his head up and down, a hard affirmative. I led him over to the little stairs that take you up to what Red calls the Customer Service throne, and Red held out the store's microphone for him.

"I've been found, Momma! Momma, where are you?" he said, and while everyone let out a collective "aw" at the tiny voice emanating from the sound system, Red stepped in. "Gail Osteen, Blake Jarvis is at Customer Service. Please pick him up at your leisure." Within minutes, there were the same hopeful eyes, with a neat bob rather than the spiked-up hair.

"Blake Jarvis Osteen, I told you to wait outside the dressing room like a good boy, and off you go running around—you nearly scared me to death!" said Mrs. Osteen, who smelled like vanilla and was holding several one-piece swimsuits with ruffled bottoms. She hugged her little boy, and he pointed to me.

"*She* found me!" he said, and though Mrs. Osteen looked at me kind of funny at first, she clutched me in a fragrant hug while Red smiled benevolently upon the scene. Blake Jarvis was promised a new toy for being so brave, and he and his mom went off together to pick it out, holding hands.

Red gave me a high five. "Stellar job, as always!"

You know who I thought of then? Aunt Stella. My badass, beautiful aunt, the adventurer of the family, the one who refused to be pinned down by the proprieties dictated by Southern society, much less our small town. The one who understood me completely, while my conservative parents wondered how I could have possibly resulted from their chromosomal merger. I wished desperately I could tell Stel about what had just happened with Blake Jarvis, because she would have looked at me delightedly across her Diet Coke (she drank them in extra-large mason jars, with plenty of ice, pretty much incessantly) as if I really did have a superpower, as if finding lost people was something remotely special, something only I could do. She would have told me that when I'm at college and surrounded by people who appreciate me, I will be way better off than Chassie is. *Never peak in high school,* she used to say. *You need somewhere else to go afterward.* That's what she did after she graduated, but she didn't just go somewhere else, she went everywhere: traveling the world, trying out different jobs, different apartments, different relationships.

Mom was always telling her little sister to grow up and settle down, but I thought Stel was perfect just the way she was. Calling her own shots, saying *the heck what other people think.* She's the one who told me I didn't have to do everything my parents did just because they decided it was right for them. *Find yourself,* she said. *That's the only way.*

Last summer she was on a beach in the south of France when she noticed two little kids being swept out to sea. As a teenager, she'd lifeguarded at our town water park, and she dove right in after them. She brought one back to safety before going in after the other. She got him close enough to shore that he could make it on his own, and that's when the riptide pulled her back again.

They never recovered her body.

That's the thing about lost. It doesn't always mean found. The worst losses are those things we never truly get over, no matter how good we are at locating misplaced car keys. Sometimes it feels like they take over completely, leaving a hole where your heart used to be.

The grief counselor told me to hold on to the memories, that's how I keep Stel alive forever. But there are some days I'd like to pack my memories up in a suitcase, put them on a plane, and let them fly around at thirty thousand feet until I'm ready to collect them again, which, to be honest, might be never.

My job helps, though, it really does. Last summer it was the one thing I kept doing, a place I could go when everything else seemed bleak and pointless. Red treats me like an adult, and he's never judged me for anything, unlike Mom and Dad. And if I cry when I'm back here, which I did pretty much every day after we got the call about Stel, there's no one around to see me. Along with getting regular paychecks, what more can you ask for in a job?

Well, there's another thing. At her memorial service, Aunt Stella's favorite yoga instructor called her a connector. That means someone who makes the world feel more welcoming and whole, who makes people feel better together in it. I keep thinking that if I can be more like Stel, if I can bring people and things together, maybe I won't have lost her entirely after all.

I like to imagine that Stella survived and is living on an island somewhere, free and beautiful and drinking from her mason jar. Of course, that's highly unlikely, but who knows, maybe somewhere, someone is finding the things that are important to me. Being in the store makes me think about possibility, about how we only know our side of the story. Maybe there's another side to things you haven't even thought of yet.

I drop the mic. These suitcases aren't going to unpack themselves.

2
Nell

Ashton and I say good-bye in my driveway, in front of my parents, who are waiting in the car, all packed and ready to go and politely trying not to look. My little brother, Jack, has no such honor code; his face is pressed against the glass, eyes bulging and trained on us. Mom has given me ten—OK, fifteen!—minutes for this final-final-final farewell. The drive to Alabama from our town in the Chicago suburbs will take at least ten hours, and we need to get on the road. As it is, with eating and bathroom breaks and everything else, it's probably going to take two days.

But it isn't just about time. The truth is, my mom doesn't get it. *You and Ashton have been attached at the hip since school let* out for the summer last week. *What could you possibly still have to say to each other?* she asked. She doesn't understand that love isn't a matter of having to *say things* to each other. We're past that, Ashton and me. When I tried to explain, she reminded me that we could email and text all the time, as if that's anywhere near the same. She's never liked him much, anyway: *Don't get too serious; first relationships are just for practice,* she told me when we started dating. *You'll see.* My mom is a scientist; everything has to be perfect. Me, I just want to be loved, and in love.

I grab Ashton's hand and pull him toward the corner of the yard, where there's a row of still spindly trees growing at different heights. I brought each of them home from school on Arbor Day—a tree for every year we lived here, fifth grade through sophomore year—and Dad helped me dig a hole and plant them, one after the other. The oldest are taller than I am now. I've heard the Arbor Day program is being discontinued. Just like my life as I know it.

"I'm really going to miss you," Ashton says, looking into my eyes, and I once again try to memorize how his smile spreads across his entire face when something is funny; the flutter of his insanely long eyelashes; his hands, strong and calloused from sports, but soft, too.

"I'll miss you more," I say, and I know it's true. Ashton gets to stay right where I want to be, surrounded by all of our friends here at home, having the summer we'd been planning before my mom doled out her "exciting news" that was going to be "so good for us." Now, I'm en route to a place where the only people

I know are my immediate family members, and at the moment, I don't even like any of them very much.

I guess I buried the lede: We're moving to a small town in Alabama, because my mom, the rocket scientist, got a prestigious job at the Marshall Space Flight Center. And families stick together, whether they want to or not, I guess. Or at least mine does.

"You've got to come and visit me," I say.

"I'll do my best," he replies. He leans forward, and I lean forward, and we kiss just as my mom honks the horn.

I cry until we cross the Mason-Dixon Line. At that point, I think I'm out of tears.

3
Grant

When my alarm clock rings, I hit it as hard as I can, knocking it off my dresser. Something about that feels good for a second. Then I hear it, still beeping. I look at the side of my hand, which is bleeding—from the alarm clock, maybe, or maybe from something else. I turn over onto my stomach and bury my head in my pillow and drown out the noise and the tiny twinges of pain (I've felt worse), and I will myself to go back to sleep. It's summer, and there's nowhere I need to be. Setting my alarm at this point is just for appearances, even if appearances have ceased to matter.

Downstairs, I hear people moving around and breakfast sounds, like pouring cereal and the toaster dinging and the chatter of my little brothers. Here in this room, my head is pounding, and the inside of my chest feels ragged. I shut my eyes. The only thing I can do is wait for the hangover to pass. The problem is, shutting my eyes doesn't necessarily bring rest. That's when my head feels like it might explode. That's when I get pretty near desperate for another something to soothe me. Most of the time, I give in. Nothing like popping the top of a cold one, as they say.

My name is Grant. I'm seventeen years old. I used to be the captain of the football team, the most promising young quarterback in the history of my school, maybe the entire state of Alabama. I used to date the hottest girl in town. Now I'm just a guy. Don't expect too much from me. If you do, I'll probably let you down.

Don't say I didn't warn you.

4

The purple leopard suitcase wasn't alone for very long. Another flight came in shortly afterward, and all of the new suitcases it had held for its passengers were tossed onto the conveyor belt, tumbling around the left-behind bag, which was caught up in their swirl. Then everyone came and collected their belongings but one, and the purple suitcase had a friend, a neon green bag with a lemon appliqué. The purple suitcase would have breathed a sigh of relief, if suitcases could breathe, because it sucks to be left alone at baggage claim, and traveling together is almost always better than traveling alone.

At the last minute, though, a breathless, sweaty guy rushed into the terminal and grabbed the lemon-lime suitcase. "There you are!" he said. "Let's go!" And then he, and it, were out the door, and the purple suitcase was all by itself once again.

5
Nell

To my surprise, our new house is not completely tragic. It's got a sloping roof that nearly touches the sprawling top branches of a big green willow tree growing right in the middle of the front yard. The back is full of what my mom says are magnolia trees. They're squat, with oily, oblong leaves, and they're supposed to be beautiful when they bloom in the spring. There's even a tiny trickling rock pond that the former owners built. It's twenty-years-ago high-tech; you hit a button, and water flows down the rocks. The other day I saw a little frog chilling in the pond, and I said, "Hey, frog," and it said nothing, and I said, "That's my line."

I apologize to the frog, and to you. This is what passes for a joke with me at the moment. I haven't been speaking to my parents unless it's truly necessary. The only thing that's keeping me going is a constant stream of text messages from Ashton and my friends back home. (I check my phone. There's nothing new yet, but the ♡ ♡ ♡ **Miss u baby** ♡ ♡ ♡ **Sleep well zzzzz** from last night warms my heart.)

There's this playhouse in the backyard. The former owners had two little girls, and little girls, according to the widely accepted gender rules of society, must love pink. I have long preferred blue, myself, and can go on about a certain shade of lush green for at least a minute, but I hope these little girls really did love pink, because they were the owners of a bright pink shack that's got enough room in it for all the pink things I can imagine them wanting: a pink Barbie Dreamhouse and a pink Easy-Bake Oven and a ton of pink stuffed animals, or whatever else little kids are playing with that comes in pink these days.

Pink notwithstanding, I would have killed for a playhouse when I was a kid. I made do with pillow forts. And now I sound like some ancient curmudgeon complaining about trudging in the snow for ten miles to get to school, hot potatoes in my pockets to keep my hands warm. I'm fun. I promise I'm fun. Just not right now.

On our second day in the new house, I took a bunch of blankets and a pile of books and carried them out to the empty playhouse, which is large enough that I can lie on the wood-planked floor and stretch my arms as far as they can go in front of me and my legs in the opposite direction, and there's still room on each side to grow. I decided then and there that this would be my safe space, where I can retreat and be alone and think. Where I can figure out what I'm going to do with myself. I have to work on my plan, which is to get my parents to let Ashton come and visit, and to get Ashton's parents to do the same. (I'm less worried about that part. The difference between how adults treat teenage boys and girls is *real*.) In the meantime, I read books. I'm currently obsessed with noir. I've got a stack of novels with shadowy figures in trench coats trudging through the dark on their covers, which seems to fit my vibe right now.

In case you haven't heard, Alabama summers are no joke. Walking outside is like being hugged by a person who's just emerged from a pool of molasses. But under the roof of the playhouse, it's cool and quiet, and there's a woody-earthy smell emanating from below. It soothes me even more than the rock pond. So that's how I've decided I'll spend my days, book in one hand, phone in the other, keeping up with my friends and my boyfriend back home. In a week and a half of this schedule, I've plowed through seven novels. A girl cannot live on rereads alone, and it is, in fact, this lack of new material that forces me to finally have a conversation with my mom that goes beyond "Please pass the salt and pepper, and btw why did you have to ruin my life?"

It's Sunday, so Mom's in the kitchen, sitting at the table reading the newspaper and sipping coffee. I'm guessing Jack is playing video games in his room and my dad's probably in his office, working as usual, even though it's the weekend.

"Hi," I say.

"Nell!" she says. "Does this mean you're talking to me again?"

"I am right now," I tell her.

"Honey," she begins. I can sense she's about to try to give me a hug, possibly paired with the worst of the worst—*comforting words*—so I step back. I want her to hurt like I do for a minute. It's the only power I have.

"You've always adjusted so well when we've moved before," she says.

"I was in fifth grade, Mom." That was when we went from Houston to the suburbs of Chicago. "And before that, kindergarten." Those two moves had been for my dad's job—he's a consultant for a huge oil and gas company. He figured out a work-from-home arrangement after my mom was given this "once-in-a-lifetime opportunity." The thing is, I barely remember the first time we moved. The second time, I hadn't known how hard it would be. Now I do.

"I don't see how you can't understand the difference between then and now!" I say. "You ripped me away from my entire world, with barely any warning. Right in the middle of high school. When I finally had really good friends, a boyfriend, and everything! That's brutal! It took me forever to feel good there, and I finally did, and now we're here. . . ." I'm on the verge of crying.

"Shhhhh," she says, and right on cue, Jack comes wandering into the room.

"What's wrong?" he asks. We tell him nothing, even though something clearly is.

"I was just asking if Mom could take me to the library," I say. Libraries are the same everywhere, I'm thinking. Maybe this one will feel a little bit like home, even if it's in a new town.

She glances at her watch. "Those nightstands we ordered are

supposed to be delivered this afternoon, and Dad's got an important work call scheduled. What if I loan you the car and you go yourself? It's not far." Back in Illinois, I would have jumped at the chance to get behind the wheel of her Mercedes on my own. But now taking her car seems like accepting that I'm stuck in Alabama and might as well embrace it. I'm not ready to do that yet.

"I'll go by myself next time?" I wheedle. "Pretty please?" She folds after I promise to make it fast, which isn't difficult. The town's so small! To get to the library, we drive by a big church, a scattered array of small stores, and the high school. (It nearly sends me into a panic to think about *that*.) Jack and I both pick out a stack of books, and we're home again before the nightstands have arrived.

Back at the kitchen table, Mom passes me a section of the newspaper. Circled in black ink are a bunch of want ads.

"These seem like they might be good for you," she says. "And a job will help you meet some other kids!"

"Oh," I say. "I'm not really into a job right now, to be totally honest. I'm still . . . adjusting."

She smiles with her mouth, but her eyes stay serious. I know that look. "Nell, I'm not making a suggestion."

"Mom, *come on*," I protest. "You really expect me to work at a Waffle House? No way. That's my nightmare."

"You don't have to work at a Waffle House, honey," she says calmly. "Though I think they're pretty hip nowadays! I hear they have a hilarious Twitter account."

I groan.

"The point is, you have to work somewhere. You told me you didn't want me to help you get a job at the Marshall Space Flight Center, and I respect that. But you're going to have to find something to do with your time that doesn't involve moping around reading romance novels."

"Mom."

"You may not feel like talking to me for the rest of the summer," she says. "But you are going to talk to *someone*. You're going to get a job, and that is not up for debate."

"I'm not reading romance novels! I'm reading *detective fiction*!" I yell. I toss my current book, which is, for the record, Raymond Chandler's *The Big Sleep*, on the counter and stomp out to the pink playhouse, where I lie on the floor for a while feeling sorry for myself and angry that I sacrificed my book when I could now be finishing it. I skim through one of Jack's dumb kid magazines—he's always trying to hang out in the playhouse and read with me—and cry. *How many tears am I going to shed in this place?* I wonder.

I reach for my phone and call Ashton, but he doesn't answer, so I leave him a quick voice mail. "Everything's terrible, I miss you, call me back!" I say. Next I try my friend Morgan, who picks up. "Nell!" she shrieks so loudly I have to move the phone away from my ear. "I'm with Nisha and we're giving each other pedicures and we wish you were here!"

Nisha grabs the phone. "Come back!" she says, and I feel even worse. "You should see this color Crankincense and Myrrh;

it's this vile green that looks totally rad. Oh, dammit, Morgan, you just spilled polish on my white shorts! Ugh, Nell, we gotta go. Love you!"

I'm holding the phone to my ear like it's a shell, listening to the echoes of my friends carrying on with their lives without me. Something in me shifts, ever so slightly. I stand up, shaking myself off like I've been in a fight but I haven't given up yet, and head into the kitchen. My mom is sitting there drinking a glass of wine and talking to my dad as he makes dinner. They both turn to me.

"OK," I say. "I guess I'll need the car tomorrow. To look for, you know, jobs."

"Fabulous!" she answers, breezy as can be. Jack is helping shuck corn my dad brought home from a nearby farm. He asks, "Can I come?" and my mom interrupts, "Oh, Jack, honey, Nell's got to do this on her own. But I bet Dad will take you to check out that toy store at the mall after you two drop me off at work."

She winks at Dad, but he gives her this look. "Just because I'm working remotely doesn't mean I'm not working," he says. "You know I can't just be gone for half the morning."

"I thought you were going to take things a little easier for a while," she reminds him.

"Fine," he says, but he seems about as psyched as I've been since the move, and I wonder if my dad isn't so thrilled about this upheaval, either. But then he smiles and looks at my little brother. "Jack, wanna check out the toy store at the mall tomorrow?"

Jack nods eagerly, and I manage a smile, too, and I guess that's how it all begins.

6
Doris

On Monday, I find a new girl. She's not that hard to find. She's driving a Mercedes with an Illinois license plate, which I notice when I pull up next to her at the traffic light at what passes for a busy intersection around here. Out-of-state travel isn't that common in our town, with the exception of the bargain hunters heading to Unclaimed. Neither are German cars. Somehow I doubt she's a bargain hunter. She's got blond hair pulled back in a ponytail and pale skin and probably freckles, though she's on the other side of a car window, so it's hard to see exactly.

I turn toward Unclaimed, and she heads in the other direction—yep, definitely not a bargain hunter. Maybe someone's relative visiting from up North? I pull into the lot, parking my car and locking it, even though the last break-in around here was an only slightly exaggerated fifty thousand years ago and a lot of people don't even lock the doors to their houses. For me locking is just a habit, like brushing my teeth in the morning. It's a way to keep precious things safe (and cavity-free).

This is supercorny, but every time I see the store, I still get a little bit excited. Sometimes when I'm the last person there, I walk around touching things, imagining the stories. Who owned this stuff? Why'd they leave their carefully packed possessions behind? Did they die? Develop amnesia on the plane? Go into witness protection midflight and have to discard their bag along with any connection to their former selves? It's the stuff of great mystery novels.

I have a system, separating out the bad stuff and making a list of what's good so Red can price it, have it professionally cleaned if necessary, and put it out on the floor. Some days I can get through the boxes at light speed. It all depends what's inside.

The bell over the front door tinkles as I enter.

"Hey, Red." I greet my boss, who's arranging dress shirts neatly on a rack.

"Hey, Doris!" he says, pushing his ginger hair out of his eyes and waving me over. "Guess what just came in?"

I'm good at finding things, not reading minds, but I take a stab anyway: "A brand-new billiards table?" (The other week we got a Ping-Pong table.)

"Nope," he says proudly. "A big container of stuff from

32

Huntsville International that a custodian found in a broom closet. The bags have tracking labels from eight years ago! What do you make of that?"

Huntsville is one of the airports that's closest to us—we get stuff from there pretty regularly—so the long delay is especially weird. Most of our shipments are a year or two old, max. Last summer I did open a bag that had been lost in Italy, flying a perpetual circuit from Rome to Bologna to Venice and back again for something like five years. When it finally got to us, it was full of moldy biscotti.

"Yeesh," I say. "I hope whatever's in them isn't perishable. All right, I'm going in," I tell him, and head to the back room, where I crank up the Spotify playlist called "Unpacking 2.0" that I'm rocking out to. Last summer I made "Unpacking 1.0," and I'm not going to lie: My mixtape talents are only improving with time. "I'm Bound to Pack It Up" by the White Stripes comes on—Aunt Stella turned me on to them—and I start sorting. The playlist is at the end of its second round when I take a break. I've made my way through four suitcases. A lot of stuff is in pretty good condition, despite the length of time it's been stashed away in a broom closet. (That's another mystery novel right there!)

I always make a list of whatever's worth reselling so we can track the items as inventory. For fun, I also draw little pictures of what I find in the margins:

1. 1 rhinestone bracelet and necklace, good condition
2. 1 leather jacket, worn, still looks really good, fits me perfectly

3. A pile of different-colored T-shirts that we will resell at a buck a pop
4. 6 plain white button-downs, 1 blue with embroidered sunglasses all over it
5. A snorkel, a pair of goggles, and, in the same suitcase, a dog collar (?)
6. A well-worn paperback romance novel published in 1976 titled *Lords of Love*

Discards go in the dumpster in the corner of the stockroom. (I always throw away deodorant, as some things should simply *not* be shared.) Food also goes in the dumpster, because we're not allowed to resell it, though if something unopened and unexpired comes through, it's fair game for staff to snack on. My stomach growls right on cue, but there's nothing remotely edible in any of these bags. When I'm done with each suitcase, I add it to the row of emptied luggage we also resell if it's not too beat-up. I unzip my fifth suitcase, a tiny pink hard case with a picture of Hello Kitty on the front. I am *not* expecting a giant gray stuffed manatee to pop out, and when he-it-she (?) does, I scream. There's also a flashlight in the suitcase. And nothing else.

Note: This is not even the weirdest thing I've ever found at the store.

The flashlight doesn't work; it's got two corroded batteries inside. The manatee is in as mint condition as a stuffed manatee can be. I throw him—it's a boy, I've decided—over my shoulder. He hangs nearly to my waist.

"Red, you're not going to believe what was in those boxes

from Huntsville!" I'm saying as I jog up front again. Then I notice he's not alone. He's talking to the new girl, the girl from the car. It's been a couple hours since I saw her, but I don't forget a face.

Red doesn't even do a double take at the stuffed animal on my shoulder. "Doris, I was just telling Nell here about you," he says, and his phone rings. He pulls it out of his pocket. "Oh, it's the wife—I gotta take this," he says. "You two. Talk amongst yourselves. I'll be back." He puts his phone to his ear and walks away, leaving me and the new girl to size each other up.

"Nice manatee," she says. There's no trace of Southern in her accent. She crosses her arms across her chest, and I'm not sure if she's cold or standoffish. She's in a pretty, floaty blue sundress, and the store's kept at a chilly sixty-five degrees because Red is one of those guys who starts sweating when it hits seventy. I usually wear a hoodie and jeans with Converse sneakers and wool socks to work, and strip down to my underlayer of T-shirt and shorts when I go outside. I keep flip-flops in my car to wear for the drive home, but I may have to rethink that plan. A pair melted in my backseat last week.

"So you met Red," I say. "I'm Doris." I raise my hand in the air, somewhere between a wave and a high five and a "halt!" Then I bring my hand back down and look at it. "Sorry. I just touched a bunch of questionably clean clothes."

She's looking around at everything, perplexed. "What is this place? I thought it was a store that sells suitcases, but—"

"We do sell suitcases," I explain, "along with what's been left inside them. Well, whatever's good, anyway."

"You sell other people's *stuff*?" she asks. "Is that even legal?"

I get asked this question a lot. "After ninety days, lost luggage becomes the property of the airlines, and they sell it to us," I explain. Her face is still a blank, so I continue with my spiel. "The semibrilliant idea for a store selling lost luggage was thought up by Alabamian Doyle Owens in 1970. He drove to Washington, DC, where he picked up a bunch of left-behind bags for three hundred dollars, brought them home, and sold the contents on card tables in his house. Soon he had enough cash to move the operation into an actual store. He named it Unclaimed Baggage. Over the years, a chain of them sprung up in Alabama. We're a privately owned satellite of the flagship store, which is about an hour and a half east of here. Even though we're a smaller store, we get a decent amount of inventory and shoppers coming from all over the country and even the world—and plenty of regulars, too."

"That stuffed animal was in a suitcase?"

I reach up and pat its soft fur. "Yeah. First time for a manatee. We get a lot of teddy bears. One time I found one of those plastic baby dolls you practice resuscitation on. I screamed, and the whole store came running."

"That's pretty hard-core," she says. She grins, and I can't help smiling back.

"So, how can I help you?" My fingers are itching to start unpacking again.

"I need a job," she says. "Or at least, my mom says I need a job. I already went to Waffle House—"

"Did they give you the Scattered, Smothered, and Covered Test?" Waffle House makes their hash browns about fifty-seven different ways. "Scattered, smothered, and covered" means they're covered in onions and cheese. "Chunked" means they've got smoked ham on them. I'd applied there before I got the job at Unclaimed last summer, and in my interview I'd been asked to define each of the terms on the spot.

"I failed the Scattered, Smothered, and Covered Test!" I tell Nell. "But you don't want to work at Waffle House. You get all the truckers asking if you're married and trying to grab your butt."

"I didn't get that far," says Nell. "As I was talking to the manager, a guy tried to grab my butt, and I smacked him."

"Good for you," I said.

"He looked pretty stunned." She glances down at her knees and smiles ever so slightly. "I ran out of there. Then I tried the grocery store down the way, and they said they needed someone with experience."

"You dodged a bullet," I say. "The assistant manager throws raw chickens at people who clock in late."

"So actually I dodged a chicken," she says, and I laugh—the new girl is funny. She keeps going, checking off the no's on her fingers. "According to your local newspaper, the bowling alley only hires people who are over eighteen. The water park, unsurprisingly, wants you to have lifeguarding experience *and* your CPR certification, and I don't have either. I can't work anywhere that serves booze 'for consumption on premises' because I'm sixteen. I can't work at Baskin-Robbins because I'll spend all my money on ice cream. I was driving by and I saw this place, so I came in. And Red said maybe you needed help?"

Typical Red. He'll hire anyone who knocks on his door begging for work.

"Do you mind waiting here a second?" I gesture to the velvet couch that came to us after a cruise company went out of business. I hustle to the front of the store, where Red is off the phone and showing an old lady items from our "luxury fur collection." I have told him again and again that we should get rid of these mangy pieces of mink and raccoon, which are not very PC and also make me so sad. He argues that since the animals are already dead, it would be far sadder to waste the furs.

This old lady has hair that's a little bit gray and a little bit blue, and she's clutching a shaggy piece of something between her fingers and haggling like she's on her very last dollar, even though her purse has a brand name on it and her fingers are covered in diamonds.

"Excuse me, ma'am," I say, giving her my most charming smile. She stares back at me, and I remember I've still got a manatee on my shoulder. "The latest in new fur looks!" I say. "May I speak to you for just a second, Red?"

"Just one itty-bitty moment, ma'am," he tells her. He follows me to a corner of the room where we huddle.

"Do you want me to hire this girl?" I ask.

"Do you think we should?" he whispers back. "It's your call."

"Since when am I the head of personnel?" I say, and he smiles.

"I was figuring you might want to take on a little more responsibility."

"Were you planning on telling me about this promotion?" I ask.

"How about it?" he says. "Want to be my head of personnel for the stockroom this summer? I can bump up your hourly a buck. The back room is all yours. From my perspective, seems like you could probably use a little help? We have a giant order from Kansas City coming in next week. They're sending a piano!"

"Who loses a piano?" I ask.

"The same sort of person who loses a brand-new set of golf clubs?" He and I glance over at the sports equipment. "I'm thinking we put it right out front, where people can take a load off and play a little, if the spirit so moves 'em." Red grins. "That'll give us some real atmosphere."

The old lady clears her throat. "Have you seen my sunglasses?" she asks. "I seem to have misplaced them."

I nudge Red.

"Oh, ma'am, they're right on top of your head," he tells her. "I do that all the darn time!"

"Oh my!" she says, touching the glasses. She giggles and goes right back to pawing through the raggedy remains of former living creatures. I turn to my boss.

"OK, then," I tell Red. "I'll interview her. If she's cool, I'll offer her the job."

"Excellent," he says.

"And . . . thanks for the promotion, Red. You're kind of the best, you know that?"

He flushes the color of his hair. "Just tell the new girl I don't take any guff, and she can be responsible for bringing in doughnuts for the next staff meeting. Have her start as soon as she can. We gotta move some more product to the front again. Business is booming!"

As he returns to the old lady, who has now moved on to a set of puke-yellow Fiestaware, I could swear he very nearly jumps in the air and clicks his heels together.

7
Nell

All of a sudden, Doris is in front of me again. "Come with me," she says. "I want to show you something." She takes my hand and pulls me to the back of the store, where there's a door to another room.

"Why don't you have a look around?" she suggests, pushing the door open. "This is probably the way to get to know us fastest. Go ahead, wander!"

It's almost overwhelming, but I obey, heading partway down one of the aisles, which contains rows and rows of shelves. At one end is a full skeleton; at the other, a set of armor. Sitting on the shelf in front of me is a bust of that Beatle with the funny name—Ringo!—which I know because, there, at the bottom of the bust, it says RINGO. There's a full set of Harry Potter, and when I open up one of the books, I see it's been signed by J. K. Rowling. I keep walking. There's a pile of rainbow-colored wigs; I resist the urge to plop one on my own head. On the next shelf, there are more socks than I've ever seen in one place in my whole life, rolled into balls of two, separated by color. Old albums by a guy named Lightnin' Hopkins. About a million T-shirts, some with tags still on—a lot are the kind they sell at the airport: "I ♡ NY," "Follow Me to Tennessee," "Virginia Is for Lovers." Everything is sorted neatly, though what the ordering principle is, I couldn't say. The entire effect is like a costume store combined with a Walmart combined with your creepy-but-maybe-cool aunt's attic.

I pause next to a beat-up Magic 8 Ball, one of those black plastic toys that looks like it belongs on a pool table. It's got an *8* in a white circle on one side, and on the other, a little window where a variety of answers pop up for whatever questions you pose. It's a totally hokey thing, but Nisha's older sister, Jasmine, had one in her room, and we'd ask it whether we'd pass certain tests, or if we'd ever be famous, or if the boys we liked would notice us. *Signs point to yes*, it would say, or, frustratingly, *Don't count on it*. I reach up to the shelf and pull this one down, holding the cool plastic in both hands for a second. *Does Ashton really love me?* is what I think. When I turn it over, the answer sends a surge of happiness through me: *You may rely on it*.

I stare at it hazily for a minute, thinking about how I'd always dreamed of having a boyfriend, and then I did. I hold the toy close to my face, and on a whim, I press my lips against it. I hear a light cough and turn around to see Doris. Great. Way to impress strangers, Nell.

"Oh, the 8 Ball!" she says, not even acknowledging that I was just caught making out with it. "I've asked it so many dumb questions. Will I get into Brown? Will my parents let me go if I do? Will I ever be kissed? By someone not horrible?" She sticks out her tongue and makes a face. "The answer to that one: *Very doubtful.* Every single time! I think it's trying to tell me something." She laughs. "What did you ask?"

"Um." I think fast. "Just, well, if I would get this job."

"What did it say?"

"You may rely on it?" I look at her hopefully.

"You're in luck. It's my living wish to make Magic 8 Ball predictions come true. Presuming you haven't been convicted of a crime?"

"Pretty much the worst thing I've done was cheat on a seventh-grade history test about the different types of Greek columns," I admit. "I still feel bad about that. It was like trying out a new look, and then realizing Goth is just never, ever going to be your style."

She gazes at me for a second too long, and I wonder if I've said too much.

"Not that there's anything wrong with Goth," I add.

"Doric, Ionic, and Corinthian," she says.

"Huh?"

"Those are the types of Greek columns. That must have been a really short test!"

I start laughing.

"I got called Doric for half a year of middle school, so I know the columns up and down or left and right or whatever. But I agree with you, I can't pull off a Goth look, either."

"So . . . are you going to ask me some more questions?" For the first time since I arrived in Alabama, I dare to hope for the best.

"I've never interviewed anyone before," she confesses. "I just Googled 'best practices for hiring new employees' on my phone while you were checking out the merchandise. So now you're going to have to be patient as I put you through a real-life interview. Ready?"

I nod, and she ushers me to the big table in the stockroom. "This is where we have our staff meetings," she tells me. I pull out a metal folding chair and sit on it, facing the manatee in the middle of the table. It's cold back here, and I rub my arms for warmth.

"Here, put this on," says Doris, passing over a navy blue sweatshirt with AUBURN written across the front in big orange letters. "It's clean! As long as you're not a Crimson Tide fan, that is."

"Huh?" I say, slipping on the sweatshirt. "Is that some kind of . . . period reference?"

"Football," she says, shaking her head. "You really are new here, aren't you? So, Nell . . ." she begins. "What's your last name?" She's got the clipboard in front of her with some official-looking paperwork in it, and as I talk, she writes.

"Wachowski," I say, and then spell it out, because no one ever gets it right the first time.

"If hired, can you produce proof that you are sixteen years old or over?"

"Yes. I'm sixteen and three-quarters. My birthday is in October."

"I'm sixteen, too, but my birthday's in April." She looks at her paper again. "If hired, can you produce proof that you have a legal right to work in the US?"

"Yep. I was born here. I've never even left America, to my great sadness."

"Me either. Can you perform essential job functions like lifting boxes, moving heavy objects, and carrying out the duties of the work here, as you are aware?"

"I think so!" I flex an arm. "I was on the field hockey team at my old school."

"Do you currently use illegal drugs?"

"No way. Not ever."

"Wise," says Doris. "Are you generally available for shifts between the hours of nine and five, or ten and six, Monday through Friday and some Saturdays?"

"I'm basically free for the rest of my life right now," I say. "At least until school starts. We just moved here, and I have no friends."

She lifts an eyebrow. Just one. I'm doubly impressed. "You and the 8 Ball looked pretty close."

Oh, here it is. "I was . . . um . . . imagining . . ."

"Are you one of those boy-crazy girls? Or . . . I watched this YouTube video about people who eat metal—is it like that? They can't help themselves—"

"No! I was thinking about my boyfriend," I say. "I really miss him."

"Does he look like a Magic 8 Ball?"

Because this seems like maybe the only way to prove I'm not lying about my "Canadian boyfriend" or utterly unhinged, I show her the screensaver on my phone. It's a picture of Ashton. He's waving at me, a toothy grin on his face. I feel a pang, remembering taking that picture just a few weeks ago. How is it that a phone can make a person seem both so close and so incredibly far away?

"Ohhhhhh," she says. And for some reason I get the impression that she thinks he's dead. That my beloved boyfriend died tragically, and we moved to get away from the pain, and I'm carrying him around in my heart and my phone because I can't bear to let go. Is that a tiny tear welling up in the corner of her eye?

"He's alive!" I shout, and she jumps a little in her seat.

"That's comforting," she says, "because he appears to be calling you right now."

I look at my phone and there's another picture of his face, along with ASHTON and the heart-eyes emoji, which is how I programmed his name in my phone because, well, I'm that sort of cheeseball.

"Oh, I thought . . . um," I say, wondering why I *did* assume she thought he was dead in the first place. What's wrong with me? But she gestures at me to take the call, so I do. "Hi," I say, and his voice comes through so loudly I'm pretty sure Doris can hear it: "Hey, Pony!" It's his nickname for me. Practically all of freshman year I wore my hair in a ponytail, and that's when he says he first noticed me, even though we only started dating sophomore year. I get up and walk back through the aisles of inventory, gesturing to Doris that I'll be just a second. She nods and writes something on her forms.

"Hey, Ash! I can't really talk now," I say. "I'm at a job interview." That's when I realize that probably the worst thing in the world to do at a job interview is take a phone call from your boyfriend. Even if he lives six hundred miles away and you're not sure you're ever going to see him again, or that he's even still your boyfriend.

"You're getting a job?" he asks. "Does that mean you'll be too busy to hang out with me if I come visit?"

Aware of Doris in the other room, I drop my voice to a whisper. "Ashton, I gotta go. I'll call you later?"

"Wait!" he says. "I need to show you something. Hang on!" There's silence on the line, and I look at the shelves in front of me. The Magic 8 Ball is right there. Is this where we'd left it, or is it following me? Holding my cell phone between my shoulder and my ear, I pick up the toy and shake it. I silently ask, *Is this job going to work out?* and slowly turn it over.

Signs point to yes, it says. I smile. I add another question for good measure: *Will Doris and I be friends?*

It is decidedly so, answers the 8 Ball.

"You there?" asks Ashton. "Did you get my photo?"

I look at my phone again. He's sent me a selfie. And in his hands he's holding what looks like a printed-out plane ticket.

"No way," I say. My heart starts racing, but I try to remain cool. "You actually used a *printer*?"

"I did it!" he says. "I'm coming down to the BIG BAD SOUTH in August. Tell me this is a good idea."

"August! Oh my God! That's amazing! And . . . so far away," I say.

"I've got baseball camp before that," he says. "And my parents say I have to pay them back for the ticket before I step on the plane, so I need a job, too! I think I have an in at the sporting goods store that just opened at the mall. I'm psyched. You're psyched, too . . . aren't you?"

"I am, I am!" I say. I hear that cough again. "Hey, let me call you later, OK? I love you. You're literally the best boyfriend ever."

"Love you, Pony," he replies, and I hang up the phone and walk back out to face Doris.

"I'm really glad he's not dead, because this would be super-weird if so," she says.

"I'm so, so sorry," I say. "It's just—"

She holds up her hand. "I have some follow-up questions."

"Go for it."

"How long have you been dating this guy?"

"Like, three months. But I've known him since freshman year, kind of."

"And he's coming to visit you?"

I smile again. "Yes! That's what he just said."

"And you're kissing 8 Balls and imagining they're him?"

I can't deny this.

"Show me another picture of him?"

I open up my camera roll and display a recent photo, which she inspects.

"He's cute," she says. "Very cute."

"He's the most adorable boy in the world," I say.

"You're in love, aren't you?" she asks, but it's more of a statement than a question. "With Mr. Cute Sexter Boy."

"Hey!" I say. "That wasn't a sext! He sent me a picture of his plane ticket."

"Was it wearing clothes?" She laughs.

"Stop!" I say.

"Sorry, sorry, but it's just . . . that's why you're so hung up on this guy, even though you only dated three months and you just moved hundreds of miles away. Right? You're totally in love." She pauses and gives me a suddenly bashful smile. "I'm sorry. Sometimes I'm way too direct. My aunt Stella used to say I have the gift of gab, but my parents think it's more like the gift of sticking my foot in my mouth."

"It's OK," I say. And maybe it's because I haven't had an in-person conversation with anyone resembling a friend in at least two weeks or that I'm in happy shock at Ashton's news, or both, that I spill way more than I should. "I *am*," I admit, "in love." Even though it's only the two of us in the room, I lower my voice to a whisper. "We lost our virginity to each other before I left Illinois. It just felt right. We didn't know if we were ever going to see each other again. And now he's coming to visit!" I

49

can't help it, I want to shout it from the rooftops. "I'm just really, really happy."

She stares at me intently.

"Was that TMI?" I ask.

"Maybe," she says. "Or maybe you have the gift of gab, too. So, *was* it right?"

This is where it gets complicated. The truth was, it was fine. Good even. Strange. The worst part was that it felt like it had to mean so much, that your first time always means so much, and there was no way for that not to be a tragedy, given my departure. I don't know how to explain any of this. It doesn't seem like the sort of thing you're supposed to say about your boyfriend, or to a girl you barely know.

The first time is supposed to be perfect, right? So that's what I tell her. "It was wonderful," I say.

Doris is still gazing at me, her expression serious. "We have a lot to talk about, Nell Wachowski," she says. "But for now, two things. First: There are two ten-minute phone breaks for each eight-hour shift, in addition to lunch. Otherwise, you have to keep your phone in the locker you'll be assigned. And second: As the newly minted head of stockroom personnel, I would like to offer you a job."

"Yay!" I wave my phone in the air, and then realize I should stop drawing attention to the thing that nearly stopped me from getting hired at all. "Thanks," I say. And then I blurt out, "Don't worry, I'm on the pill. My mom made me to go the doctor and get a prescription when I turned fifteen, just after

50

she sat me down and lectured me about sex for an hour. Again. TMI."

"Ha," says Doris. "My parents still think I believe in storks, or maybe immaculate conceptions, and they certainly do not think anyone in this town is having premarital sex, so long as we're talking about the proper Christians. The heathens will go to hell, so it doesn't matter. I learned everything about the human body from reading stuff online, plus Coach Deeson's health class. If you can call that 'learning.' He thinks the uterus is a 'baby holder.'"

"Oh no," I say.

"All the jocks call him Coach Deez-Nuts, which is actually still sort of funny after the fiftieth time, only because it makes about as much sense as he does."

I laugh.

"Anyway, work stuff," says Doris, her tone suddenly brisk and professional again. "The pay is eight dollars an hour. You'll go through shipments and separate out what you think we can sell, listing it on the sheet. Then you stock the shelves and put items in the to-be-cleaned section, if necessary."

"Cool," I say.

"I can explain the shelving system; it's kind of quirky. Red brought his six-year-old daughter, Freddie, in one day and had her point to different spots and say what would go where, if you can believe it."

"She actually said 'bust of Ringo'?" I gesture toward the shelves.

"That's a mystery," she answers. "I think it might be something from an ex-girlfriend that Red moved in here to get out of Heather's sight but can't bear to sell because, you know, nostalgia."

This place is weird. I like it.

"Heather is Red's wife," Doris continues. "She's tough but cool. She does our bookkeeping. If there's a little girl running around, it's probably Freddie. She pretty much gets free rein of the place, and is allowed to play with all the toys, so don't worry about that. She's really well behaved. And you've got to meet the rest of the staff: Byron was a big University of Alabama football player until he blew out his knee and moved back home, but he's not the asshole jock type at all. Nadine brings us homemade lemon pie and is always showing off pictures of her grandbabies. Cat plays drums in a band and does Roller Derby. Everyone is pretty great."

I nod again. Doris seems so adult—together and on top of things. "Do you have any questions for me?" she asks.

"Have you ever had someone come and reclaim an item?" I've been wondering how that works. "Like, show up saying it's theirs and they want it back?"

"Not once!" she says. "Even when we've found pretty amazing stuff. Jewelry, expensive coats, whatever. I guess once it's gone, it's gone."

"Maybe people just give up after a while," I say. "They move on."

"Or they don't know where to start looking. If you call the airline and they can't find it, what do you even do, besides submit a claim and eventually get your money back, if you're lucky?" she says.

"Maybe ninety days is some kind of threshold for forgetting." I think about this with regard to relationships. It's the three months of summer. It's the time I've been with Ashton, boyfriend-girlfriend serious. It's close to the amount of time we'll have been apart before seeing each other again. Will we still want to find our way back together in ninety days?

"One final question." Doris interrupts my train of thought. "When can you start? Oh, and one *more* question: Have you ever had a Krispy Kreme Doughnut?"

The 8 Ball was right about me getting this job. I cross my fingers that it might be right about everything else, too.

8
Grant

When I wake up, my stomach is growling. I don't remember how I got home last night, but I know I'm hungry. My alarm clock is officially broken, so while I have no idea what time it is, at least I don't have to deal with its infernal beeping. I listen for voices, but it's quiet. I roll out of bed and wander to the bathroom, where I've left my cell phone. It's past noon; no wonder I'm starving. I walk downstairs in my boxers, and there on the kitchen counter Mom has left me a plate of waffles. They're cold and hard from sitting so long, but I gnaw on one anyway as I peruse the fridge.

There's a casserole with aluminum foil over it, and a Post-it on top that says, DON'T EAT! FOR JR. LEAGUE MEETING, but guess what I do anyway? I pull it out and yank off the foil, just to see. It's my mom's famous sausage-egg-and-cheese casserole, and before I can stop myself, I'm using my hand to scoop it up and shove it in my mouth, one step above animal. I think about going the whole way and putting my lips right on top of it, eating like our old Lab, Rusty, spraying chunks of food left and right, but I stop myself.

Here's a fact to chew on: I have not been feeling like myself these days.

I've heard my mom say it to her friends on the phone: "Grant's not feeling like himself these days!" her cheery tone covering up the darker truth. I've heard her say it to my old girlfriend, Chassie Dunkirk, who dumped me in April. Chassie won't respond to any of my messages, but she calls my mom every now and then to check in. At least they have each other, because I'm a huge disappointment to them both. "Grant hasn't been feeling like himself, boys," I hear my stepdad, Brian, tell Bobby and Michael, my three-year-old half brothers, twins so cute that of course they get all the attention in the house, especially when Grant hasn't been feeling like himself.

The reason I'm not feeling like myself, the reason I'm lurking around the house like a ghost instead of killing it at football camp, the reason Chassie dumped me, the reason I'm standing in front of a refrigerator devastating my mom's casserole when she's told me not to *and* made waffles for me, is because I am a total and complete shithead.

And possibly an alcoholic. The internet says definitely—I answered seven out of their ten questions "yes," and that means I should seek help, ASAP. But I'm already getting help, so the laughs are on you, internet. The psychologist Mom and Brian and Coach are making me go to, a woman who insists I call her Dr. Laura, says I have "adjustment disorder." According to her professional opinion, I'm a normal teen simply "experimenting with the limits of what I can and cannot do."

This is because I have been giving her exactly what she wants to hear. I say, "I realize I've been excessive, but there's a lot of peer pressure." I tell her, "I am going to keep a sense of awareness about me when offered alcohol, and not simply say yes to fit in." When she asks if I crave the taste or the way it makes me feel, I muse and say, "Not really." Dr. Laura isn't one of those TV psychiatrists with a couch in her office. She sits in a chair in the corner of the room, and I sit facing her on another chair, which swivels. The more I bend the truth, or annihilate it completely, the more I tend to swivel, which is something she's never seemed to catch on to. You'd think she'd see through the lies. Part of me keeps hoping she will.

But it's a better look for her, for everyone, if I'm just "not feeling like myself." It means the situation is temporary and that my real self—the high school quarterback, the role model to his little brothers and every other kid in the whole damn school, the guy who was on track for a full scholarship to the college he's dreamed about playing for since he was a little kid watching games with his (real) dad, the guy with the perfect girlfriend and flawless life and impeccable future—will one day just be back, and this misfit, out-of-sorts asshole will, *poof*, vanish and be forgotten forever.

That everyone but me seems to believe this only makes it feel worse. No one wants to admit I have a real problem. That's how, when what happened happened, they managed to keep it quiet. No one said a word to anyone outside of the tiny containment circle that dealt with the information and my hush-hush punishment. God knows, the one thing everyone can agree on is that I have to play football—if I'm out for the spring or summer, no biggie, but when the championships come around, I better be on the ground, back to my old self. So this has to be a phase. I'm the only one who seems worried that it's not.

For now, I'm taking a private little "leave of absence" for "health reasons," says Coach, no need to get everyone—aka, the whole town—worked up about it. No football camp for me this summer, I'm grounded till the next century, and my driving privileges are a vague memory, but as long as I "take care of things" and do right by Dr. Laura, I'll be reinstated on the team come September. But how can I take care of things when I'm not sure I won't do what I did again? That I won't be able to help myself, or even know what I'm doing? That's the sort of question that can drive you to drink. Two things you shouldn't do together. Ha. Ha.

I know, not funny.

Drinking has always been something that I've done, it seems like. Back when we were in eighth grade, Chassie's big brother, Deagan, would get us beer and those spiked lemonades she liked. He was on the football team then, so he had a hookup for booze, even though he was just a few years older than us. We drank and got goofy, mostly. Chassie and I would fall all over each other, kissing and touching, and maybe we went further than we should have, but it was OK, because we've known each other forever and we really were in love. I think we were in love. I tried to be a good boyfriend. When I was sober, I really, really tried. But drunk Grant is another story.

All I know is, something changed in me freshman year. Coach saw me at JV tryouts and put me on the varsity team. The team had sucked for years, but we won the very first game I played. Afterward, these crazy sensations were coursing through my brain and body, and wouldn't stop. It was more, even, than sex, and almost too intense to feel good. Later that night we were partying at my friend Brod's house, and Leroy Coggins handed me an ice-cold Bud. I popped the top to release the beautiful noise that now triggers saliva to well up in my mouth (I really am a dog), drank it down in a giant glug, and asked for another. I couldn't get enough. I was so thirsty.

After the next game, which we won, too, someone had a bottle of Jack Daniel's. When I walked into the party, people were passing it around, chugging straight from the neck. I took my turn, and whoa: I was a hard-liquor convert. Beer helped, but whiskey and vodka and gin would really take the edge off. I'd feel just like everyone else for a little while, normal and happy and cheering the team for another victory that I'd helped achieve. And then I'd feel *better* than everyone else.

I started drinking more, not just after games but other times, too, and I got wilder. There was always alcohol available; no one deprives a football player in this town, especially not one who guides the team to victory every damn time. Sometimes I didn't make it home at night—I'd crash at Brod's condo, or sneak into Chassie's bedroom, and once when the weather was nice, I slept the whole night in our neighbor Mrs. Humphrey's flower bed. I always told my mom I was staying over at a friend's house, and she believed me. She was too busy with the twins, who were teeny-tiny babies then, to notice much, I guess. The funny thing is, no one seemed to mind. I was just being a guy, a football kind of guy, and it never affected my game. Until the thing that happened happened.

Now here I am, a prisoner in my own house. So far, progress has been more backward than forward. I don't know how to talk about what went down. And I don't know if I can stop drinking, but if I tell Mom or Brian or Dr. Laura that, wouldn't it prove that I really am as bad as I'm secretly scared I might be? Then maybe I really am an alcoholic, and not just an alcoholic as identified by the internet.

I finish the casserole and debate re-covering the dish with foil and putting the Post-it back on top, an empty platter in disguise in the fridge, but I decide that omission is less of a sin than a full-blown lie, so I shove the tray into the dishwasher and go back to my room. My sheets are starting to smell, but I don't care enough to get up and change them.

9

Eventually, the purple leopard suitcase wasn't alone anymore. A human came and collected it and put a new tag on it, then delivered it to a large, gray, mostly dark room where a bunch of other suitcases resided. Some had been there for weeks, even months.

Not a lot happened in this room. Every so often, the door would open and a new suitcase would arrive, and sometimes, one or two of the suitcases that had sat there so long would be taken out. Of course, the humans never told the suitcases where they were going. And the suitcases couldn't very well ask.

The suitcases didn't yearn for their owners, exactly. After all, having someone use you whenever they feel like it and shove you under a bed for the rest of the year doesn't necessarily endear them to you. But what the suitcases did mourn, in whatever way suitcases could, was how they'd gone so far off course. For a minute, they'd known exactly where they were headed and what their purpose was. They knew what they contained and who it was for. But now everything was up in the air, except they were down on the ground, no longer en route to wherever they were supposed to be.

What would happen next? No one could say.

10
Doris

"They're kind of a tradition in this town," I explain as Nell picks up her very first Krispy Kreme Doughnut, an original glazed, which is the classic and also my personal favorite. They're still warm from the oven, and as she takes a bite, the pastry collapses in her mouth and she lets out a little gasp.

"Oh my God, this is so good," she says. "Why have I never had these before?"

We're sitting in one of two booths at the tiny store, which is really more of a drive-thru operation. I asked her to meet me here after my shift ended partly because everyone should taste a Krispy Kreme Doughnut as quickly as possible once they step into a town that has them, and partly because, well, I think I might kind of want to be friends with the new girl.

"They started as a Southern chain," I tell her. "Mostly as a fund-raising business. At first, people sold them to make money for churches and schools. Later, they opened some retail stores. Luckily, we got this one. It's one of the true perks of living here."

"It is an utter tragedy that I've spent sixteen years of life without knowing of their existence," she says. "Is it wrong that I want another?"

"The first time I had them, I ate six," I confess. "I'd say it's pretty normal."

She smiles and reaches for a chocolate iced glazed from the variety box we have opened in front of us; I grab my second favorite, the strawberry iced.

"I've been really angry at my mom for making us move here," she admits. "Ripping me from everything I knew the summer before junior year. I had great friends! I had a boyfriend, finally. I was happy."

I nod. "I don't know what it's like to lose a boyfriend—or find one, for that matter. But I do know what it's like to lose someone you love." I decide to just come out with it. "My aunt died last summer."

"Oh, I'm so sorry," she says, and reaches out and puts her hand on my arm. "My grandpa died a few years ago, and it was really, really sad. What happened?"

"Well," I begin, and suddenly tears are flowing down my

cheeks as I tell her how my aunt Stella saved two kids from drowning but died herself. I'm full-on sobbing by the end of the story, and so is Nell.

The cashier shuffles over and looks at us kindly. (Last summer I located a pair of Crocs for her in her favorite color, Krispy Kreme green.) "You girls OK?" she says, pulling a pack of Kleenex from her pocket and setting it in front of us. "Take these. I've got plenty. You never know when you'll need a good cry." She pats me on the shoulder and heads back to her post.

"Thanks, Myrna," I manage, and reach for the tissues, passing a wad over to Nell. "Stel lived with us for a while when I was a little kid, and then again when I was in middle school. She was 'between things,' figuring out what she wanted to do next. I'd come home from school, and we'd sit and talk. I told her everything. You know how some people just get you? She got me. This sounds lame, but in some ways, she was my best friend. She was in her thirties, but she seemed like a teenager sometimes." I grab a tissue and wipe my eyes and nose. Fortunately, I've stopped crying. "I'm sorry."

"Don't be," says Nell. "I get it. Really."

Another "thanks" is all I can think to say.

"Why do people have to *leave* us?" asks Nell. "Why do we have to leave people? It just *sucks*."

"It really does," I say.

We end up sitting in that little booth for another hour talking about everything we can think of, everything and nothing

64

all at once. I guess when you're getting to know someone you might really click with—a potential new friend—it's like it is with Krispy Kreme Doughnuts. Once you get started, you don't want to stop.

· · · · ·

"Hi, honey," my mom says quietly when I walk in the door. The room is dark. Mom works at a catering company that does Southern party food like deviled eggs and chicken salad and cheese straws. A lot of nights I figure out what to eat for myself because she's busy figuring it out for other people. But right now she's home, which means she must not be feeling well.

I sit next to her on the couch, where she's resting with her eyes closed, her hand holding a cold cloth to her forehead. "Another migraine?" I ask.

"The new prescription isn't much better than the old one," she says. My mom has always gotten headaches, but after Aunt Stella died, they got worse. Which is weird because Mom was never really close to Aunt Stella—in fact, it seems like her relationship with Stel was mostly based on criticizing her. Stel would listen patiently as her older sister scolded. Then she'd turn around and do whatever she felt like.

My mom, well, I love her, but she has a lot of hang-ups about how people, especially women, are supposed to behave in the world. Her favorite words? *Proper*, and *ladylike*, and *sweet*, which, barf. If I were a therapist, I'd tell her she's internalizing years of repression and shame and it shoots straight to her brain, where it twists and turns and causes pain and blurred vision and stars. But I'm just her wayward daughter with the views she says Stella put in my head, and she wouldn't listen to me anyway.

"How was work today?" she asks.

"Pretty great, actually," I say. "Red promoted me! I'm in charge of stockroom personnel. And I made my first hire!"

She sets the cloth down and looks at me. "Does that also mean a raise?"

"Yeah," I say. "He bumped me up a buck an hour."

She nods, satisfied at this. "That's my girl. Any good things come into the store?"

Even when she's got a headache, my mom, like most people, loves to hear about bargains. She cheers up even more when I tell her about a new KitchenAid mixer that came in a box with a card on it to "the happy couple," and starts speculating about whether the guest is obligated to send another gift, and what the legendary etiquette expert Emily Post would have to say if she were still alive.

"The hire is a new girl from Illinois," I tell her, mostly to change the subject. "Her name is Nell. She'll be in my class at school, too."

"Where in Illinois?" asks Mom.

"Near Chicago," I tell her, and she makes a face that means "Ew, the big city" and/or "Ew, Yankees." My parents are the perfect town cheerleaders, regardless of some of the obvious flaws of where we live. Not that there isn't good stuff, too, but my parents gloss over the bad—like how black and white people rarely interact socially, or even go to the same restaurants, or how Maya Bloom's family never gets invited to certain events on account of their religion, or how the country club didn't even let in women as members until the '90s.

One of the things I like about Unclaimed is that pretty much everyone in town shops there. Red won't stand for intolerance; once he kicked out a guy wearing a T-shirt with the Confederate flag on it. But my parents didn't exactly get the memo. I'll hear them talking about how things were so much "nicer" way back when. I want to ask, *Nicer for who, exactly?* And *What does "nice" mean, anyway?*

A lot of the time, I feel like I was born into the wrong family. Especially now that my aunt's gone.

"You got some mail from your friend," says my mom. There on the coffee table is a postcard with a picture of a bunch of girls wearing riding helmets and hugging each other. "Greetings from Camp Sunshine!" it says across the front. Maya loves sending postcards, but it can take weeks for them to arrive, so it's hard to have a real conversation that way. Plus, I'm sure my mom reads them, though I'm also sure she doesn't understand what they're really about. I slip the postcard into my pocket to look at when I'm alone.

"Oh!" says my mom, and at this she's more excited than she was about the misdirected KitchenAid: "I almost forgot! Lydia

Collins—you know, the football boy's mom?—she called and left a message for you earlier today." She gives me a big grin, migraine temporarily forgotten, because if someone related to *the* Grant Collins is calling her daughter, her daughter must finally be doing something right. My mom's most public secret is that she desperately wants me to be popular like she was in high school.

"Weird," I say. This is the second time I'm finding myself thinking about Grant Collins in less than a week. And just like I don't understand why Chassie would be kissing someone who's not Grant—at the store or out of it—I can't for the life of me guess why Grant's mom would be calling me.

Mom glances around. "Now, where did I put that phone number?"

I look past her to the table, then back to the pocket of her shirt, then next to the TV remote. I glance down in the crease of the couch for a telltale corner of paper, and I'm about to get up and walk to the kitchen to check the refrigerator when I see my mom's note poking out from under the cloth she'd been using to soothe her headache.

She follows my gaze and looks at me with an apologetic expression, then hands me the message, which is slightly damp. I shove it into my pocket along with Maya's postcard, and excuse myself to my room.

There, I flop onto my bed, my feet dangling off the edge, and examine my mail. It's funny because Maya's not even *at* a place called Camp Sunshine; she must have found this postcard in a shop somewhere. On the back, she's written,

Dear Doris,

This is not my camp experience but that doesn't mean I'm not having a good time. BTW I still hate horses. All of my girls are great except one of them only eats chicken nuggets and another one refuses to sleep at night and ANOTHER lost her retainer and you weren't around to find it. FML. There's a hottie counselor in the next cabin, though, and I think there might be a spark! How are you doing? Miss you terribly, tho I can't say I miss home. TELL ME WHAT'S GOING ON WITH YOU. It gets lonely in the wilderness JK JK.

XOXOX MB

I always write back immediately; that way the conversation doesn't stall quite so fast. Conveniently, I have a bunch of post-cards with the Unclaimed Baggage logo on them that were made for a promotion years ago. I found them in an old file cabinet in the store, and Red let me take them home. I pull one of those out of my desk and start writing, adding pictures in the margins, as usual.

MAYA!!!!

Miss you too. Summer without you and Stella is weird. But! There's a new girl in town and she might be cool. I'm investigating. Also, Grant Collins and Chassie might have broken up? Is the world ending?

P.S., send me updates about your crush, and don't clam up around her the way you usually do! Make a move! Notify me immediately if something big happens. I wanna know!

xoxoxoxo Doris

I stamp and address the card and slip it in my bag to put in the mailbox tomorrow on my way out. Then I pull out Grant's mom's number and hold the piece of paper in my hand for a few moments. If I don't call back, I'll never hear the end of it from *my* mom, so I punch in the digits, my heart beating a little bit faster than usual. I'm picturing Grant picking up and what I'll do then, but a woman answers on the first ring. It's Mrs. Collins, who I used to see regularly when she'd drop Grant off at Sunday school, back when I used to go, too, before I officially decided that church wasn't my thing. That was the summer before seventh grade, which is, not coincidentally, around the time I started thinking Grant Collins was a huge jerk.

"Oh, Doris! Thanks for calling me back so quickly," says Mrs. Collins. It comes out *callin'*, her words dripping with verbal molasses the way some women here do when they're fixin' to ask a favor. "Can you hold on just a sec, sweetie?"

"Yes, ma'am," I say. I hear some muffled conversation and rustling, and then everything is quiet.

"Doris?" she asks.

"Yes, ma'am," I repeat.

"Sweetie, can I trust you to keep something just between us?"

"Sure," I answer.

"Well, it's about Grant. . . ."

Duh.

"He's found himself with a bit of time on his hands, and Red Finster tells me you're the person to talk to about getting Grant a job. I'm sure it would help him to be around people, to have some structure, and I thought maybe—"

"You want me to hire Grant?" I ask. The guy must be in some serious shit if she's having to call in favors with me. What happened to football camp? Or Chassie? Or being king of the world?

"Well, isn't that so sweet of you?" she answers, even though I haven't actually said I'd give her son a job. "He's very strong, as I'm sure you can imagine. You won't be disappointed."

The last thing I want is Grant Collins in my space, in my store. In fact, I'd be perfectly fine never to see Grant Collins again, even if most of the female student body of my high school feels differently. But I can't help thinking about Aunt Stella. How she was a connector. How she saved those kids, even at the cost of her own life. I guess that's why, instead of telling Mrs. Collins it will be a cold day in hell (which is where I'm sure at least a few people in town think I'll end up) before I hire her son, I say, "Can he come to the store at ten tomorrow morning? I can talk to him about the job then."

"Wonderful," says Mrs. Collins, relief in her voice.

I wish I felt the same way.

11
Grant

I may not remember everything, but there's one thing I can't forget. The last conversation I had with Coach. Lately whenever I'm alone and quiet—and sober—there's a chance of it starting to run through my head again.

"Grant," he says, beckoning me into his office, which is really just a supply closet they converted because he's the coach of a public high school's football team, not Paul "Bear" Bryant. He's sitting on an exercise ball instead of a chair because he says he's starting to get fat, but really he's solid as a rock, a barrel-chested man with sturdy arms and legs, the kind of guy you could see running through a line of defense without breaking a sweat. There's a photo on his desk of him doing just that when he played for the University of Alabama back in the '80s. It's turned around to face whoever's sitting in the chair across from him, which in this case is me.

"Grant," he says again, "I'm gonna talk to you like you're a man."

I guess I appreciate that, even though I've never felt less like a man than I do sitting across from my huge coach on his plastic ball of a chair.

"You know I never wanted you off the team. Hell, I still want you on the team," he tells me. "There's plenty of leeway I gave you. But then you had to go do something like this." He frowns. "You had to get the police involved."

I can't say I meant to. I can't say much of anything.

"Boys drinking, hey, it happens. Boys messing around with girls, it happens, too. And plenty of people drink and drive around here, you and I both know that. But the administration has decided to crack down this year, harder than ever. Zero tolerance policy. Not to mention, you made yourself a spectacle. How do I explain you falling all over the field, weaving everywhere, scoring for the wrong damn team? Or operating a motor vehicle, drunk, with the head cheerleader in the front seat? Or crashing that car in a ditch and fleeing the scene? Good Lord, boy. I need this job. And I need our team to win, and I certainly don't need any nasty rumors swirling about my starting quarterback."

Even, apparently, if those rumors are true. "I'm sorry, sir."

He pounds his fist on the desk, and the photograph shakes

in its silver frame. "We're all sorry. Damn sorry. But it doesn't change anything."

It sure doesn't.

It's been a warm winter, and it's an even hotter April. He wipes at the sweat forming on his upper lip. "Here's what we're going to do," he says. "For now, you're off the team. With the new policy, I'm not supposed to give you a second chance."

I nod. I understand.

He leans in close.

"You're gonna need to see a headshrinker. Don't worry, I know just the right person. I've already talked to your parents. The police department is on board, too; I've been friends with the police chief for a long time, and since you're Grant Collins and this is *most definitely a one-time thing*"—he stares at me hard—"they'll write up the incident as a vehicular problem. Lucky for you, Chassie's not interested in pressing charges. We've convinced her to keep things under wraps. You need to keep this under wraps, too. Don't tell a soul about what really happened after the game, and I can make it go away. As far as anyone knows, this is a leave of absence due to injuries. If you can get the all clear from Dr. Laura by the time senior year starts, we'll take you back and you can help us win the championship. Which I know, son, is what you want to do, too."

I don't know if it's what I want to do, but going along with Coach's plan sounds a lot better than the alternative. Who am I without football?

You know what I'm afraid of? That I'm no one at all.

12
Nell

It's my first day at my new job, and I'm sweating my butt off in the parking lot. At nine a.m. it's already more than ninety degrees of the exact opposite of "dry heat," and, per Doris's instructions, I'm wearing jeans and a long-sleeved T-shirt *plus* a hoodie. I'm also carrying two boxes of Krispy Kreme Doughnuts—as instructed by Doris, who gave me the money from petty cash—for the staff meeting. Red's change is perched precariously on top. I can see the accident before it comes.

"No!" I yell as the money plummets to the concrete below, and then the top box is going, too. I try to save it while keeping the bottom box steady, but it's a leaning tower of doughnut, and there's sweat trickling into my eye, and it's going *down*. I wonder if Krispy Kreme would be interested in sampling my new artisanal asphalt and gravel flavor? Then an arm reaches out, and it's attached to a boy, and suddenly both boxes are securely in his arms. There has been no doughnut carnage. We have been saved. I squat down to pick up the loose change and grin up at him. And I blush because, dear God, this boy is cute. I may be taken, but I can still acknowledge beauty.

"Hi," he says. "Looked like you needed some help."

"Thanks," I say. "You're like a doughnut superhero." He has this thick, wavy brown hair streaked with reddish-gold highlights. I can see his triceps rippling where they extend from the arms of his faded blue T-shirt, which he's wearing with ripped jeans and pale green Chuck Taylors. His hands are tan, with clean fingernails that aren't bedraggled like some teenage dudes. He's basically the kind of guy you'd dream up just so he could put his arms around you. His lip curls up, just a hint of a smile, or maybe a smirk, and again I feel heat rushing to my face.

"I'd shake your hand and introduce myself, but you're kind of occupied," I joke. "I'm Nell. This is my first day at my new job, and you've saved me from disaster, so I probably owe you my firstborn."

"Nah," he says. "But maybe I get the first pick of the doughnuts. I hope there's a lemon-filled in here."

"I would have pegged you for more of a cruller guy," I say.

"I'm a cruller virgin," he says, smiling. "Maybe today I'll finally get lucky."

We're at the door to the store when he stops and looks in my eyes. "I'm Grant," he says, pausing to let the information sink in, as if he expects some reaction other than simply "Nice to meet you."

"Nice to meet you," I say.

"You're new here, huh?" he asks then.

"Straight from the suburbs of Chicago," I say, holding the door open for him so he can walk through with his armful of pastries.

"Well, then, welcome to 'Bama, Nell," he says, and we're inside, the rush of cool air tickling my skin. Now I'm glad I have the hoodie.

Doris is already there, hanging some T-shirts on a rack. She waves at me and then her eyes turn to Grant and the smile disappears from her face.

"I thought you were supposed to come in at ten," she says to him.

"My mom had to drop me off early." He shrugs like we're lucky to have him whenever he turns up and for however long.

"I guess you'll have to join us for the staff meeting, then," Doris tells him in kind of a stony voice. Resuming her normal cheery tone, she shouts, "DOUGHNUTS ARE HERE, EVERY-BODY!"

"Wait, do you work here, too?" I ask Grant, and he shrugs again.

A woman with a topknot plucks the doughnut boxes from his hands. She's got to be Heather. There's a little girl with a matching bun running around after her—Freddie. She smiles shyly at me and follows her mom to the doughnut table. I pass

Red his change, and he gives me a hearty "Welcome to the team!" The group of us trail after Heather into the stockroom. She sets out paper plates and opens the boxes, gives a doughnut hole to Freddie, and pours herself a cup of coffee from the Dunkin' Donuts box sitting on the table. She notices me watching.

"We do Dunkin' for coffee and Krispy for doughnuts, and I try to resist until midafternoon on the latter," she explains, sliding into the folding chair at the head of the table.

"I don't!" says Red as he sits and grabs a chocolate doughnut. Doris files in next to him, taking a plain glazed, so I find a seat across from them and help myself to one, too, even though this morning Dad made a special nonweekend weekend breakfast, eggs and bacon and everything. A few other people file in: Nadine is the cozy-looking sixty-something woman in black pants and a silky polka-dot blouse; Byron is the youngish, muscular guy wearing a blazer over a T-shirt and a funky necklace with a dangling elephant charm; and Cat has purple hair and a pierced nose and could be twenty or forty-five, it's hard to say. Freddie grabs the stuffed manatee off the table and carries it around, cradling it like a baby and talking to it.

Everyone's sitting and chatting and eating and drinking when I notice Grant standing in the corner of the room against the wall like he's waiting for detention to be over. He's got his arms crossed against his chest and this too-cool-for-school expression on his face. No one seems to have noticed him, which could be his intent. I decide to be bold: I stare at him until he raises his eyebrows back at me in a question.

"Cruller?" I mouth, holding one up for him. Doris watches with a curious expression as Grant slouches over and takes the pastry out of my hand. He goes in with a big bite, revealing that his left front tooth is chipped. This does not detract from his looks. "Not as good as lemon-filled," he says. "But decent." He finishes in three more bites, returns to the wall, and resumes his pose.

Red starts talking. "Good morning, Baggage Heads!"

I glance around to see if anyone else thinks this is as corny as I do. Grant is rolling his eyes, but everyone else is smiling and paying attention. "I'd like to begin with a special announcement," Red continues. "We have a new member of Team Stockroom starting today." He points at me: "Meet Nell Wachowski!" The room is full of warm Southern greetings; my first name almost sounds like it's pronounced with two syllables here. I wave and try not to feel silly. Grant, across the room, catches my eye and then he starts to slow clap, loud and pointedly. Oh no. I shake my head at him, glancing around the room to see what sort of reaction this cute boy who may be a monster has incited. Doris looks infuriated, Red looks confused, and most of the rest of the people at the table simply seem amused.

"She brought the doughnuts," Grant says, by way of explanation.

"Grant," says Red, "how can we help you?"

It's almost as if Doris is in pain. "He's here . . . for an interview," she says. "With me."

A brief look flashes across Red's face. "Oh, yes," he says. "I spoke to your mom about that the other day. Glad you may be joining us, Grant. Let's save any remaining clapping for the end of the meeting, thanks. You and Nell, y'all are with Doris, so do what she says! Byron and Nadine, you're on the registers. Cat, can you handle Customer Service this morning, and we'll meet this afternoon to talk about the new shipment schedule?"

Everyone nods, mouths full of sugary deliciousness and caffeine, and Red briskly addresses some new store initiatives, goals for the month, and other businessy things. I tune out a little because I'm trying to figure out why Doris seems so angry and why Grant is mostly staring at the wall.

Red finishes off. "We have about fifteen minutes until the store opens to customers, so eat up, and let's have another awesome day! New folks, remember to fill out your paperwork with Heather before you leave. We'll meet back here at the same time tomorrow. Nadine has offered to make us her famous casserole, so bring your appetites! Thanks for the doughnuts, Nell," he adds. "*Now* we can do this." He initiates a round of applause, and everyone else joins, including Grant, while I grin and stare down at the table.

Everybody's standing up and chitchatting when he interrupts again: "Oh, also, please be on the lookout for my master keys—especially you, Doris. As Heather says, I can't keep track of anything unless it's attached to me."

"Speaking of which, go check on your daughter, babe," answers Heather. "She just told me she was taking her new manatee friend on a tour of the store. You'll probably find her in Toys."

"Yes, ma'am," he says as he grabs another doughnut, which he tucks into his mouth, and motors out of the room. Nadine follows, giving me a kindly pat on the shoulder and a slow, Southern "Nice to meet you, honey." I intercept Doris while Byron talks with Grant.

"What's up with that guy?" I whisper.

Doris leans in close and talks low and fast. "Total bad news. Grant Collins is exactly the kind of teenage boy everybody warns you about. He's all about football, thinks he's the hottest human on the planet, et cetera, et cetera . . . and it looks like you've caught his eye, so watch out. He's inextricably connected to one of the meanest girls in town, and I don't think you want to bring on her wrath. Even if they aren't currently dating. They have always been together; they *will* get back together."

"That clapping was pretty embarrassing," I say.

She nods. "Guys at school do that sometimes when they think a girl is hot. It's humiliating. They always play it off like it's about something else, and teachers let them get away with it. But it's like their secret code."

"Gross," I say.

"I'm already regretting telling his mom I'd talk to him about a job."

"Why would you do that?" I ask. "It seems like you hate him!"

Her face goes kind of pale. "She called me last night, begging me to let him work here. Something must have happened because he's not at football camp like everyone else on the team. But she wouldn't tell me what it was about . . . I didn't know what to say, and for some reason, I agreed."

There's got to be more to it than that, but she stops as Byron and Grant part and Byron heads out to the front of the store, shooting Doris and me a thumbs-up as he goes. Everyone else clears out, and Grant saunters over casually.

"So," he says, "what exactly do we do here at this . . . garage sale?"

Doris brushes doughnut crumbs off her shirt and stands and gives him a hard look. She's not very tall, but she has presence. "OK, y'all," she says. (I make a mental note to start incorporating *y'all* into my vocabulary.) "Nell: You'll be helping me go through inventory, separating the sellable stuff from the junk and listing everything on these clipboards so we can enter it into the master list on the computer later. Why don't you start with those?" She points to a leaning tower of suitcases and hands me a clipboard.

I stare at it like I've never seen such a thing in my life. What I'm really looking at, though, is the sheet of paper attached to it, already covered in what I guess is Doris's handwriting, line after line of items of various worth that all went missing at some point and arrived here. Her list isn't just numbers and words—it's art, with tiny but intricate pictures in the margins and notes to the sides that make me laugh.

"I can't . . . draw," I say.

"You don't have to, just do it whatever way makes sense to you—as long as it's legible, it's cool," she tells me.

Still admiring her work, I head over to the suitcase pile, choose a big, bright yellow one from the top, and dig in.

"Grant," says Doris, "since you haven't even been properly interviewed, why don't we do that?"

"I thought I had the job," he says.

"I told your mom I'd interview you. I can't just give you a job. It doesn't work that way here."

"Cool, cool, whatever," he says, and sits down at the table like he's the bad boy in an '80s movie, turning the chair around so he looks over the back of the seat.

Doris groans.

"What?" says Grant.

"Who does that? Is it even comfortable?" she asks.

Grant, shockingly, has turned red. He gets up off the chair and turns it around the right way and sits in it. "Is that better?"

"Yes," says Doris. "Thank you. Let's get started. If hired, can you produce proof that you are sixteen years old or over?"

"Yeah," he says.

"If hired, can you produce proof that you have a legal right to work in the US?"

"Yep." (Grant is a master of the one-word response.)

"Can you perform essential job functions like lifting boxes, moving heavy objects, and carrying out the duties of the work here, as you are aware?"

"Sure."

"Do you currently use illegal drugs?"

"What counts as illegal, exactly?"

She gives him a stare-down.

"Fine, fine, I have been known to drink and smoke, on the occasion," he admits. "Not currently, as in not this moment."

She shakes her head but pushes on. "Have you ever been convicted of a crime?"

"Not yet," he says.

"My next question was going to be are you honest and trust-worthy, but I'm pretty sure you just told me the truth," says Doris. She marks something down on the paper in front of her, then glances over at me. I dig back into my bag, pretending like I'm not totally eavesdropping, and pull out a bunch of sequined tops with the tags still on them, which I start to sort through. This person just went on some kind of shopping spree. I've named her, and her suitcase, Natasha.

"Do you promise never to steal from the store, because that would be really, really shitty, and then we'd have to fire you, and I've never fired anyone before?"

I sense that Doris is going off-the-cuff with these questions.

"I will definitely not steal from the store," says Grant. "What would I even take? Somebody's moth-eaten old polo shirt? A delightful bag of nails?"

In fairness, there's one of each right on the table in front of him. Doris frowns again.

"Do you promise not to drink or do drugs while you're on the job?"

"I promise," says Grant.

I find a pair of gold lamé pants. Natasha is a dancer, I've decided.

"Are you generally available for shifts between the hours of nine and five, or ten and six, Monday through Friday and some Saturdays?"

"Yes," he says. "Baby, I'm free whenever you want me to be."

She puts down her clipboard and gazes at him coolly for what feels like forever. He returns her look. I pull a pair of shiny high-heeled platform pumps from the bag, log them on my clipboard, and put them in the sale pile.

"Grant. I'm going to say it. Your mom wanted me to give you this job, and she's a nice lady, and she's old friends with Red, so I will. You and I, however, are not friends. And that's fine. We can work together peacefully. But if you start drinking or smoking whatever it is you smoke here or being a . . . sexist *jerk*, I will not hesitate to fire you. You can't just act like you're the king of everything the way you do at school. You do not get to call me, or any other woman here, baby. And no more of that clapping crap."

Doris has balls. Or whatever women have that's way more powerful than balls—*strength*. I watch and wait for him to explode back at her, but Grant just nods and says, "Yes, ma'am," and I don't even think it's sarcastic. I reach into the yellow bag again, and this time it's empty, so I put the suitcase in the for-sale luggage stack, say my farewell to Natasha, and start on the next.

"OK," says Doris. "OK." She puts a clipboard next to him. "Good stuff goes on your list and in the sale pile. Bad stuff, anything that's truly garbage or so gross you can't even tell what it is, goes into the discard receptacle over there." She points to a huge waste bin in the far corner of the room. "We don't resell food, so it's up to you what you want to do with it. There's an even bigger dumpster out back if we need it. If you aren't sure about anything, just ask."

Grant raises his hand.

"Yes?" asks Doris.

"Do you have a pen I can borrow?" he asks. He turns his grin on her, but she stays stoic, handing him a Bic from the table.

He picks up his clipboard, and we all get to work.

·　·　·　·　·

An hour and a half later, I've gone through an Amanda, a Parker, and a Roy. I've found:

1. A rolled-up *Titanic* poster (Vintage!)
2. 2 brand-new dog toys in packaging: a chew-thing that looks like a giant sausage and a stuffed eagle with an American flag in its claws
3. 12 pairs of socks, different colors, no holes
4. 6 books of various types/conditions, children's to adult
5. 2 designer purses, leather (They're full of what Doris tells me are "the usual accoutrements": Kleenexes, old lipsticks, grimy loose change, a wallet with the cash and cards missing.)
6. A new lavender bikini, still with the tags (In my size! I ask Doris if I can buy it, and she says yes. We even get a discount as store employees. Perks!)
7. Half a bag of rock-hard gummy bears (I throw those away, though I'm tempted to try one, just for the experience.)
8. 5 tank tops in white, gray, and black
9. 6 pairs of jeans, men's and women's

Yesterday Doris and I couldn't stop talking, but the presence of Grant has changed things. We're shy all of a sudden, or maybe it's that two of the people in this room seem to kind of hate each other. I turn my head back to my latest suitcase, which I've dubbed a Marvin. It's full of men's business suits, each in the same dark gray color; periwinkle blue boxer shorts (thankfully clean); crisp white button-downs; and an array of muted, solid-color ties. It's like walking into my dad's closet, except even my average-businessman-dressing dad has that purple tie with skulls on it that Jack and I bought him last Father's Day.

Doris breaks the awkward silence. "Grant, you're tall, can you get the box up there? That top one marked 'Tucson'?" She points to a shelf in the stockroom where a row of big cardboard containers have been stashed, different airport cities written on them in Sharpie. We watch as Grant stretches his arms up to grab the box with both hands and sets it gently down by her feet.

"Thanks," she says.

"You're welcome," he says.

I take this as a positive sign.

Then she grabs a knife and slices across the box in one brisk, badass motion. I look over at Grant, and he's looking at me with wide eyes, and I can't help it: I smile, and he smiles back. I turn back to Doris, hoping she hasn't caught this—I feel my loyalty should go to her. But she's busy pulling suitcases from the box and lining them up in a row for us to tackle. One of them is especially cute, in a purple leopard print—the sort of bag you imagine someone stylish using for weekends off in Vail or Miami.

"That's a total Daphne!" I say.

"Huh?" says Doris.

"I've been naming them," I confess. "The bags. They all seem to have a personality, you know? Right here, this is a Marvin, probably owned by a banker or someone in another dull but respectable job, a dignified family man"—and then I let out a scream, because as I pull out the last business suit, something drops out of it that is definitely not conservative or well-pressed or boring like you'd expect from a Marvin. I've clearly underestimated Marvin, because it is a sex toy designed all too realistically like a man's you-know-what.

"What is it?" shouts Doris.

"Are you all right?" asks Grant, who is suddenly right next to me, looking down at the plastic man-part that that has fallen to the concrete floor of the stockroom. It rests there casually as if it's totally cool being a representation of a penis, like it hasn't a care in the world, which it probably doesn't. "Jesus," he says. "You found a . . . dick?" Then Doris is on the other side of me, taking my hands in hers and squirting them liberally with a bottle of hand sanitizer.

"I should have given you gloves!" she's saying. "We have a whole box of them, just in case something like this—"

"I didn't touch it!" I say, though I accept the Purell anyway. "It dropped out of the suit!"

"You're lucky," she says. "I touched a dirty diaper a year ago, and I still haven't gotten over it. I've never found a penis, though."

"It's not a *real* penis," I say. "In fairness."

Grant nods. "She's right. *That* would be a truly disturbing thing to find in a suitcase."

Doris drops my hands, and she clutches her stomach. I'm worried she's about to throw up, but instead she lets out an earsplitting howl, with some snorts to go along with it. Grant joins her, and suddenly I'm leaning over, too, straight-out ugly guffawing. I realize it's the first time I've really laughed since I moved to Alabama.

"Stop, my abs hurt!" I say, wiping my eyes, and Grant says, "Well. I certainly was not expecting *that* on my first day on the job," and Doris adds, "I really want to know why he didn't pick up that suitcase!" and snorts again.

"Is this a regular occurrence?" I ask, and Doris shakes her head.

"It's never happened before. Usually the weirdest-slash-grossest thing is, like, um, boxers with skid marks." She blushes and looks at Grant.

"I don't know why you're looking at me. *I* don't poop in my pants," he says, and that sets off another round of laughing. This time, when we get quiet, we all stand there looking down at the dildo, nearly as embarrassed for it as we are for ourselves.

"What should we do with it?" I ask.

Grant pokes it with the toe of his sneaker. "Ladies, ladies," he says, putting an arm around each of us, "I have an idea." He smiles like the Cheshire cat, his eyes lifting up at the corners slightly, and he looks both angelic and so beautifully evil. "Let's hide it in Heather's car."

Doris shakes her head violently. "No. You do not want to see Heather mad. I've only seen her truly furious once, and that was enough."

"What happened?" I ask.

"Red lost Freddie," she said. "She'd been running around the store, and then she just wasn't. Turned out she'd gone next door to Baskin-Robbins, where they were giving out free samples. I found her there eating enough to give herself a stomachache. But she could have gotten kidnapped or hit by a car. . . . Heather's face was as red as Red's hair. You should have heard her yell. . . ."

"Hmmm," says Grant, this time looking directly into Doris's eyes. "What about putting it out in the store? We can say it's a personal massager, see what happens. Some of the women of this town might really be into it."

"Don't stereotype," says Doris, frowning again. "Maybe some of the *men* of this town would really be into it."

"It *did* seem like a guy's suitcase," I offer.

"Maybe they would," says Grant. "Far be it from me to judge."

"I'm the boss, and I'm pulling rank. We are not putting the dildo in anyone's car," says Doris. "Nor are we putting it out in the store for sale. Did you know it's illegal to buy or sell sex toys in Alabama?"

"Really?" I ask. "Not that I've ever bought or sold one, but why does anyone care?"

"Morality," says Grant. "The concept is very big around here."

"No sale," says Doris again. "No car. Any other brilliant ideas, aside from putting it in the trash?"

"I know!" I shout. It's one of those rare moments when I feel like I have exactly the right thing to say, and it comes out of me at the perfect time, not seven hours after the fact. "Let's give it a proper burial."

That's how the three of us end up burying the dildo in the store's shaggy back lot, just underneath an azalea bush. Grant uses a tiny plastic shovel, part of a beach set we found in the stockroom, and as he digs into the red Alabama soil, Doris and I sing "Taps," or at least, the one stanza we can remember. Doris, who had grudgingly put on a pair of latex gloves, places the dildo in its shallow grave, and Grant and I cover it up with dirt. We leave a tiny little gravestone made of a piece of cardboard box to mark the location for posterity. HERE LIES DICK, it says.

13
Daphne

After departing the big, gray room, the purple leopard suitcase had traveled from place to place for what felt like an interminably long time in a plastic container with a bunch of other suitcases. The wheels churned underneath as the driver drove, and it seemed this was simply the suitcase's life now, on the move forever but never getting anywhere at all. The only thing to do, it seemed, was accept it.

But then the truck had stopped, and a human had lifted the plastic container out, and removed several of the suitcases. They were put in a large cardboard box and stored in a smaller gray room. Another human picked them up and put them in the back of another vehicle and toted them to a building where they were placed on a high shelf in a stockroom, along with many other items. The suitcases waited some more in this new place. And waited. Until a boy had reached up high for them and brought them to the floor, and a girl had opened the box and lifted the suitcase out, and another girl had given—her—a name. Daphne.

14
Grant

After a week at my new job, my argument that my bosses
might need to get in touch seems to have worked. Mom's
stopped taking my cell phone away at six p.m. every night in
an effort to keep me from coming into contact with any of my
"bad influences"—it's way easier to blame other people than it
is to blame me, even if she doesn't know exactly who to blame.
So after she picks me up at the store and drops me off at home,
before going back out to her Junior League meeting (I got
reamed for the casserole, but I think it's also what ultimately
got me out of the house), I head upstairs to my room and start
making calls.

The first is to Chassie, who, not surprisingly, doesn't answer.

When her phone goes to voice mail, I leave a short message: "I'm sorry, Chassie. Please call me back." I'm not even sure why I'm still trying, but it seems important that she know I feel awful about what happened. Then I call Bad Influence #1: my buddy Brod, short for Broderick, who was on the football team about nine hundred years ago, never left town after he graduated, works at the local grocery store as the assistant manager, and nowadays mostly buys booze for high school kids so he'll stay in with the popular crowd. Brod is one of the few people who knows about what happened in the spring—I was at his house that night, for a while at least—but he's never acted different or anything. I guess when your main thing is selling alcohol to minors for friendship, reproach is not high on your list.

Call me old-fashioned, but I like to make actual phone calls rather than texting (and don't even get me started on sexting) because, guess what: If you text, what you've said is traceable, especially if your mom is like my mom and has been known to check up on you through your phone. I mean, I'll text, too. I just have to stay on top of deleting anything incriminating.

Broderick doesn't answer. He'll hit me back; he always does. For now, I lie on my bed and wait. I start thinking about Unclaimed Baggage. Pawing through other people's crap that they never picked up from the airport, deciding what secondhand thing is worth selling, isn't exactly the dream of the high school quarterback. But in a way, it calms me. There's no booze around. I have something to do with my hands. And after Doris called me out for my Grant Collins act, I decided to try something new and just be myself. It's actually kind of nice.

My phone beeps with a text from Brod. Like I say, I've learned to stay on top of deleting messages.

What up, buddy? he says. **Just got tacos. Hang later?**

At least he's using the code. "Tacos" is Brod's word for alcohol—usually a case or two of Bud. We implemented it last year before the shit really hit the fan. If he says "burrito supreme," it means he's got his hands on a fifth of Beam. "Doing a Taco Bell run" is exactly what you think, though he might pair it with an actual Taco Bell run to keep his energy up.

The thing is, I don't really want to meet up for fake tacos or even real tacos. What I'd like to do is be normal. Have a family dinner and tell my mom and Brian and Bobby and Michael about my day, and hear about their days, and talk about what the next day might be like, too. I want to be the Grant Collins who is feeling like himself again, whoever that guy actually is. But I don't know if I know how.

My phone rings, and I pick up.

"Hey, man," I say, thinking it's Brod.

"Grant," answers my dad. I consider hanging up immediately, but I know he'll just call me back, and then he'll probably call my mom, and that will upset her, so I stay on the phone, but I say nothing.

"How you doing?" he asks.

I remain silent.

"Talk to me, son."

"Are you driving?" I finally ask, just to fill the void. He only calls me when he's on the way to somewhere else, which is appropriate, considering how he left our lives.

"I'm picking Gwen up from her shift at the hospital," he says. Gwen is his new wife, the one he left us for. She's a nurse, he's a doctor—talk about clichés—and they live in South Carolina and have two little girls I've never met. About a year after he ditched us, when I was ten, he wanted me to come and visit. He bought me a plane ticket, and I went so far as to get on a plane, but then I freaked. I started screaming and crying, and they had to let me out before we took off. Afterward, my mom told me I didn't have to do anything I didn't want to do. Then I got busy, and I guess Dad got busy, too.

"Your mom called," he says. "Sounds like you've been having a rough time."

I grunt. This kind of pisses me off. I know he's my dad, and I know he still sends his monthly support checks, but I feel like he kind of relinquished his fatherly role when he moved five hundred miles away.

"You're always welcome to come out here for a while," he says. "If you need a change of pace. Small towns can be rough, all those same stories circling around with nowhere to go. All the rumors—"

I'm pretty sure he's talking about himself and the gossip that followed when he split with Mom, and I'm over it. It's always been about him.

"I gotta go. Brian needs me," I lie. It's an attempted dig, mentioning my stepfather, not that Dad seems to notice.

"OK," he says. "Be good, son. I'm here, whenever you want."

"Sure you are," I say, and hang up. I stare at my wall a few seconds before picking the phone right back up again.

Pulling an all-nighter, I text Brod, which as a code doesn't really work that well, now that school's out, but old habits die hard. It means that after I put in an appearance at the dinner table, and after Mom and Brian turn in at around ten, I'll sneak out of my room, climb out on the big old tree with branches that stretch right outside the window of my second-floor bedroom, shimmy down, and jog the six blocks over to Brod's condo, which is on the edge of all the too-expensive, echoey houses in the fancy section of town. He'll be on his recliner. I'll let myself in because this is a small town in Alabama and no one locks their doors. He'll offer me something to drink, and I'll say yes, and help myself. I've done it a million times before. It's easy. It's all so fucking easy.

PS, I write. **You know there's an emoji for those things now?** 🍪

15
Doris

"So what's the deal with you and Grant?" asks Nell. It's been a couple of days since what I'm secretly referring to as the Dildo Detente, because even though I'm certainly not about to become a full-on Grant Collins fangirl, the tensions between us have been cautiously eased.

He's not in the store—he said he had a doctor's appointment this morning—so I guess now's the moment. I could tell Nell why I have such a grudge against Grant and his friends, why there's no way I'm letting him get too close, why I was so hard on him the day I hired him, and why I probably shouldn't have hired him at all. But how do you know when you can trust someone enough to tell them the truth? If you share your deep-est secrets, what might you lose?

So I hedge. "Oh, you know," I say, reaching into the black-and-white-checkered wheelie bag between us—Nell has dubbed it the Lauren—and pulling out a long, red velvet cape. "We were friends when we were kids, everyone was. But things changed in middle school. And ever since he got football-famous, he's been impossible. He hangs out with this sketchy crowd, including this guy Brod who graduated years ago but who buys everyone beer so they'll go to his parties. He's the chicken-throwing assistant manager I mentioned."

Nell wrinkles her nose. "Ew." She takes a couple silk shirts out of the bag, unfolding them for inspection and then folding them again.

"Grant drinks; I've heard stories. He flirts; you've seen it. And probably a lot more. Why would he stop, you know? Just because he's working here? I just think we should be careful," I say, and before she asks more questions, I change the sub-ject. "What's the latest with Ashton?" Most mornings Nell tells us how he texted her the cutest thing the night before, or how they talked on the phone for hours, or that she's counting the days until his visit, but today she hasn't mentioned him at all.

"He's at baseball camp," she says. "They take their phones away and only let them use them once a week." She makes a sad face. "I'm, like, a baseball widow."

"Except he's not dead," I remind her, and she laughs.

"What about you?" asks Nell. "What's your boyfriend situation? There must be a ton of guys in this town who want to go out with you—"

"Ooh, check out this, um, cool headband," I say, holding up a herringbone hair accoutrement that matches the Lauren perfectly.

She raises her eyebrows at me.

"My 'boyfriend situation' is nonexistent. And no, they don't."

"Are you sure?"

I press my hand against my heart, a vow of truth. "I swear to Cupid and Venus and Saint Valentine and the host of *The Bachelorette* that there are definitely not 'a ton of guys in this town who want to go out with me.'"

"Why not?" asks Nell. "You're funny, you're pretty, you're smart, you're an incredible artist. . . . I bet lots of guys would be into you." She pauses. "Oh no. I'm sorry. Is it that you aren't into guys? I shouldn't assume—"

"I do like boys," I admit. "Even though I frequently wish I didn't."

"Yeah, sometimes it seems like it would almost be easier to be gay, right? So many guys are awful, but all of my friends who are girls are totally great," says Nell. "If only I were attracted to them. I mean, I know it isn't actually easier—"

"My friend Maya is gay," I tell her. "I wouldn't call it 'easy' in this town."

Nell frowns. "People are shitty about it?"

"Depends who you're talking to, but for some people, if you don't 'fit in'—if you're not hetero, cis, white, a cheerleader, a football player, a Christian—well, you're an outcast. Maya's Jewish and gay, which is a double whammy."

"I want to meet her," says Nell. "If you like her, I bet she's awesome."

I come out with it. "Boys don't want to date me because I'm so far from the head cheerleader I might as well be captain of the girls' football team, but of course there would never, ever be a girls' football team here. I stopped going to church. Freshman year I organized a pro-choice rally, for which my parents nearly disowned me. I tried to get the school to stop having a prayer before each football game. It didn't work. I don't know exactly what I believe about God, but I definitely don't think it's right how some people around here use him to justify acting like small-minded bigots."

"Or use *her*," says Nell. "Why is God necessarily a he?"

"You're preaching to the choir. Or not preaching. You know what I mean."

"Ashton is biracial," Nell says. "His mom is black, and his dad is white. There were a few kids at school who said awful things when we started dating. I tried to just ignore them. I didn't know what else to do."

"You don't see a lot of that here, different races dating," I tell her. "When it does happen, certain old-school Southern folks will talk and talk and talk. They'll be nice to your face, maybe, but you'll be shunned. Everyone's supposed to stay in their proper place, whatever that means. White people go here, black people go there, and if you break the rules, you get the silent treatment—or worse."

103

"Byron and Nadine are black, though," Nell points out. "And everybody at the store is really friendly with everybody else."

"Red doesn't stand for any racist stuff," I say. "And everyone who works here is cool. I mean, there are plenty of people who live in the South who aren't racist. And plenty of people up North who are. It's not about where you live. It's about how you think."

"Yeah," says Nell. "Sometimes I would get comments from strangers, like when I was with Ashton at the mall or something. Usually from white dudes. I always wondered if that was why my mom thought I could do better. Was she scared? Did she think I should date a white guy?"

"Did you ever ask her?"

Nell shakes her head. "I don't know if I really want to know."

"You can't help who you love," I say. "And even if you could, you should still be able to date whoever you want. Consensually, of course."

"Where do you think Grant fits into all this?" Nell asks. "Is he a Southern person who's racist . . . or one who isn't?"

"I don't know," I say.

"We should find that out before Ashton visits," says Nell, and then she looks at me with a smile, like she's planning something. "And then we should find you a boyfriend. There must be someone worthy! We could double-date."

"My aunt Stella always told me 'Never get stuck on one guy—men will break your heart,'" I recall. "Better to play the field and do all the things you really want to do. I need to get into college! I have to get out of this town. Out of this state, ideally."

"Well, you can have a boyfriend and also leave your state," says Nell. "Look at me."

I laugh.

"It's embarrassing, but before I had a boyfriend, I wanted one so much. Nisha and Morgan and I would talk about it constantly—who we liked, what we imagined kissing them would be like, how we could get them to like us," she tells me. "We'd ask the Magic 8 Ball questions about it! And when I first started hanging out with Ashton, I couldn't believe it. That he actually wanted *me*."

"You *are* kind of a secret nerd," I say, patting her on the back.

"I know!" she says, laughing. "He doesn't even know how much I love detective fiction, or that I want to learn how to code, or anything. Why do we do that, hide our true selves?"

"Because the scariest thing in the world is showing someone who you really are. Because then if they don't like it, it feels like your fault! How did you meet him?" I ask.

"I first noticed him freshman year. I played field hockey, and he played baseball, and we practiced in adjacent fields. But we didn't talk until sophomore year. He said he'd wanted to ask me out the whole year before; he'd been so distracted by my ponytail swishing around that his game had suffered. But he was too nervous to say anything, plus, he needed to have a car to actually take me somewhere. That day he'd finally gotten his driver's license. We went to a movie the next night, and the rest, I guess, is history."

I smile, because this is all pretty romantic, and she smiles, too.

"He chose me, and that felt so good. It made me feel like I was a different person. More interesting than before. Beautiful. Cool. The kind of person who deserved a boyfriend."

I nod. I can see that, I guess. Having someone else value you means you don't have to work so hard to do it yourself—or at least, it can feel that way, even if it shouldn't. "But, Nell, you are interesting, on your own. You are choosable! I know that, and I've never even met your boyfriend."

"You think so?"

"Yes. I would choose you! I do choose you." I reach out and squeeze her hand for a second, and she squeezes back.

"I choose you, too," she says. "I'm really glad we're friends."

"Me too," I say.

She smiles and leans close to me. "Can I tell you a secret?"

I nod.

"I thought leaving Illinois was the worst thing ever to happen to me. I was so angry, but I also felt like my heart was broken. And then I met you. I've kind of started to like it here. I never thought that would happen. Now he seems so far away. He *is* so far away. I try to picture his face, and it's there for a second and then it kind of fades away. I miss him, and I really do love him, but can it ever be the way it was? Do we even have a chance? We're sixteen!"

We're done with the Lauren, so I pick it up and walk it over to the empty baggage stash. Next I grab the purple leopard suitcase that Nell named the Daphne. I lug it over and set it down in front of us, but I don't unzip it yet. I'm thinking.

"Maybe you do," I say. "My parents started dating when they were sixteen, got married at twenty-one, and they're still married. Or maybe Ashton gave you something in one place, but it no longer applies. Not every relationship is meant to last forever. I mean, we're only in high school."

"Maybe," she says. "But that breaks my heart."

"Just like Stella said," I tell her, smiling. "But, you know, when people aren't in your world, sometimes you lose their place, I think. They don't quite fit anymore. Or it hurts too much to think about them not being there. Like with my aunt. I'm scared my memories of her are fading, but sometimes I don't want to remember—"

"You can't forget!" says Nell. "That's how you keep her alive!"

"But she's not alive. She's dead."

Nell flinches. I forget how people react to that word. But what am I supposed to say? It's the truth.

"What if the whole 'keeping her alive' thing hurts too much?" I ask.

Nell gulps. "I'm sorry. I'm such a jerk. I mean, I still have my boyfriend, and your aunt Stella . . ."

"It's OK," I say. "Ashton is alive, and he's coming to see you. Unlike Stel, which is good, because as much as I really, really miss her, I'm not down with ghosts. Hey, have you told your parents he's coming to visit yet?"

"No. I'm scared my mom is going to tell me he can't come," she admits. "Part of me is also scared that if he does come, and I feel the same way about him, it's going to be too hard to let

107

him go again. Or . . . what if he gets here and it turns out I don't feel like I used to? What if I can't stand him?"

"That probably won't happen," I say. "But either way, you'll know."

"I just wish it wasn't all so hard." She looks at the Daphne. "Ooh, yay, I've been waiting for this one," she says. "I've decided she's a PR executive and was on her way to Bermuda or Miami or Paris for a big meeting, and all her stuff went missing, so she just bought a whole new wardrobe and decided whoever found this would be better off for it."

I unzip the suitcase. "Um," I say.

"Not another dildo," says Nell, leaning to peer inside.

"Even weirder." I feel around in the empty suitcase.

"There's . . . nothing in it?"

I turn the bag upside down and tap it, expecting sand or rocks or *anything* to emerge, but there's really nothing. I shake it, and there's a rattling sound. "What's making that noise?"

"Did you check all the pockets and zippered compartments and everything?" asks Nell, so we do that, too, but the search is fruitless. In all of my time working at Unclaimed, there's never been a suitcase that arrived with absolutely nothing in it.

"Witness protection!" says Nell. "She had to change her identity midway through her trip and took her clothes and left the suitcase behind."

"Amnesia," I suggest. "Not only did she forget to pick it up, she forgot to put anything in it!"

"She's a PI, and she's being tailed, and she left this suitcase at baggage claim to put everybody off her trail. It's a MacGuffin!"

"What's a MacGuffin?" I ask.

"It's a thing that moves things forward in a story but isn't *really* the thing that matters at all," says Nell as Grant walks in. "It was used famously in *The Maltese Falcon*. This statue was the MacGuffin all the characters wanted, but it was really a symbol for other things, like greed and temptation and money and stuff."

"Hellloooooo, ladies," he says. "What have we found today?"

"Emptiness," says Nell.

"MacGuffins!" I say, and he gives me a blank look. "The Daphne is full of air," I add. "And we want to know why."

He leans over to see and shrugs like only Grant Collins can. "Maybe someone brought a second suitcase with them because they wanted to do a lot of shopping at their destination. My mom has done that before, but she usually puts the smaller suitcase in a bigger one. Then they forgot it because it didn't have anything important in it."

"Wow, you really know how to ruin fun," I say.

"Can't you at least humor us?" says Nell. "This is a matter of intrigue, not Packing Tips 101! Like: Why does it make a rattling noise?"

"That's the sound of the spinner wheels moving around on their axes?"

"You're why we can't have nice things," Nell tells him.

"Sorry," he says, though he's clearly not. "Maybe she realized the suitcase was totally last year and upgraded for a new one, midtrip. Or all the clothes were so expensive they were stolen by TSA. Or everything fell out and got run over by a plane. Maybe it doesn't matter, because we're never going to know."

He's probably right. Still, when I lift the suitcase to put it in the rack of sorted luggage, I can't shake the feeling that it contains some secret we have yet to discover. What's the noise about? And it seems heavier than it should be if there's really nothing in it. I think about opening it up and searching again, but Nell's moved on to a hunter green Samsonite and Grant is breaking into one of the cardboard containers of miscellaneous goods left at airport security and never reclaimed, so I push the Daphne to a far corner of the room behind a bunch of other bags and get back to work, too.

A few minutes later, Red comes in to say hi. "Just checking on the gang," he says, but he sits down at the table like he plans to stay awhile. "What do y'all know about this thing people are doing, 'social media'?"

We stop unpacking and look at him. Grant stifles a laugh.

"My parents only just upgraded my flip phone!" I say. "Don't ask me!"

"Did it give you a direct line to the 1900s?" Grant asks.

"Yes," I say. "They called and told me they want their jokes back."

"I'm pretty good with that stuff," Nell tells Red. "Ashton and I Snapchat a lot."

"Well, Cat is leaving us to go back to school in August and get her combination business degree–MFA," Red says.

"Cat's leaving?" I say. "No!"

"I can't convince her to stay, even with the promise of first pick on doughnuts," says Red glumly. "So I need some savvy person to manage the Instergum for us."

Even I'm finding it hard not to laugh at that one, though it's mixed with the sadness of finding out about Cat's impending departure.

"Don't mock an old man," he tells us as we giggle. "Y'all are the digital generation! It's like breathing for you."

"I don't know if it's like breathing," mumbles Grant.

Nell's eyes are wide and excited. "I'd love to do it!" She turns and looks at me and Grant. "If you all—y'all—will help me."

"Sure," says Grant, shrugging.

"I can try," I say. "Wait, was that your first *y'all*?"

"Yes!" says Nell. "How did I do?"

Red gives her a thumbs-up. "Y'all are true heroes to an old man who doesn't even have a Tweetster account."

We manage to keep straight faces as he gets up from the table. "I'll send Cat back after lunch so she can give you a tutorial and get you all the passwords you need," he says. "And stay tuned. Heather's planning a little going-away party for Cat in August—everyone's invited."

"We'll be there," I say.

Red gives us a wave and is out the door, but when we burst out laughing, he pokes his head back in. "I know you're having a hoot at my expense, I just wanted you to know that I know." He waves again. "Later, taters."

"That guy is really the most cheerful person in the world,"

marvels Grant. "I wonder what he was like when he dated my mom."

"Red dated your mom?" Nell opens her eyes wide in surprise. "Oh my God. I can't imagine. . . ."

"Small-town life," I say, just as Grant says exactly the same thing. He looks at me, and I look at him, and we say the same thing next, too, that silly joke from when we were kids playing together and football and popularity and puberty hadn't changed anything yet: "Jinx. You owe me a Coke." He gives me a big smile, and I find myself hoping that maybe, just maybe, Grant isn't just like everyone else in this town. Maybe deep down he's a little bit like me.

16
Nell

It's my day off work, but after I send a **MISS U** ♡ **U CAN'T WAIT TO C U!!!!** text to Ashton—he may not have access to his phone, but when he gets it back, I want him to know I've been thinking about him—I spend the morning checking the store's Instagram account from bed. Cat's not officially gone until August; I'm her trainee until then. We met the other day, and she gave me free rein to post as I see fit. So far I think I'm nailing it. I upload a photo of the disco leggings and sparkly platform shoes that were in the Natasha, and I throw on a quick caption: *Who's ready for a DANCE PARTY? #summervibes #disco-sensation #baggageclaimed.*

I can't believe my luck in getting to run this account. Unlike my personal Instagram, which is basically just my friends back home, it has thousands of followers already. The experience is going to look great on my college applications. Plus, it's fun.

I spend some time reading all the new comments. Everybody loves the skeleton from the inventory closet; I posted his picture with the caption *Meet the official new Unclaimed Baggage mascot. Who wants to name this guy?* Options range from Mr. Lost 'N' Found to Skele-Store to Unclaimed Bag-a-Bones. Where do people come up with this stuff?

After I finish 'gramming, I lie in bed a few more minutes, trying to psych myself up to tell my parents about Ashton and his plane ticket. When I finally go downstairs, my mom is reading the paper and wearing, for the love of God, a bikini. It's actually kind of embarrassing how good she looks, given that she's closer to fifty than she'd like anyone to know. Dad is next to her in a T-shirt and swim trunks, finishing a stack of pancakes. "Are you two going to the beach or something?" I ask, grabbing a plate for myself.

"We thought we'd check out the water park," says my mom.

"It's practically in our backyard," Dad adds. "We have to go at least once this summer. What if it's so great we want to go twice?"

"*Have to* is a strong word," I say as Jack walks into the room. His little-boy barrel chest emerges from the waist of baggy neon yellow trunks, which engulf his skinny legs. On his face there's a bright-yellow mask, and he's pretending to put his face in the water as he walks, his arms churning imaginary waves at the sides of his body.

"Mmmrph," he says, from behind the mask, which I lift off his face. "Hey!" he yells, pulling it back down over his eyes. "Do I just rip things off *your* face when you walk into a room?"

"Sorry," I say, laughing. "I wanted to see who the merman was."

He lifts the mask on his own and fixes me with a fierce, presumably mermannish, look. "*Have to* is two words," he says.

"What?"

"You said *have to* is a strong word. *Have* and *to*—that's two words. Just sayin'." He grins and puts the mask back on his face. My brother. Sometimes it's nice to have an adorable baby brother who's way too smart for a seven-year-old. Sometimes it's annoying as hell.

"Go put your suit on," my mom tells me, and I make a face. "Come on!" she pleads. "We haven't had a family outing since we moved here! Spend some time with us! You're so busy *working* all the time." She smiles and winks, but a surge of anger rises in me. First she makes me get the job, then she tells me I'm doing too much of it? And what about *her* relationship to work?

"*Mom*," I say, but Dad gives me a look, and I know I can't argue. "Fine, fine, fine. Can I ask a friend to come?"

Their eyes light up in unison.

"Why, sure," says Dad, and Mom smiles as Jack spins around in a circle wearing his dumb mask and sing-chanting, "Have to, have to, have to!"

The talk about Ashton will have to wait.

17
Doris

I used to love my days off, especially Sundays. But ever since Aunt Stella died, I've sort of dreaded them. She'd been a Buddhist since she was eighteen, so she never went to the church in town. And then I stopped going, too. Instead, we'd binge-watch teen dramas, or she'd tell me about what it was like to fall in love, or she'd read me poetry from one of her favorite writers, Mary Oliver, who was "spiritual," she explained, but not "religious." We'd cook and eat lunch together, and she'd listen to whatever I had to say. Sometimes we'd even sit and meditate together. My parents would come home and call us two peas in a pod, and we'd look at each other and smile because we knew it was true.

My parents didn't like that I decided to stop going to church, but Aunt Stella defended me. She said it was my choice and that no belief should come out of being forced to do something. And they listened to her, though I could never figure out why. I'm surprised they haven't changed their tune now that she's gone, but maybe they think I'm too far gone, too.

Today, I've already read Stel's favorite Mary Oliver poem, "Wild Geese," twice, and then reread Maya's last postcard, wondering what's happening with her and her crush at camp. I'm bored and sitting in the living room by myself, flipping channels on the TV, when my phone beeps. I've got a text from Nell.

What r u doing? it says.

Hi, I write back. **Not much, u?**

My parents r INSISTING we go 2 water park. Come w? PLS? she writes.

I don't think I can, I type. I have been to the water park, and the results were disastrous.

Why not? she writes. **Please please please please?**

I don't write anything for a minute, and she sends a string of sad-face emojis.

My parents will pay for your ticket! she writes. **Seriously, they're so excited I have a friend . . . PLS?**

I look at the phone, remembering our conversation about choosing each other from the other day. And before I know it, I'm writing, quickly so I can't change my mind, **OK! I can be there in 45** ☺

My phone buzzes back immediately. **Yay! I'll b out front** ♡

I get up from the couch and run upstairs; I need to keep up

the momentum if I'm going to go through with this. I dig through my dresser drawers to find the two swimsuits I own. One is a conservative navy one-piece, the kind of bathing attire you might rely on if you were a practical, sporty type who really liked doing regular laps in pools, which I do not, but my mom bought it for me when she decided—without asking—that I should join swim team as an extracurricular to help me make more of the "right kind" of friends. I shudder at the idea of being near naked around so many people, plus, I hate getting water up my nose, so that never happened. The other suit is a bikini. I bought it myself on a whim from the store; it was such a good deal, and it seemed like the kind of thing I'd eventually want to wear, or become the sort of person who wears. It's black and strappy and so new it still has the sticker on the bottoms that says FOR YOUR PROTECTION.

I hold the two pieces in my hands and take a deep breath. I tie on the top, then yank off the sticker and slip my legs into the bottoms, gasping at how vulnerable all my exposed skin looks. Then I throw on jean shorts and one of my softest old T-shirts, slip my feet into flip-flops, and grab a beach towel from the hall closet. I write a quick note to my parents telling them where I'll be, and I'm out the door before I can change my mind.

I've always thought it funny that the water park promotes itself as having "America's First Wave Pool." Other water parks around the US make the same claim. So who was actually first? And—do you really *want* your wave pool to be the very first built?

Ours is huge, with this underwater mechanism that churns up a crashing surf at various intervals, sort of like the ocean if it were on a timer. At least once a summer, a rumor starts up that a kid has gotten stuck in the mechanism. According to Aunt Stella, these suburban legends swirled even when she was a lifeguard, but it's never actually happened, thank goodness. In another section of the park, there's an Olympic-size pool with five diving boards at various heights, the top one dubbed "The Suicide." (No one has ever killed themselves on it, though I've seen a few drunk kids come pretty close.) Then there's the part of the park known as the "beach"—a small patch of sand adjacent to the river, its murky water roped up in a section with a platform you can swim to. At the far end of the park, there's the waterslide, a set of tubes and tunnels with looping twists and turns that drop into a smaller, oddly warm pool you just know all the little kids pee in.

The waterslide was where the thing happened that stopped me from going to the water park. It was also the thing that stopped me from going to church, and, I guess, it's one of those things that really changed the course of my life.

OK, enough suspense. Thanks for following along. As your reward (though maybe not mine), I will tell you about what happened at the water park, the reason I stopped going there, the reason I bailed on church, and the reason I consider Chassie Dunkirk my nemesis and still am not sure Grant Collins can be trusted.

Imagine your flashback *doodly-doodly-doo* music here. I am twelve years old. I have a crush on a boy from our church group, Teddy Scruggs, who moved away a couple of years ago, which is handy, because if I had to see his face, I think I might die or vomit, or die while vomiting. It's a sticky-hot July Sunday, and after service, the whole group has an outing to the water park. I have on an old swimsuit with Minnie Mouse on it that I'm starting to realize might be embarrassingly babyish, what with the cartoon character and the straps that tie in little pink polka-dot bows at the shoulders. I'm too oblivious to realize I'm supposed to suck in my stomach, however, so it just juts out there, my torso convex rather than concave like the midsections of models. The rest of the girls have on sleek, multicolored one-pieces or, in the case of Chassie, a tiny floral bikini that my mom would say is way too grown-up, even for the sixteen-year-old me. Chassie and Grant are already acting more like adults than kids. Despite the rules, they ride down on the same mat together; they are cool enough for the lifeguards to let this go on. I have heard that they kiss, and more, in the dark tunnel.

Teddy has a wide, open face and a sly smile that churns up my stomach. Sometimes I think about him before falling asleep at night. He's been paying attention to me, teasing me, tugging my hair. Then Chassie pulls me aside and whispers in my ear.

"Hey, Teddy is into you," she says.

I don't know what to say back, so I just grin.

"Did you hear me?" she says louder. "Teddy likes you. He's hot. You should go for it." She starts to walk away, and then she turns back and offers me a warm smile. These are rare from her now, even though we used to be the kind of childhood friends who attended each other's birthday parties. I have felt her growing away from me, moving in directions I don't understand. This gesture, though, reminds me of when the old Chassie would split her Hostess CupCake with me at lunch if I'd give her one of the ham-and-cheese biscuits my mom had packed for me. There is friendship in it.

"What should I do?" I ask her, and she smiles again.

"Oh, Doris, you're such a noob. He's going to ask you if you want to go down the waterslide together. Just say yes."

I make up my mind that I will. What do I have to lose?

At the top of the waterslide, it happens. He's in front of me in line, with Chassie and Grant ahead of him. "Hey, Doris," he says quietly. "Wanna do something cool?"

I silently thank Chassie for preparing me for this.

"What is it?" I ask, playing like I don't know.

"I'll go first, and I'll wait in the tunnel for you. When you see me, you get off your mat and onto mine. Tag-team water-slide. It's really fun."

"That's against the rules, though," I say, pointing to the sign posted right in front of us. "We could get hurt."

"I won't let you get hurt," he says. And I leave it at that, because this is way more exciting than anything I've ever done, and it seems like Teddy Scruggs might really like me.

Grant and Chassie go first. A few seconds later, Teddy flops onto his mat and turns back to wave at me. "See ya," he says, and he's gone. I pause, but the lifeguard pushes me on: "Don't hold up the line!" he lectures, so I sit on my mat and go.

My ears are full of the sound of water rushing by, strange echoes that seem to come from all around me. I start to enjoy the way I am being moved on this mat by powers other than my own, the lapping of the pleasantly lukewarm water at my sides. Then, suddenly, I am no longer moving. Teddy Scruggs is in the tunnel, where he has stretched his legs and arms out wide in an abrupt curve and stopped himself to wait for me.

"Hi!" I say in surprise, and he says, "Hi," and then his mat is partly on top of mine, and he's on top of me, kissing me, his hand down the top of my Minnie Mouse bathing suit. I struggle underneath him because this does not feel right at all. I say, "Stop!" but he keeps going.

"I know you like me," he says. "Chassie told me."

I try to wriggle away, but there's nowhere to go, and he is stronger than me, his boy-grip on my wrists. I try to scream, but it comes out "Mmmfhhhfrrr" because he's kissing me again and grabbing different parts of my body, and we're moving down the tunnel. After what feels like ages, we finally pop out of the end, face-to-face with Grant and Chassie, who are standing knee-deep in the water, watching. I am so embarrassed, as if it's me, not him, who has done something wrong.

Chassie starts laughing, and I realize my swimsuit top is halfway down; he's ripped one of the babyish bows in half. I hold the swimsuit up to my chest and try to run out of the water, which, have you ever tried to run in water? It's slow-motion hell, especially when all you want to do is get away.

Grant says to Teddy, "Scruggs, your technique needs improvement," and Teddy laughs and says to Grant, "Naw, she liked it. She'll be back for more."

I feel like I'm going to be sick. After I drag myself out of the water, not looking back, I run to the bathroom, where I throw up once, then again. When I compose myself enough to emerge,

I find our church youth-group director, Mrs. Stokes, and tell her I need to go home, something bad happened. Instead of listening to my side of the story, she launches into a talk about appropriateness in the eyes of the lord. "Teddy told me everything," she says as everyone watches. "This is an embarrassment to our group, young lady. I don't know what got into you, cajoling that boy to go down the waterslide with you!" She eyes my swimsuit—which I'm holding up with one hand—suspiciously, as if Minnie Mouse, with her peppy stance and cute gloves, were some kind of temptress. "We women must behave as God intended."

I am too scared to say a word to defend myself. What if this was my fault? I *did* break the rules. I'm terrified I'll cry, and that will make everything even worse. What I wish I could do now is go back in time and shout this: *Why don't boys get blamed or held accountable when they put their hands on girls' bodies? Why are girls the ones who have to look or act a certain way so they don't "entice" the boys? Aren't boys capable of doing the right thing, even if a girl is wearing a swimsuit, or leggings, or a crop top . . . even RIGHT IN FRONT OF THEM? And if they're not, why do we let those boys out of the house?*

Instead of uttering any of that, I throw up a third time, right on the ground next to Mrs. Stokes's polished toenails, and she looks down, purses her lips, and—get this—rolls her eyes, as if I'm puking for attention. "You should have your parents come and get you," she tells me. Beyond her I see Teddy and Grant and Chassie staring at me. I know I'll never forget their faces.

I call home in tears, and I'm lucky enough to get Aunt Stella, who's been living with us since moving back home after a year of working in New York City. "I'll be right there, honey," she says, but it's not until I see her, storming toward me with rage in her eyes over how I've been treated, that I start to feel like I can breathe again. She hugs me and wraps a towel around me, and then gets me a ginger ale and tells me to wait for her by the picnic tables. Then she marches over to Mrs. Stokes and starts talking fast and low. I can't hear what they're saying, but Mrs. Stokes keeps trying to interrupt, and Aunt Stella is not having it.

Finally, Aunt Stella returns, grabs my hand, and says, "Let's go!" Her face is flushed and sweaty. "This town," she says, shaking her head. "It never changes."

"What did you say to her?" I ask.

"That was for adult ears only," she tells me. "I'll explain when you're old enough, I promise."

"Do I have to go back?" I ask. "Do I have to see Teddy Scruggs again?"

"No." She grabs my hand and holds it, squeezing hard.

When we pull into the driveway at home, my parents are outside waiting for us. My mom's got her hands on her hips and that look on her face that says, *This is not acceptable.* My dad, as usual, is going along with my mom.

"What did you do?" my mom yells at Stel as we get out of the car.

My aunt is unapologetic. "Something that should have happened a long time ago. I told Priscilla Stokes that Doris was quitting youth group."

"I beg to differ," says my mom, who is now as flushed and sweaty as her sister. For two people who share genetic makeup, they sure act like polar opposites. "I just got a call from the church saying that you used profanities while speaking to Mrs. Stokes. And that Doris had broken the rules at a youth-group outing. It is not in your purview to quit youth group for Doris—or to make other decisions for her, may I remind you."

"It's just wrong, Anne," says Stella. "Doris was assaulted by a boy on the waterslide. Instead of listening to her side of the story, Priscilla took the boy's side and blamed Doris for causing all the trouble! Priscilla has always been a hypocrite, even when she was a teenager. I can't believe they made her the youth-group director. Those poor kids. It's irresponsible is what it is. It's religious abuse!"

I'm dying to know what Mrs. Stokes did back in high school, but it doesn't seem the time to ask.

My mom turns to me. "Is this true?" she asks. "About what happened?"

I nod.

"Are you OK?" she asks.

I nod again, wondering if I am. "But he touched me. He ripped my swimsuit."

She wraps her arms around me.

"I don't think she should have to give up going to church," my dad says in a rare intervention into Mom–Stella drama. "The boy did wrong, not Doris."

"How do you expect her to go there and have to look at the face of the boy who groped her, who, by the way, smirked at us the entire time we were in the park?" asks Stella. "Teddy Scruggs is a little shit!"

"Language, Stella! I'll have a talk with the Scruggs family," my mom says. "You've done enough."

I notice that old Mrs. Peachtree, who lives across the street, is staring at us from her front window, and my mom sees, too. "Let's all go inside," she says. "We don't need to get the neighbors involved."

Stella sniffs. "The neighbors might as well know the truth, too. Keeping all this stuff secret never helped anybody. You know that as well as I do."

I want to ask what she means, but I'm quickly shushed. Mom tells me to go take a long bath, that I'll feel better after that, and that I can use her bubbles. I know this is so the adults can talk privately, but I do what she says—even if the conversation they're having is about me and I should probably get a say in it. The bathroom isn't too far from the kitchen, and I try my best to listen in on their conversation, but all I can hear are muffled voices, and at one point, something that sounds like crying. I can't tell who it is, though. When I come out, all strawberry smelling and fresh, Mom and Stella are cooking dinner together and seem at ease, at least, for them. There are no visible tearstains. Dad's on the couch watching some show recapping the greatest moments in Alabama football. I sit down next to him, and he pats me on the knee.

"Watch here, Dori," he says, using his nickname for me. "This is from the Sugar Bowl in 1993. I was at that game! The move this guy's about to do is called 'The Strip.' It's a classic!" I swear there's nothing that makes him happier than this.

"Wow," I say, watching a guy rip a ball from another player

and run down the field only to be tackled. "Interesting." I stay and watch a little longer, because even if I will never understand why he cares so much about what brawny guys wearing tight pants and shoulder pads do on the football field, he's my dad and I love him, and I feel safe next to him. When I've had enough, I get up and help set the table for dinner. It's not until we're slicing into the pie for dessert that my mom tells me I can take some time off from church, for a while, if I want, while they get things straightened out.

"This is your own decision, though," she says. She gives my aunt a look, but Stella only smiles calmly.

I imagine walking into church, everybody's eyes on me, or Teddy Scruggs getting me alone and trying to do what he did again—or worse. I think of Chassie, laughing at me, and the disgusted look on Grant's face. I picture Mrs. Stokes. What she thinks goodness is isn't what I think it is. It isn't what goodness *should* be. Something in me churns, and I'm not sure I can eat my pie.

"I want to take a break," I say.

My mom's mouth turns down, and her forehead wrinkle creases deep. My dad seems like he's about to say something, but instead he just coughs abruptly. Neither of them fights me.

"Want whipped cream, honey?" asks Aunt Stella.

I nod, and she squirts a shot of Reddi-wip onto my pie. I take a big bite. It tastes great.

. . . . .

That night, Stella comes into my room after my parents have said good night, each of them hugging me an extra-long time. She sits at the side of my bed, and she touches my cheek, tucking my hair behind my ear. "I want you to know you can always come to me if you have a problem," she says. "Whatever it is. I will listen to and support you, and we will figure it out. Even—especially—if it's something you're afraid to talk to your mom and dad about. I will always believe you and do my best to help."

"Was someone crying earlier?" I ask her. "When I was taking a bath and you were talking? And what did you mean about Mrs. Stokes always being a hypocrite?"

"I'll explain all that to you someday soon," she says.

"Why not now?" I ask.

"It's better if you're a little older. It's some pretty grown-up stuff." She rubs my shoulder. "I know, that's the worst, making you wait to hear the truth. Just know . . . sometimes people in authority positions don't do the right thing, not in the slightest. A lot of things aren't very fair, honey. But the most important thing you can do is be strong and not worry about what everyone else says or does. You do you."

"How, though?" I ask. "How can I go back to school?"

"You walk in there, and you hold your head high, and you show them what you're made of," she tells me. "It's hard to be brave. But every time you do it, it gets a little bit easier."

At school I got called Dor-pukus, which isn't even a pun or a funny joke. Teddy would stare at me in the halls, and sometimes make faces, but I steered clear of him, and by the end of eighth grade, he'd moved away. Chassie alternated between ignoring me and smiling at me knowingly. Grant avoided me entirely. Every once in a while, my parents would get after me about going to church again. I'd fight them, or Aunt Stella would fight them for me. Eventually it seemed like they'd dropped it. I couldn't believe they'd just forget, but I wasn't going to bring it up if they weren't.

For a while it seemed like the waterslide incident was all I thought about, and then, like all memories, it started to fade. I threw the Minnie Mouse swimsuit away, got new ones, got older. But a memory like that never goes away entirely, and as I turn my Honda into the big parking lot that runs along the entire front of "America's First Wave Pool," everything that happened that day feels achingly clear.

18
Grant

At 10:30 last night, I shoved a couple of pillows under my covers—the oldest trick in the book—and climbed out my window, my backpack strapped on tight. I swung my legs around one of the hardiest upper tree branches and maneuvered my way down, muscles aching, because even though I'm digging through boxes every day at work, it's hardly the exercise I'm used to. I miss running and lifting weights, even if I don't really miss playing football. Having it gone, you'd think, would mean something, but what I long for isn't the game, it's feeling my muscles and my brain connecting and orchestrating this complex action that seems so simple if done right. And it's who I am when I'm doing that. *Someone.*

I touched lightly on the grass and sprinted out of my yard, hunched over and tight, like I had a football clutched between my arms and was headed for the end zone. By the time I got to the Humphreys' backyard, six doors from mine, I'd broken a light sweat and felt pretty good. I slowed down and started walking, traipsing through the sprinkler systems that folks had set to go off after dusk, for peak absorption. (This is according to Brian, who runs a lawn recovery service.)

Brod's condo is part of a neighborhood that my mom always lifts her nose at a little. It's not that far away, but it's different: a few rows of attached townhouses with carports rather than full garages, and tiny little slips of backyards. They're each about a third the size of our two-story house. "Houses like that are for divorcées and bachelors," I heard Mom tell a friend on the phone when the condos started going up a few years back, cheaper housing for "transitional types," as she put it. "They're going to bring down the value of the neighborhood."

My mom's concerns are founded, even if she doesn't know exactly why. After Brod graduated, back when I was still in middle school, his parents moved to Florida, and he took over his parents' lease and stayed around to run his own little 24-7 party house in their absence. I guess my mom was right: He is definitely a bachelor.

Brod's parties started out pretty awesome. There were people his age there, which lent a level of excitement beyond the regular high school party vibe, though plenty of sophomores and juniors and seniors and even a few popular freshman showed up, too. Why wouldn't we? There was always so much beer, so many tacos (ha, ha), so many hot girls, and you could do whatever you wanted, no chaperones, no rules. *Especially* for me. Whenever I walked in, someone would hand me a drink, pat me on the back, say something nice. If the team had just won a game, people would actually stand up and cheer. After homecoming sophomore year, a bunch of people lifted me in the air and hailed me as the reigning champion of the school, the town, the world.

Now when I walk in, it's different. With the team off at camp, it's pretty sparse. Which is actually a plus. When I arrive, Brod's still wearing his collared Family Mart shirt and khaki work pants, but he's put on his flip-flops and is leaning way back in his dad's old La-Z-Boy recliner, his feet in the air. The room is cloudy with smoke. There are a couple of guys I kind of recognize who have long since graduated. They're playing *Grand Theft Auto One Million* or whatever, and they all look like they have a raging case of pink eye from something that is most definitely not pink eye.

"HEY, BUDDY!" Brod yells, raising a beer at me with one hand and lowering his legs to the floor as he works the recliner knob with the other. Drunk Brod gets effusive. "It's been a while!" He stands up and grabs me in a bear hug around the waist and lifts me in the air. I pat him on the back a couple times before I extricate myself from his grip.

It's been only a few days, but I guess in Grant and Brod time that translates to practically a long-distance relationship. This girl walks into the room then, and I try to place her. Long, dirty-blond hair. Long, tan legs in ratty cutoff jean shorts. A bunch of thread bracelets around one thin wrist.

"Brod, you got any rolling papers—oh, hey-o!" she says when she notices me. "Grant Collins! Where you been hiding yourself?"

I must have a blank look on my face, because Brod interjects, "You remember Mercer," he says, and it's a statement, not a question.

"Maybe I'm not that memorable," says Mercer, confident that she most certainly is. "Grant's a big shot; he gets what he wants." She comes up close, draping a sinewy arm around my shoulder. Her nails are long and pointed and have pink polish chipping off them. I can smell her perfume, and underneath that, her sweat. Despite myself, my body is responding. I laugh and head to the kitchen, where I grab a beer from the fridge. This girl's gotten me rattled because I have zero recollection of hooking up with her, but it's clear that I must have. I pour myself a bracer of Jack in one of Brod's mom's old Christmas mugs, chug it, and go out back to get some air.

"Hey, Grant," says this kid from my class, Nicky Weaver, who's standing there in calf-high grass (no lawn recovery service for Brod) staring out at the sky. He's one of those superachiever student-government types, so I'm surprised to see him, but I guess summer changes things. He lifts his beer toward mine, and we let the aluminum cans ting against each other.

"Whatcha been up to?" he asks. "Last time I saw you outside the hallways of our humble high school, you were scoring for the wrong team." He raises his eyebrows at me. "Sorry, bro."

Since I've been pretty much in hiding lately, I haven't really had to deal with too many people who saw me mess up the way I did, running the wrong way down the football field and ultimately scoring for the other team. After that, I remember falling. I remember my head feeling like it was on fire. I remember the sound of cheering, but also the sound of booing.

Later, I remember walking into the party and how different it felt from all those times when we'd won, when I'd been the hero. The faces around me were hard and cold. I drank anyway. It felt better to drink. I think I finished a bottle of whiskey. I don't know. I remember leaving and insisting on driving, and the fear on Chassie's face when I started to lose control of the car. I remember the moment of clarity as I hung from the seat belt, suspended upside down. I hated myself as much as I thought I possibly could—except it turned out, I could hate myself even more.

From then, everything's a fog, but I know what people told me in the hours and days that followed. I took off running from the car, even though Chassie was hurt. Leaving the scene of the crime after breaking my girlfriend's arm by driving drunk makes me about the most massive coward in human history. I don't want that to be the guy I am, but people say it's true, and you can't argue if you don't remember.

Chassie dumped me the next day from her hospital bed. In one night, I totaled both my car and my relationship.

Now Nicky's practically daring me to talk about it. I wonder how much he really knows.

"Yeah, man," I say, taking another swig of my beer. "Don't rub it in." Maybe I'm having sympathy pains for that night; I swear I can still feel my head throbbing.

"You scored, and then you literally flipped over on the field; it was like you tripped on air," he says. "You were airborne, and then you were facedown on the field, and then a bunch of other huge dudes were right on top of you. Damn."

I nod and force a light laugh. He doesn't know about the car accident, at least.

Brod pops his head out.

"Y'all in for bong hits?" he says.

"Yes, sir," says Nick. He looks at me. "You coming, too?"

I nod and we go inside. We all sit in a circle, and Mercer plants herself on my lap, and pretty soon I stop thinking about football or much of anything at all.

· · · · ·

I head back to my house when the sun is just peeking over the horizon. I leave Mercer sleeping in Brod's guest bedroom, kissing her forehead as I go because it seems the gentlemanly thing to do, even though I'm pretty sure nothing about me counts as a gentleman at this point. I climb back up the tree, and Lord help me, I think I'm still drunk, but I hang on tight and don't fall. I make it to my window, and there's a moment when I think

I see a shadow of my mom sitting in my room, but no, it's just the reflection of the tree. I get into bed and pass out until the sun starts streaming hard-core through my bedroom window. I've forgotten to close the blinds.

After I get up to shut them, I can't fall back to sleep. It's Sunday, and even though I've got a dull ache in my brain from the whiskey, I have this funny idea: What if, instead of rolling over and closing my eyes like usual, drifting in and out of consciousness for the next few hours, I get out of bed, go downstairs, and eat breakfast with the twins and Mom and Brian before they go to church? This thought is so compelling that I actually rise and plant one foot in front of the other until I reach the bathroom, where I brush my teeth thoroughly, adding some Listerine for good measure and splashing cold water on my face. I notice a hickey on my neck and go back to my room to put on a shirt with a collar I can pop to conceal the evidence.

When I get to the bottom of the steps, which face the kitchen, the twins see me and start shouting, "Rant! Rant! Rant!" my home version of the cheers I used to get back in the stadium, except they still can't pronounce their *G*'s. I see the surprise on my mom's face.

"Morning, honey. I didn't think you'd be joining us!" she says. "There's toast and eggs, still warm. Help yourself."

I'm ravenous. I pile some food on my plate, then go sit next to the twins. Brian's on the other side of them, reading the paper. He looks up at me and smiles, offering me the sports section.

"No, thanks," I say quickly, taking the local news instead.

"Rant!" the twins shout again. It's like a spike in my head, but I ignore the pain. Mikey tries to feed me a spoonful of egg.

"Nom nom nom," I say, pretending to eat it, and they giggle. Brian sets aside his section of the paper.

"So, how's the new job going?" he asks. My mom is pouring herself more coffee in the kitchen and turns to look at me as I answer.

"It's pretty good," I say. "You know, it's weird. . . ."

"Oh?"

"Well, we unpack all these suitcases that people have lost," I say. "So we never can predict what we're going to find. The other day, there was this one suitcase, and when we opened it, there was nothing in it."

"Your mom packs like that!" says Brian.

"That's right," she says, walking over to wipe the twins' mouths. They're babbling at each other with yellow egg all over their faces. "You never know when you're going to need a little extra space for shopping."

"Well, we really think you're doing great," Brian adds. "We're very proud of you."

I can't really accept this praise, but I can't exactly tell them the truth, either.

"You know what we were thinking?" asks my mom. "What if you call your dad and tell him everything you've been up to lately? I know he'd love to hear from you." She comes over and puts her hand on my shoulder.

"I don't think that's such a great idea," I say, shrugging her off.

"Honey," says my mom. "You two should have a relationship. It's important. He *has* been reaching out, trying to mend things."

I stand up, dropping my fork on my plate with a clang. "Why should we mend things? So you can get rid of me?" I say, and my voice gets louder as I go. "I'm not going to forget what he did just because you have. Why should I talk to him? *He* is the asshole. Him reaching out doesn't change a damn thing."

"Please don't use words like that in my kitchen," says my mom. Brian is frowning at me.

"Why not, Mom? He cheated on you and left us both and decided to have a whole new family. I think that makes him an asshole, and I'm not going to stop saying it just because it's not 'polite.' Did you put him up to calling me the other night?"

She presses her lips together and breathes in slowly through her nose. I notice the twins staring up at me. Mikey looks like he might cry.

"Aw jeez," I say. "It's OK, buddies." I put my hand to his little cheek, and for a second, everybody's quiet.

Then Brian stands up. He's putting an end to this nonsense. "Ready, honey?" he says, looking at his watch. "Let's get the twins in the minivan."

Mom wipes her hands on a dish towel. "I need to fix my lipstick," she says, and heads into the bathroom, pulling the door closed behind her, hard.

Brian takes a kid under each arm like a football to tote them outside. He looks at me half-angry and half-apologetically, like he, too, is bummed I got the dad I did, or maybe he's just bummed about me. "You should think about what your mom said," he tells me. "Giving your dad a call could really help things, in ways you don't even know right now. And it would give your mom some peace of mind. She's hurting from all this, too. Don't take your anger out on her. There's no call for that."

For the peace of the family, I nod, even though I plan to think about my dad as little as possible. Brian goes outside to put the twins in their car seats, and Mom comes out of the bathroom. I wait for the yelling to start, but she's surprisingly calm.

"You know I don't want curse words in front of the boys," she says. "I expect you to respect those wishes when you're living under my roof."

"I know," I mumble.

"Maybe it's my fault. Maybe I haven't been there enough," she says. "I'm trying to do the best I can. Everything since your accident has been . . ." Her eyes well up, and I feel like a shithead yet again.

"It's not you," I say, because it's really not, and the last thing I can deal with is this guilt on top of everything else. "It's me. I'm sorry. It's all my fault."

This is why I'm better off hiding out in my room, hiding out at the store, hiding out at Brod's. Other people shouldn't have to deal with me.

Brian honks the car horn. "We can talk about this more later," she tells me. "But will you do me a favor?"

"Nothing to do with Dad," I say. "I just can't."

"Maybe you can talk to Dr. Laura about it, then?"

I nod again. It's so easy to nod. Nodding doesn't mean a thing.

"And maybe you'll think about coming to church with us again? When you're ready?" She's so hopeful I hold off from saying there's no way that's going to happen. They've let me off the hook for a while now since my weekends were usually taken up by football, and now that they're not, I'm too fragile to push, or so they think. I'd like to keep it that way. With everything I've lied about, I'd feel like a hypocrite sitting in the aisles and praying.

Once she's gone and the house is quiet, I glance down at the paper. There's a new recycling program the town is trying to get off the ground. Somebody's Shiba Inu has been stolen from outside the Family Mart. (I glance down at Rusty sleeping under the kitchen table and feel grateful for the nonjudgmental nature of dogs.) Cops are cracking down on speeding motorists on Main Street. Two drunks got in a fight outside the hospital, but handily, when one cracked the other's ribs, the emergency room was right there. *Ba-da-bum.* (I'm here all week, folks!) Aspirin is on sale at the drugstore. The town theater is putting on a performance of *Jesus Christ Superstar* next week. That reminds me of how Calvin Buttress stole the baby Jesus doll from the nativity back when we were in fifth grade. Not only did Doris locate the doll, she also found Calvin Buttress hiding in a stack of choir robes. (Because he was only eight, he was forgiven.)

Oh, and here are the DUIs.

All of a sudden I'm grabbing my phone, looking for a number I've never used. On my first day at the store, I watched her type in her digits carefully, admiring the way she was so purposeful about everything. I'm sure she meant me to have it for work reasons. But I really need to talk to someone, and none of my current friends can provide that service.

I text, **Doris—it's Grant. You around?**

I barely expect her to respond. I'm pretty sure she hates me for any number of reasons, even if lately in the stockroom things seem OK between us. A long, long time ago, back when we were kids, we were friends. Then, for a handful of years, I was somebody girls like her tend to hate. Now I'm not sure who I am.

It's a milestone, I think wryly. This may be the very first time in the post-puberty history of Grant Collins that I'm getting in touch with a girl without the intention of trying to get in her pants.

19
Doris

I catch up with Nell and link my elbow with hers, and she hands me the paper wristband that grants me admission to the water park.

"You didn't have to do that!" I say.

"My parents insisted," she tells me. "They're already inside with my little brother. Want to meet them? I don't think you really have a choice—they're adamant about getting introductions to all of my 'new friends,' and, um, you're kind of the only one."

"Of course I do," I say, and Nell leads me over to the section of the wave pool where her mom and dad and brother are sitting in lounge chairs. They're this perfect, adorable family; they even have matching towels with a fancy insignia on them. Nell sees me looking. "Those are from my dad's alma mater," she says. "He's obsessed with college merch."

They all stand up to meet me and shake my hand, Jack included, which takes me by surprise. In my town, you're more likely to get hugged than to have your hand shaken, and when I see a hand coming at me, it takes a second for me to remember to put mine out, too. Then Jack goes, "Mah pleasure, dahling. It's so very nice to meet you," in a faux-Southern accent, and I nearly burst out laughing.

"The pleah-shuh is all mine," I respond, in equally plummy Southern tones.

"Do you like wave pools?" Jack asks, his voice returning to normal.

I glance over at the water. It's a virtual sea of kids, yelling and floating and bumping into one another atop a film of sunscreen and whatever else is in that murky blue. I have to admit, it's less enticing than it once was, but I don't want to be one of those people who grows up and starts hating everything they used to think was cool. I still love stickers and teddy bears and chocolate pudding, so why not be a wave pool enthusiast, too?

"I bet it feels really good to jump in on a hot day like today," I tell him.

"Will you go in with me? Please?" he's asking, and I'm about to say, *Damn the grossness, forget about the chaos, I'll do it.* But Nell is dragging me away.

"Mom and Dad will go in with you," she tells him. "We're going to wander around and check stuff out."

"Yeah, buddy, stick with us," says Mr. Wachowski. He's sat back down on his deck chair and is paging through what looks like a school catalog. "Help me figure out if I'm an Auburn or an Alabama fan. What's better, orange and blue and tigers, or red and white and elephants?"

"I don't know," says Jack kind of dejectedly, and my heart breaks.

"Hey!" I say, kneeling next to him and whispering in his ear, "I'll tell you a story about the wave pool later."

"I like you, Doris," he says, patting me on the shoulder.

I look up at Mr. Wachowski. "Go with Auburn if you love an underdog with a cult following; pick 'Bama if you want to be a part of mainstream Alabama's storied football tradition. Don't tell my father I said that. He's a diehard 'Bama fan and would disown me for saying there's even an option—Roll Tide! But if you go with Auburn, start saying 'War Eagle!' as much as possible."

He grins at me. "Who do you like?"

"I'm a conscientious objector. I only watch synchronized swimming," I say, smiling back.

"C'MON!" says Nell, pulling me up.

"Wait!" shouts her dad, digging into his beach bag and pulling out a twenty-dollar bill. "Ice cream on me," he offers. Nell snags the money and tucks it into her pocket.

"Doris, you should come over for dinner soon!" adds Mrs. Wachowski, lifting her sunglasses to see me off. "Don't be a stranger!"

"OK, OK, OK, guys," Nell says, grabbing my hand. "Enough.

She likes you! You like her! We will see you again. We are teenagers who must roam and be free!"

And we're off.

"Ugh"—she's talking a mile a minute—"I think I terrified my parents into thinking I was turning into an elective mute when we first got here, so they're being embarrassingly supportive about any friendship efforts on my part."

"They're adorable," I say. "And so is Jack. Maybe we should introduce him to Freddie."

"Great idea," she says. "He doesn't really have anyone to play with yet. He just hangs with Dad, or me, because Mom's so busy at work. Sometimes having a brother is a pain. You're lucky you're an only child."

"I never really cared about having a brother or sister," I say. "I always had Aunt Stella. She was my built-in person. Maybe that's how Jack feels about you."

She stops and looks at me, just for a second.

"You're right," she says. "I should do more stuff with him. But first, let's explore!"

Then we're off again, Nell cracking jokes as she drags me to get ice cream—chocolate for her, strawberry for me—which we order in waffle cones. We do our best to eat faster than the ice cream can melt as I tour her around the water park, pointing out important sites and key information about the people we see. She listens with an intent expression, like she doesn't want to forget a single detail, so I go all in: how Tricklin Vendee peed himself in front of everyone at this very concession stand when we were in first grade (poor Tricklin, not least because he was named Tricklin); how Whitney Jefferson broke her wrist jumping off the high dive and then strutted around showing off her cast, which she claimed had been signed by Justin Bieber but turned out to be forged by her sister, for the entire first month of sixth grade; that behind the lifeguard lockers is where everyone goes to make out; and, oh yeah, that's the waterslide where I was groped by Teddy Scruggs. OK, I don't say that last part. But the ease with which it nearly floats off my tongue makes me wonder if I should go ahead and spill.

We've finished our ice cream and are sitting at one of the picnic tables that overlooks the pool the waterslides feed into. Kids are shooting into it from the end of the slides at regular intervals and hollering with glee.

"Remember when we were talking about boyfriends?" I ask.

"Yeah," she says, and waits.

"Well, something happened to me the last time I came to this water park. With a boy. He wasn't my boyfriend, though," I start, and the whole story comes out in a whoosh, like its own little waterslide.

Nell gets as mad as I've ever seen her. "Your aunt Stella was right," she says. "That awful woman who blamed you should not be in any kind of authority role, Doris. That is sexist and *wrong*. Where is she now?"

As far as I know, Mrs. Stokes is still in charge of the youth group at the church. I never wanted to see her again, so I haven't thought about how she might be shaming other girls, now. The thought makes me feel sick.

"She should be fired," says Nell. "And then can we track

down Teddy Scruggs and beat the crap out of him? Or at least scare him until he poops his pants? I'm very good at revenge. I have lots of ideas."

I smile. Even though I guess I always knew I hadn't done anything wrong, it feels so good to hear someone else say it, too.

So I tell her something else.

"Grant was there," I say.

"What?" she asks, her eyes wide.

"He was friends with Teddy," I explain. "He and his girl-friend, Chassie. They saw me with my top down. They laughed."

Nell just breathes, quietly. "He's your friend now. You should talk to him."

"Is he my friend? I don't know if that's true. What if he was part of the whole thing? It was so humiliating. It made me feel like I was nothing, a joke. That's partly why I stopped going to church."

"So that's why you've hated him for so long," Nell says. "You're not a joke, Doris. I promise."

"Thanks," I say.

She puts her arm around me just as my cell phone beeps.

"Oh my God," I say, looking at it.

"What?" asks Nell.

"It's Grant Collins. Texting me."

"What is he saying? How? Why? Oh my God!" says Nell. She stands up, so excited she's nearly running in place. "This is fate. Doris! You have to talk to him. What did he write?"

"He's asking if I'm around," I say. "Sit down, you're making me nervous!"

147

"Tell him we're here." She looks at the waterslide, and then takes a seat next to me on the bench. "I mean, if you want to? Remember what you said: that whatever happened with Ashton, either way I'd know. Don't you want to know with Grant, too? It's your chance to find out the truth!"

Do I want to know? I get out a "hi," before I delete it. "What do I even write?"

Nell grabs my phone. "I can do it for you," she says, dictating to herself: "Hey, Grant, I'm at the water park with Nell! What's up?"

I lean over her shoulder to watch the words come out. She throws in some emojis. I watch the bubbles that indicate that he's writing back. I feel nervous, and pukey, and . . . totally curious to find out what's next.

Mind if I come meet y'all? he writes, and Nell and I look at each other in semi-astonishment.

"Grant Collins wants to hang with us," she says. "The question is, do we want to hang with him? Here? After what you told me?"

"I guess there's only one way to find out," I tell her, and she smiles.

"Thatta girl."

Sure, she types, and gets a thumbs-up in reply.

Nell and I look at each other. She's exuberant; I'm slightly panicked. That's when a voice on the water park's loudspeaker interrupts this surprising development.

"Attention!" announces a woman. "Attention, park-goers.

May I have your attention! We have an urgent announcement. A seven-year-old boy is lost in the park."

This happens a lot. Pretty much every summer weekend, a kid will go missing at the water park. Everyone freaks out looking for him or her, and that terrible rumor about getting squished by the wave pool mechanism rears its head once again, and most of the time, the kid's off eating a Popsicle at the edge of the river. In the old days, I found several of them there.

"Jack Wachowski, your parents are looking for you. Jack Wachowski, age seven, please meet your mom and dad at the ice cream stand immediately. If anyone has seen Jack Wachowski, please contact the nearest park employee immediately. Jack has brown hair and blue eyes and is about four feet tall. He's wearing a neon yellow bathing suit."

"Maybe he was following us. He used to do that sometimes." Nell looks around, and I track her gaze, but there's no sign of him.

"Let's go back to the ice cream stand; by then I'm sure he'll be there, too," I suggest. She bites her lip. "Don't worry," I say.

My talent is about to come in handy.

20
Nell

Doris leads me through the crowds. In just a few minutes, we're back at the ice cream place, and there are my parents. Mom has her face scrunched up in worry, and Dad is tapping his foot, looking around like he's about to jump out of his skin. I run to them like I'm the one who's missing and hug them while Doris watches.

"You better put on more sunscreen," Mom tells me, touching my forehead. "You're burning!"

"The sun is too hot here," I say, which means nothing and everything all at once.

"What happened?" Doris asks my parents. "When did you last see him?"

"We were all in the wave pool together," says my mom. "And then he started playing with some other kids. We were watching and watching, and all of a sudden we didn't see him. There were so many waves, and so many kids. We told the lifeguard, and they got everyone out of the pool."

"But there was no sign of him," says my dad. "He wasn't in or anywhere near the wave pool, and he wasn't at the car, either. After that, we came straight here and reported him missing."

"Where's his stuff?" I ask. "Did he bring his mask with him?" This seems very important to me.

"That's gone, too," says Mom.

A tan, serious-looking lifeguard with a whistle around her neck arrives to give us an update. They've closed the wave pool temporarily and are searching the water. Nobody's found anything, and that's good news, but my mom goes pale. I can't stop thinking about how much I've ignored Jack since we moved. I even talked about wanting to be an only child! If Doris and I had gone into the wave pool with him like he asked, this never would have happened.

Then I have another horrible thought: *What if he's been kidnapped or, oh my God, drowned?*

Doris and my dad are talking quietly, and at some point, my dad puts his hand on my mom's shoulder and she nods, an unspoken communication between the two of them. Doris and my dad leave to go look for Jack. I'm crying and even though I'm neither wet nor cold, my mom is holding a towel around me. The announcement for my brother to come to the ice cream stand has been repeated more times than I can count.

I'm sobbing, with snot pouring out of my nose, when Grant Collins shows up.

"Hey, I've been looking for y'all everywhere!" he says. My mom straightens up as he says in his boy-almost-man voice, "Nell! What's going on? Are you OK? Where's Doris?"

"She and my dad went to look for my brother. He's missing," I mumble, and my mom glances from me to Grant and offers him her hand.

"I'm Nell's mom," she says. "Diana Wachowski." Grant takes her hand and shakes it gently. Suddenly I realize: He is flirting, or Mom-flirting, because he says in this voice that's him but not really him, "I can see the resemblance, Mrs. Wachowski. Good looks don't fall far from the tree."

Normally, I would groan loudly at this, but even in this moment of worry, my mom has the funniest little blush on her face. None of us are completely immune to the charms of Grant Collins, I realize. My *grandmother* would probably swoon around Grant Collins.

"This happens, Mrs. Wachowski," says Grant, and his Southern drawl picks up, so he sounds soothing as can be. "Every summer weekend since I've been coming here, which is basically forever, a kid will wander off, and management will check the pool and make announcements and look everywhere, and then they'll find the kid asleep on a towel at the beach, or with a bunch of other kids in line at the waterslide. This place is crawling with lifeguards. One of them found me ages ago, too." He shrugs like he's embarrassed by this confession. "I was five and licking a mint-chocolate-chip ice cream cone, right where we're standing now."

"I hope you're right," she tells him, and looks at me. "Why don't you two go search the park? I'll stay here in case he shows up. It would make me feel better if we're covering as much ground as possible."

"OK, Mom." I give her another quick hug before turning to Grant. "Do you want to help look?" I ask. I've finally stopped crying, but my voice comes out all quivery.

"Sure," he says.

"He's seven and has brown hair, and he's wearing yellow swim trunks," I tell Grant as we start walking. We're all business, scanning the crowds as Grant leads me to the small section of sand at the water park's edge that dips into the gray-brown Tennessee River, a portion of which is roped off for safe swimming.

"Hardly anyone comes over here," he says when we arrive, standing in the warm sand and surveying the beach. "Just families with babies and old people, mostly." I look out at the water, wishing for a glimpse of my brother's hair, or the splash of color indicating his mask. As Grant said, there are only a few families with little kids sitting on towels around us, and some senior citizens—ladies in sun hats sitting in beach chairs, letting the water rush up to their toes and bantering like they don't have a care in the world.

"Have you seen a little boy in yellow trunks?" I ask them, but they shake their heads apologetically. "Sorry, hon. We'll keep an eye out. God bless!"

"Let's go," I tell Grant. "He's not here."

Grant, however, is gazing at the entrance to the beach, where two teenagers have just walked in. It's a girl and boy. She's wearing the smallest string bikini I've ever seen in my life, and her hair falls in waves down her back. She could pass for a swimsuit model, minus the sling on her arm. The boy is tall and handsome and carrying beach towels and an umbrella. Grant draws back for a second, almost like he's been slapped.

The girl sees us and her eyes narrow. In an instant, she's facing her boyfriend again, and they're in an epic lip-lock. OK, then.

Grant is frowning.

"What?" I ask, and he shakes his head and lifts his shoulders again in the universal "it's nothing" gesture that he's so good at.

"Let's keep looking," I say, and we avert our eyes as we walk around the couple, who are still making out ostentatiously.

"Tell me about your brother," Grant says. As we walk to the next section of the park, I let loose a torrent of Jack info, how he loves bagels with peanut butter and banana and hates sleeping in the total darkness and always wants a new made-up story before bed. How he's obsessed with his dumb video games and does accents to make us laugh. How he's one of the people I love the most in the world, even if I don't always act like it.

"I feel so guilty about everything," I say, and Grant nods.

"I get it," he says. "I feel the same way about Mikey and Bobby. They got the shitty end of the stick having me for a big brother."

"No way," I say. "How is that possible? You're Grant Collins. I'm new here, and even I know that's something."

"That's kind of the problem," he says in this harsh way that prevents me from asking more. "Look, you didn't do anything wrong," he finally adds with quiet intensity. "It's not your fault. We're going to find him."

"I hope so," I say. My throat feels clenched tight.

"Maybe we should head for the waterslide. That would be an easy place for him to go unnoticed; it's thronged with kids. And you can't hear announcements when you're in the tunnel."

"OK," I say, glad to follow someone else's suggestion.

"I can take a look in the men's locker room on the way," Grant adds. "Maybe he went in there to pee."

"Good idea," I say. We're traversing concrete to the next stop, surrounded by blissfully unaware park-goers with zinc swiped across their noses and towels under their arms, bags with the latest *Us Weekly* poking out of the top.

"So, um, this is weird," says Grant. "But I feel like I should say something."

"OK," I say. I'm positive he's going to tell me about Doris, and what happened at the water park that day, and how it haunts him. I will then advise him to talk to her about it, and she will forgive him—because who can stay angry at Grant Collins?—and we will all be friends forever and no one will ever ruin it by moving away. Maybe the two of them will even fall in love. That would be quite the romantic twist.

But I'm wrong.

"When we were at the beach . . . did you see that girl, the

one with the long hair and the world's tiniest swimsuit, with that guy?"

"How could I miss her?" I say.

"Yeah. Well, she's my ex-girlfriend. Chassie. She broke up with me in the spring. Apparently, she's found a replacement." He laughs in a bitter kind of way. "Not that I blame her."

"Oh no," I say. "I'm sorry." I would have guessed Grant Collins was the kind of guy who was immune to heartache, a boy who got whatever he wanted and didn't worry about who he hurt.

He looks at me like he's waiting for me to say more, so I come out with the lamest, most insensitive cliché of my life: "Well, there are other fish in the sea."

Immediately I hate myself, because that's what my mom said to me when she told me we were moving, when I told her that she was destroying my life irrevocably by separating me from Ashton.

I didn't think Grant could feel the way I did.

He looks at me. "You had a boyfriend back at home, right? What's his name again?"

"Ashton," I say. "We're still together. Long-distance, and he's at camp now, but he's coming to visit in August—"

"Well, how would you feel if you saw him with someone else? Would you be like, hey, that's cool, plenty of other fish in the sea? Or would you feel like there had been a fishing crisis and salmon had dwindled to an endangered population and it's pretty much all your fault because you're the one who eats salmon?"

Fortunately, I'm rescued from answering this impossible question about love and marine life. Doris and my dad are walking toward us, and between them, holding their hands and swinging back and forth, is a kid in a yellow merman mask.

"Jack!" I scream, and run to them.

21
Doris

Afterward, everyone asks me how I knew. How did I go straight to Nell's dad, who, unlike some adults, actually listened and believed me enough to go along with my suggestion? What magic was it that gave me any idea, having met Jack only once, where he would be? (Duh, my greatest power, as discussed.) But how had I possibly known that Jack wouldn't be at the water park at all, which is why he wasn't responding to the announcements on the loudspeaker? How had I known, immediately, that he had gone . . . home?

We found him in his room playing a video game. One of those noisy fantasy parables in which cartoon characters compete to do something underwater, collect gold coins, save a princess. (Could a princess ever save a prince, for once?) You could hear the music from down the hall, the *bloop-bloop-bleep* of canned gaming noise. Mr. Wachowski's shoulders loosened, and he got a big smile on his face.

"Of course," he said to me. "Doris, you're a genius." I grinned, too, because even though I'm not a genius, it does feel good when I can use my talent to help someone else.

There Jack was, sitting in his room, his small hands manning the controls, his swimming mask dangling around his neck. We walked in, and he casually held up one finger, like, no biggie, he's in the middle of something, right? As if there hasn't been a search party called out for him?

"Just a sec, guys," he said, placid as pie. "I'm about to make it to level ten." We waited for a second or two, and he did. Then Mr. Wachowski picked him up in a laughing-crying hug, and Jack put his head on his dad's shoulder and patted his back and said, "Hey! It's OK, Dad. It's OK."

"How did you find your way back here?" asked Mr. Wachowski. "How did you get inside?"

"Remember, I have a really good memory. And the back door was unlocked," said Jack.

Mr. Wachowski shook his head. Now that Jack was safe and sound, it was time to lay down the law. "This will not happen again, son."

I walked out of the room to give them a second. Across the hall was Nell's bedroom. I wandered inside. She'd told me that before they moved, her parents said she could have it painted any color she wanted. She picked navy blue with glow-in-the-dark stars on the ceiling.

"If I couldn't live where I wanted, I wanted to feel like I was living in the sky," she said. The dark blue and faint pinpricks of light gave the room an otherworldly feeling, like I was orbiting outside of myself. There was a big collage hanging over her bed—printed-out photographs of Nell with friends she'd told me about, and a photo-booth strip of her and Ashton, cheek to cheek in one, kissing in the next, gazing at each other in the third, and laughing hysterically in the last one. Around those images were bubble-letter messages saying things like "MISS U ALREADY" and "Don't ever Change! xoxoxo" and "I ♡ u pony, ♡ ash" and "#teamhashtag #teamblessed #teamteam." I didn't know what it all meant, but it was clear she left behind something important.

· · · · ·

We're in the car driving back to the water park, and Mr. Wachowski is giving Jack another lecture about the rules, along with a stern eye in the rearview mirror.

"No more taking off," he says. "You cannot do that. You have to tell us where you're going. You cannot just leave because you feel like it. Do you understand?"

"Yes," says Jack.

"Do you know how worried we all were? That we thought something terrible might have happened to you? Do you know what your mom said when I called her to say you were at home?"

"No," says Jack in a small voice.

"She said, 'Tell him I am never letting him out of my sight if he does anything like this ever again.' Do you want to be under supervision for the rest of your life?"

"No," says Jack. His voice is getting wobbly. "I didn't mean to scare everyone. I just wanted to play my video game."

"*You do not get to just play video games without asking,*" says Mr. Wachowski, and his voice is quiet, but so intense I almost jump out of my seat. "It is not safe for a little boy to walk home alone. If you need to leave, you tell us, and we will go with you. We are a family, and we stick together. Got it?"

Jack nods. "I'm sorry."

"Good," says Mr. Wachowski, his voice softening. "I know moving has been hard, on all of us. I love you, buddy. Your mom and sister and I wouldn't know what to do if something bad happened to you. We need you!"

Jack and I both breathe deep, relieved that the scary part of the conversation is over, and Mr. Wachowski turns into the parking lot of the water park. We pass my car, still there from this morning, which now feels like a thousand years ago.

"Doris, tell me the story about the wave pool?" Jack asks me, reminding me of my promise to him earlier.

"You really do have a good memory," I tell him. As we walk into the park I share the tale of how Aunt Stella and her friends used to dive to the bottom of the pool after the park closed each night to collect stuff that had been lost by visitors. They found so many things, ranging from swim trunks (how did someone leave the pool without their swim trunks?) to a deflated unicorn floaty to a pair of high heels (what? how? why?). One time she found a diamond necklace, and the next day a rich lady from Birmingham came to the park to claim it and thanked her personally with a check for five hundred dollars.

"Wow," says Jack, his eyes big and round. "That could buy a lot of ice cream."

That's when old stories are forgotten in favor of current reality, which also happens to include soft serve. Nell and Grant—who I'd almost but not quite forgotten in all the drama—shout and start running toward us when they see Jack with me and Mr. Wachowski. Nell hugs her little brother in a tight embrace, and Grant shakes his hand solemnly. Then Nell peppers Jack with the same sort of questions their dad has already asked him, but Jack just answers patiently as we head for his mom, who's waiting by the ice cream stand with tears in her eyes. She wastes no time laying into her son for leaving the park.

"I will not let you out of the house until you are fifty years old if you ever do a thing like that again, Jackson Augustus Wachowski!" she says so loudly that people at a nearby picnic table turn and stare. "We were so worried!"

"Yes, Mom," he says, looking at her with big eyes. "I'm sorry, and I love you."

"I love you, too," she says, getting weepy again.

Gradually, the tension starts to fade, helped along by another round of ice cream, compliments of Mr. Wachowski. Jack is sitting on his mom's lap, and Nell is wearing her brother's merman mask like a headband and tickling his feet, and Grant is licking his own mint-chocolate-chip cone and not even turning his head when Chassie Dunkirk and a group of her friends stride by in teeny bikinis, their boyfriends in tow. The girls glance at us and huddle to whisper who knows what. I don't even care. I just feel happy.

How did I know where Jack would be? All I can say is, I had a feeling. I know that sometimes all a person wants is to go home.

22
Nell

After we found Jack—after Mom and Dad and I took turns hugging him over and over again until he started laughing and yelling, "Enough!"—we were all kind of ready to get out of the water park. My parents invited Doris and Grant back to our place for pizza. (I think they're hoping I'll just forget about Ashton if I've got friends here, as if I'm not capable of feeling more than one thing at the same time. But I'll take the pizza, anyway.) Mom insisted on making a salad, and Grant beamed and ate three helpings and told Mom it was the best arugula he'd ever had. For dessert, we had ice cream. It was my third ice cream of the day, but it tasted as good as the first.

After dinner, Doris and Grant and I head out to the backyard to hang out, and there's the pink playhouse looming in front of us.

"What's this?" asks Doris.

I give them a very short tour. "It's kind of silly," I'm saying, leading the way, "but at least it's a place I can go and be by myself sometimes." Grant nods like he totally gets it, and Doris acts like she's just walked into a mansion full of velvet couches and fridges of mini cupcakes rather than an eight-by-ten glorified shed with a couple of blankets on the floor, books and magazines strewn about, and a half-empty water bottle I forgot to throw away steadily generating its own colony of bacteria. It's anthropology, a look into a previous time of Nell.

"This is the perfect clubhouse," Doris declares.

She's walking back and forth inspecting everything, while Grant ducks to fit inside the doorway and takes a cross-legged seat on the wooden planks of the floor. "This is pretty cool, Nell," he says. "Your own private spot."

"It makes me want to start something, just so we can meet here!" says Doris, sitting down next to him. I join them, and we're all facing one another in a small circle. "A website. A zine—aren't zines back? Something! What can we start?"

"A babysitters club?" I used to love those books. "Not that I want to babysit."

"A bar," says Grant, and when Doris and I give him funny looks, he laughs quickly. "Just kidding."

"A detective agency? Like an Unclaimed, but for lost people!" I say. "You're the talent, Doris; Grant and I are your humble employees."

"Ha," says Doris, but she grins, and I can tell she's proud she found Jack. "Say what you will, but I *can* find a kid, usually."

I reach over and touch her arm. "I'm serious. Thanks," I say, and her eyes get a little damp.

"No problem," she says. "It's what friends are for."

She looks at Grant, but he's staring down at his hands. I remember what she told me at the water park. Are we all really friends? I'm hers, and I decide to do something about it.

"Hey, Grant, why did you text Doris, anyway?" I say. "Why did you want to come and meet us at the water park? You never told us."

Doris gives me the tiniest thumbs-up. Grant is oblivious.

"Oh, I dunno," he says, picking up the water bottle and inspecting it. "This should be a science project, dude."

I take the bottle out of his hand. "Grant."

"I just wanted to see what you were up to. Seemed like it might be fun. I didn't have anything else to do," he says. None of this is particularly convincing.

Doris gives him the eye. "Really? All of a sudden, after years of pretending I don't exist, you work with me for a couple weeks and then you decide you want to text me? Am I that irresistible?"

"You're my boss," he says. "You gave me your phone number."

"What can I help you with, then, employee? Do you want to know your schedule for next week?"

She's being sarcastic, but it's working. He puts the water bottle down.

"Would you like an explanation of your benefits?"

He opens his mouth and closes it.

"Or a tutorial on how to unpack a suitcase? We can go over that again in the store, no need to interrupt your Sunday," she says. "Though I do appreciate your dedication to the cause."

"Stop." He looks pained. "Look, I texted you because . . ."

Doris and I lean forward, as if that will help him get it out faster. "Yes?"

"I texted you because I was scared I was going to start drinking. OK?" He seems mad, but I don't think it's at us. He's still looking at the floor of the playhouse. "I needed to do something. I was going crazy in my house. And I don't really have any other friends right now, not friends I trust myself around. OK? Is that enough? Do you get it? *I just needed to be with people and not drink!*"

"Oh," says Doris.

"Oh," I repeat.

"Yeah," he says, and we're all silent for a minute.

"Well, that wasn't what I thought you were going to say," says Doris.

"You really didn't know, huh?" he asks. "I guess they actually managed to keep everything quiet."

"I think you're going to have to start from the beginning," I tell him. "I'm new here, remember?"

"And I don't know who 'they' is," says Doris. "Is this about Chassie?"

"Partly," he says. "I guess in a way everything is about Chassie. She and Mac were at the water park. Nell was with me when I saw them."

I'm starting to realize there's a lot more to Grant's pain than a breakup.

"I saw them together, too," says Doris. "At the store, a couple weeks ago. And at the water park, when we were having ice cream after we found Jack."

"Yeah, they're dating now, and she won't talk to me, and all I want to do is say I'm sorry, but she won't pick up when I call, and I know I should leave her alone just like I should leave everyone else alone and most especially leave booze alone. But I can't." He looks down at his lap, shaking his head.

"Why should you leave her alone, exactly?" prompts Doris. "Aside from the fact that if she won't pick up, you should stop calling and harassing her?"

"I broke her arm! Crashing the car in a ditch, which is why she's still got her arm in a sling." His voice cracks like he's near tears, but gets steady again as he flatly recounts what happened. "I did all of that the night of the last spring game. But that's not all: I got drunk. I ran the ball the wrong way, then found myself at the bottom of a pileup. First wrong-way run in our team's history. Luckily, when you lose consciousness, you don't hear all the boos. Later, even though I probably had a concussion, maybe *because* I had a concussion, I insisted on going to a party at Brod's, where I proceeded to drink more. Then I insisted on driving us home. Hence, the crash."

I'm silent. I have so many questions, but I can't think of a single right thing to say.

"Is that all?" asks Doris.

"Isn't that enough? We lost the game, thanks to me," he adds. "Oh, and did I mention that I ran from the scene of the crash?

168

I don't remember that part because I was blackout drunk. But I vaguely remember the cops finding me a few blocks away in a random backyard, and I definitely remember Chassie dumping me the next day from her hospital bed. I can't really blame her for that, or for having a new boyfriend."

"You really can't," says Doris.

"She doesn't respond to my voice mails, but she calls my mom to talk about whatever they talk about—probably whether I'm getting help."

"*Are* you getting help?" I ask.

"I'm going to a therapist. Coach says if I work with her this summer and she gives me the all clear, they'll put me back on the team in the fall. They need me to win," he says. "The other thing is, I'm not supposed to talk about any of this. Coach said if everyone knew about the drinking, I'd never be able to play in a state competition again. There's a no-tolerance policy that the rest of the kids 'aren't dumb enough to get busted for,' is what he said. He told everyone I was taking a leave of absence due to injuries, a concussion. He said that would explain my big mistake. Running the ball the wrong way is, like, moronic. You lose all credibility—no one wants that guy on the team." He looks at us with fear in his eyes. "Y'all really can't tell anyone I'm telling you this. Please?"

"What about the cops? Why weren't you arrested for drinking and driving?" I ask.

"They wrote it up as a vehicular problem," he explains. "So I can still play next year. That *is* pretty messed up, isn't it?"

"It's illegal," says Doris. "But also not that surprising, given how this town feels about football. Once you get a taste of winning, it's hard to give up."

"Don't say anything, OK?" he asks us again.

"But why?" I ask. "I mean, you did some really bad things. But they're doing really bad things, too. I've never heard of telling a high school kid to cover up a crime. All this for football?!"

Doris nods. "God, guns, and *Alabama football*. Welcome to the South. Or the most stereotypical version of it. Which doesn't mean some of that isn't all too real."

"You know what the worst thing is?" he asks. "I still want to be on the team."

"Why?" asks Doris.

"It makes me feel like I'm not such a waste of space, for a minute, at least," he admits. "But then it also makes me want to drink."

"You need to tell this to your therapist," I say.

"I can't." He shakes his head. "If I say how bad I am, they'll never let me play. And if Grant Collins doesn't play, who is he?"

"Maybe he's the better Grant Collins," says Doris. "You know, in the last weeks of knowing you, I've been surprised. Sure, you've been a typical football jock jerk a few times. But mostly, you've been pretty cool."

"And funny," I add.

"And sweet. You even helped look for Jack," says Doris.

"Well, you're the best friends I have at the moment," he says. "And I happen to like Unclaimed, too. My mom wanted me to have a job because I was just lying in bed all day. I thought the idea was stupid. But now that I'm getting out of the house to work with y'all, they think I'm doing better, and I am doing a little better. That doesn't change the fact that I've been lying to everybody all summer. I can't tell you how many nights I've snuck out to go drink with Brod."

"Oh, Grant," I say.

"I don't know if I can stop drinking," he whispers. "Even if I wanted to."

Doris is leaning forward urgently. "Do you want to?"

"I think so?"

"Are you drunk now?" she asks.

"No," he says.

"Good," she says. "We're not going to get in a car with you behind the wheel anytime soon, but we can be your friends. We can try to help. Right, Nell?" Doris has this determined look on her face.

"Definitely," I say. "You can talk to us."

"But if you drink, and especially if you drink and drive, know this," she adds. "I will not keep it quiet. The coach's messed-up gag rule does not apply to me. Or Nell."

I nod solemnly. We are a united front, and we can help our friend. I know we can.

Grant nods, too. "OK."

My phone chooses that awkward moment to beep. I pull it out and see that I've got a text from Ashton. **PONY I got my phone back for 5 minutes, call if you're around!** the message says. Even though I'm aching to hear his voice, I turn the ringer to silent and stash the phone in my pocket, because right now there's something more important happening than me and Ashton.

23
Grant

When I get home, it's after ten and the house is dark. I don't have any messages from Mom, and I figure it's all good. After all, I left a note that said I was with Doris, and my mom's the one who got her to hire me in the first place—how can Mom argue with that? Doris is the polar opposite of a bad influence. I'm quiet when I open the door because I don't want to wake anyone up, but when I get to the living room, a voice nearly scares the crap out of me.

"Grant," says my mom. She's sitting there on the couch, a little book light aimed at the novel she's reading. "I was waiting up for you."

"Didn't you get my note?" I ask.

"I got your note," she says. "But I kept thinking about the argument we had earlier. I couldn't sleep."

"Nell's little brother got lost at the water park," I say.

"Oh no!" she says. "Their poor family."

"They were really upset, but Doris found him. He'd wandered back home."

"Bless their hearts," she says.

"Afterward the Wachowskis invited us back to their house for dinner. I'm sorry I didn't call." I don't add that I'm sorry for everything, but I think it.

She puts her book down and comes over to hug me. I'm pretty sure she's just getting close so she can smell me, to see if I've got any booze clinging to me. But I don't. I didn't drink anything tonight, and I'm hoping I can keep from drinking tomorrow, too. So for the first time in a long time, I don't try to get away from her. I stand there, and she puts her head on my shoulder, and she holds me like she used to when I was little and scared and she'd comfort and protect me from the bad things of the world. I'm a lot bigger now, but for a minute, I let myself feel OK.

24
Things to Do When You Lose a Suitcase: A List

1. Wait for a very long time at baggage claim, thinking your missing suitcase will eventually emerge. Maybe it's still on the tarmac and someone will finally load it onto the conveyor belt and out it will pop, hooray, hooray! Maybe it's forgotten on the plane. Maybe it's on the next flight. Someone will find it. Someone has to. Right? How can a suitcase just disappear? Why is everyone so incompetent?

2. Think about everything in the suitcase that you really don't want to be without. Think about what you'll do if you are, permanently. Cry.

3. Call the airline and complain. Call many times. Talk to someone at a call center who doesn't seem to care at all about your missing bag. *Their* stuff isn't missing. Tell them things would be different if they knew how it felt. Initiate a claim. Make more calls.

4. Feel untold frustration. Scream into the air, if that helps. It does, a little. Keep calling. Yell at someone you love. Feel guilty about that. *They* didn't lose your stuff.

5. Wait some more. Buy new things, because you need what you need. Borrow a pair of shoes from a traveling companion, if you are still traveling. Steal a shirt someone left on a park bench. (Does that count as stealing?) Make do. Feel a little more OK with knowing you may never get your things back, that impermanence is a part of life, nothing is forever.

6. Scream again.

7. Maybe, just maybe, get a reimbursement for what you had to buy to replace what was in your bag.

8. Realize that some things are simply irreplaceable.

9. Vow to travel lighter in the future.

10. Move on, but don't forget. Tell your story of loss to anyone who ever talks about flying anywhere.

11. Don't check. Carry on.

25
Nell

It's the last week in June, and we're in the stockroom again.
Grant is leaning back in his chair at the table, tilting on the
legs as he checks the master list of inventory. This morning,
Red asked us to put out as much Fourth of July merch as we
could find for a last-minute holiday sale. We've dug up actual
flags as well as picnic tablecloths and short shorts and bikini
tops patterned like flags, which Doris points out is probably
not what the founding fathers had in mind, independence-wise,
back in 1776.

"Maybe it's exactly what they'd dreamed of," Grant interrupts.

"Ew," I say. "Down with the original patriarchy!" Doris and

I laugh, because *would* that you *could* get rid of the patriarchy by throwing a picnic while wearing a bikini.

"Oh, look!" I say, showing my friends a partially used bottle of black nail polish with glittery sparkles I've dug out of a makeup kit. "It's called Fireworks, does that count?"

"Let me see," says Doris, grabbing the bottle and investigating. She opens it and gives her index finger a swipe. "Ooh, I like it," she says. "If only my fingernails weren't so hideous. I really have to stop biting them."

"Try painting them," I suggest. "That worked for my friend Nisha. She couldn't bite her nails without looking at them, and seeing the polish reminded her not to do it."

"I've tried a million things, including that stuff that tastes terrible," says Doris. "I'm a nailaholic. There's no hope."

Then she covers her mouth and looks at Grant. "Whoops, I didn't mean that."

But Grant doesn't seem offended. "Whenever I drink, I look at my hands," he says, considering it. "At least, the first time I pick up a glass or a bottle. Do you think painting my nails might help *me* stop drinking?"

"But drinking wouldn't make you eat the polish, which is the idea behind painting your nails, especially with stuff that tastes bad," I explain. "That's what makes you stop. That and you don't want to mess up your manicure."

He's undeterred. "I know it's a weird idea," he says. "But it could be a signal, something to bring me back to reality, you know? A reminder. Like a red light telling me to stop. It gets ingrained in your brain, and you just do it."

"It *could* work," says Doris. "Like a placebo effect. If you believe it, maybe it *will*."

"What do I have to lose?" he asks.

I laugh. "Is it that you really want a manicure? Because I am really good at giving manicures. You may find that you love getting manicures more than you like drinking."

"I've never had a manicure," he says. "And I've drunk plenty. Let's give it a shot."

"Well, OK, then," I say, pulling some cotton balls and a nail file out of the makeup bag. "Luckily, the Vanessa's got everything we need."

"Vanessa?"

I point to the suitcase the makeup bag came in, a fancy gold hard case that matches the flecks in the polish. "Doesn't she just seem like a Vanessa?"

Both of them nod, humoring me. Grant puts his hands out flat on the table, and Doris and I peer at them.

"You don't bite them at all, do you?" asks Doris. "What's your secret?"

"I have other vices," he says.

Ten minutes and two coats later, Grant is waving his fingers in the air to dry them. "Now I see why Chassie was always going to the nail salon," he says. "This is pretty fun." He fans his hands out in front of his face and strikes a pose.

"They look really *good*," I say, and Doris nods.

"They give your whole jock-slash-boy-next-door-slash-Hilfiger-model thing an edge," she adds.

"I agree, he's shifted from football hottie to boy rocker," I say.

"Ladies, ladies, I'm right here and can hear everything you're saying about me," he protests. "But mainly I just hope this works."

"Keep the bottle," says Doris, handing it to him. "It was half gone already, so it's no good to sell. When you start to chip, you can do your own touch-ups. Now, let's get back to work before Red comes in and asks us why he's running a nail salon."

. . . . .

By the end of the day, we've added a whole bunch of T-shirts with eagles and AMERICA THE BEAUTIFUL printed on them; a stack of red, white, and blue party supplies; an American-history-themed Mad Libs; and a Jasper Johns American flag puzzle to the holiday stash. I also find a pair of personalized Keds with hand-painted red-and-white stripes on the left shoe and white stars on a blue background on the other, and Grant pulls a two-foot Uncle Sam statue, which no one in his or her right mind should have ever purchased, much less traveled with, out of a giant, rose-patterned footlocker. Cat knocks on the door of the stockroom—she's the only one who ever knocks; she says teens need "their privacy," which makes us groan—and we yell, "Come in!"

"Hey, y'all!" she says. "I just wanted to say hi, make sure you weren't lonely back here."

"You dyed your hair!" I say. It's green now instead of purple. "I love it."

"I needed a change," she explains. "Or, I guess, I'm about to embark on a big change, and I wanted my look to change along with it."

"When's your last day?" asks Doris, making a sad face.

"July thirty-first," says Cat, pretending to wipe away a tear. "I can't believe it's so soon. The going-away party is the week after that; y'all have to come!"

"We'll be there," says Doris.

"If I wasn't so excited, I'd be stressed out of my mind. I still have to pack! I need to arrange movers. . . ."

"My mom arranged our move—for a family of four—in less than a month," I tell her. "Of course, she can be kind of intense."

"She *is* a rocket scientist," says Grant.

"More important, you still have to teach me everything you know about Instagram," I tell Cat. "What am I going to do without you?"

"That's also why I'm here," she tells me. "I wanted to tell you how great you're doing! We've gotten a bunch of new followers already. I loved the skeleton post. Hilarious."

I smile and point to our recent find. "I was thinking about taking a shot of that footlocker with the Uncle Sam statue emerging, and doing an *America's Best Deals on Fourth of July Merch* caption. Grant can hold up the statue and make it look like it's really pointing at the camera."

Grant laughs. "You could say, *Uncle Sam Wants You . . . to Shop at Unclaimed Baggage!*"

"Hey, you're pretty good, too," says Cat, turning to give him a high five. "Ooh, I love your polish!"

"Thanks," he says, and Doris and I grin.

"It's always good to see a guy playing with gender norms," she says. "Especially a football hero. You have a lot of influence in this town. You could shake things up, you know. Make people a little more tolerant to differences."

He laughs again. "First I gotta fix myself. But maybe."

"Plus, it looks cool as hell." She checks her phone. "Ugh, gotta run, band practice!"

"See ya, Cat," says Doris.

"Check the Insta later!" I tell her as she walks out the door.

"I can't wait," she says, and blows us a kiss good-bye.

Around six, Byron, who has been working the registers all day, pokes his head into the stockroom. As usual, he's got on his necklace with the dangling silver elephant. Grant told us Byron started wearing it after a historic game he helped win against Auburn while he was at the University of Alabama, where an elephant named Big Al is the team mascot. Apparently, it's his good luck charm, even now that he doesn't play.

"Hey, y'all," says Byron, holding the charm between his right thumb and index finger. "The store's empty. I'm about to close up and get out of here." He looks down at the pile we've got going and shakes his head. "America, huh? What a storied history of mass-produced goods."

"USA!" chants Doris. "Land of the free-to-wear-whatever-tacky-thing-you-want-that's-got-a-picture-of-the-American-flag-on-it. I kind of like these shoes Nell found, though." She waves a Ked in the air. "Red asked us to put all this stuff out in the store for tomorrow morning, so we can stay and lock up when we're finished with that."

"Sounds good," he says. "Just make sure you have your keys. Red still can't find his. Hey, what are all of y'all up to for the Fourth? Are you going to the balloon festival like everybody else around here?"

"What's the balloon festival?" I ask, typical dumb newbie, and Doris and Grant look at me, realization dawning in their faces.

"She's never been to the balloon festival," says Doris.

"She's never been to the balloon festival!" repeats Grant.

Byron asks incredulously, "She's never been to the balloon festival?"

Doris says, "This is an urgent matter. Byron, we are taking her to the balloon festival," and Grant nods. "It's the right thing to do. The only thing to do. Nell, do you have any balloon-themed clothing? Never mind, we can find you something here. Doris, do we have any balloon-themed clothing?"

Doris jumps up and runs to the back of the aisles and, seconds later, returns with a sweatshirt that's got deflated latex balloons attached all over it. "You're supposed to blow into these," she says. "Preferably when you're not wearing it . . ."

"This store really does have everything," I say, laughing.

Byron shakes his head in that grown-up way that indicates he was not too long ago one of us, and he's glad he's not anymore. "Make sure you get there early. Shana's cousin works for the park and says they've sold more tickets this year than ever.

Thousands of people are coming from all over the country." He checks his watch. "I gotta run, I'm supposed to meet Shana in fifteen minutes, and she really, really hates it when I'm late. Lock up good, ya hear? Oh, and it's pouring out there, so don't forget your umbrellas when you leave. It's supposed to storm all night."

"Got it!" says Doris, and Byron makes his exit.

"Wait, but WHAT IS THE BALLOON FESTIVAL?" I ask again.

Grant throws his arm around my shoulder, all casual and friendly. "Nell, my friend, you are in for an Alabama *treat*. The balloon festival is an annual tradition in these parts." I raise my eyebrows. "I can tell you're skeptical," he continues, putting on a fake dramatic announcer voice. "But even the most cynical youth has been known to gasp in joy at the sight of hundreds of hot-air balloons floating off into the horizon. It's a spiritual moment, one's first balloon festival."

"People cry," adds Doris.

"There are no clowns, right?" I ask, and they both shake their heads vehemently, and Grant crosses his heart.

Last Fourth of July, my dad grilled hot dogs and cheeseburgers, and I had Morgan and Nisha over, and we gossiped about boys until the sun set and then ran around the neighborhood with sparklers. That was fun, but this is going to be something more. We'll camp out, because everyone camps out, says Grant. I have never been a camping kind of person, but now, suddenly, maybe I am.

As we talk we're still casually unpacking, because even though the store is technically closed, no one has anywhere they have to be, and we're all having too good a time to leave.

"Look what I just found!" says Grant, holding up a full bag of Doritos that came from a blue duffel bag I named the Norm. "Is it snack time? I think it's snack time."

"Can we actually eat those?" I ask, wrinkling my nose.

"They haven't been opened. And they're Doritos! How can you pass up free Doritos?" says Grant. We look to Doris for her opinion.

"What's the expiration date?" she asks.

Grant investigates. "Not until February of next year!"

"Fair game, then," she says. "I'm hungry. Who wants a Coke from the vending machine?"

A few minutes later, we're sitting there trying not to get orange dust on the items we're unpacking and sipping our ice cold RC Colas, which is all the vending machine ever has in it on account of some special deal Red cut with the company. Everyone calls it Coke, anyway, because that's what you call soda down South.

"Doritos are so good," says Doris. "How do they make them so freaking delicious?"

"There are chemicals in them that make you love them, literally," I say. "There was an article about that that my mom made me read when she was trying to get me to quit them."

"My mouth is too happy for my brain to worry about this information," says Doris.

"The article didn't work," I say, putting another chip in my mouth and crunching.

"What in the world . . . ?" interrupts Grant, pulling a long, fleshlike object from the Norm.

"What? Not again!" says Doris.

But it's far too large to be another dildo, and then there's an elbow and a hand and fingers. "It's a prosthetic arm," says Grant. "Wow. I wonder what the story is with this one."

"Finally, you're curious about a luggage mystery!" I tease him.

"Well, this is a little more interesting than an empty bag," he says.

"We actually get those kind of a lot," Doris tells us. "I mean, not a lot, but it's happened more than once! Prosthetic buttocks, however, are quite rare."

"Just think: Someday we might be able to put together a full human body!" I say. Doris laughs, but Grant is busy looking at his own freshly manicured fingers with something like a smile on his face.

PART II

PART II

26
Doris

A week later, I roll out of the comfort of my bed, head to the bathroom, and take a look at myself in the mirror. There I am, same as I ever was, dark hair, kind of a mess from sleeping, dark eyes, which I rub to wake up a little more, sixteen years of existence in human form. Sometimes when I stop and look at myself, I dare to think I'm pretty. Other times I avoid looking at myself at all, because what I look like isn't really the point. I always think it's strange when I overhear girls complimenting each other on their looks. *Oh, you're so beautiful, I'm so jealous, I HATE you,* one will say, and the other will say, *Ugh, I'm awful, YOU are the gorgeous one!* (Even if she thinks she is and the other isn't.) What's pretty, anyway? It's whatever we've been told by each other, by society, and it changes according to the decade and era. Just look at old paintings, or even magazines from the '70s and '80s. The beautiful people looked a whole lot different than they do now.

But no matter what I look like, I'm not like a lot of other girls in my town. I don't know if it's because of Teddy or if it would have happened anyway, but I'm different, the way Maya is different, the way Nell is different, maybe. The way Stella was different. Fighting against what's generally accepted hasn't helped me win any popularity contests. But it's better to do what you think is right . . . right? Even if you rock the boat. That's what Stel said, and if there's one person I truly believe, it's her. Even though it's the kind of thing Sunday school teachers will tell you—and you know how I feel about *that*—beauty really is more about what's inside than what's outside. My aunt Stella was the most beautiful person I've ever known.

. . . . .

After I brush my teeth and comb my hair and pee, I head to the kitchen, where Mom is making oatmeal, a dish she always refers to as "the breakfast of champions." (I know she didn't make that up on her own, nor does she even have the proper cereal for the tagline, but I let her have it.) Dad's outside mowing the lawn, which is his second favorite thing to do, I think, after watching football. The scent of fresh grass permeates the kitchen, and I breathe in deep. I love that smell.

"Good morning!" I say, and my mom waves her wooden spoon at me.

"You got another postcard from your friend," she tells me, pointing the utensil at the counter of the island that sits in the middle of our kitchen. A pile of mail waits there.

"Ooh," I say, and reach for the latest installment from Maya, which is at the top. This one's a vintage card that says GREET-INGS FROM ALABAMA across a map of the state, which features cartoon drawings of a guy with a gun and his dog, a guy fishing, a guy mining, and a guy with a football. You know, all the key Alabama activities. I turn it over.

DORIS, MY DEAR DORIS, this card seems to have forgotten that people other than men exist in our grand state! Can you draw me something that better reflects the current sociocultural reality, and how much time we spend reading internet articles about feminism? Speaking of realities, Hannah and I are now AN ACTUAL MOTHER-FREAKIN' ITEM! I did what you said and made a move. I asked her if she wanted to go for a walk during free time while the campers were having a canoe lesson. And she did and we talked and she likes me too and now I am kinda-sorta SWOONSVILLE. What's going on back home? I think it's time you made a move, if you can find anyone worth making a move on, that is. I know, I know. A PAUCITY OF RESOURCES. But maybe someone got cute over the summer? Miss you dreadfully but now I never want to come home. XOXOXOXOXO write back soon.

I have a million questions I want to ask Maya, and I've started writing a response in my head that includes a lot of !!!!!! and ☺☺☺☺.

"Ahem," says my mom, interrupting my train of thought. "Can you explain something to me? What does Maya mean she's 'an item' with this other girl? Is that how you girls talk now?"

My mom has never accepted that Maya likes girls romantically. She has passed it off as a phase, as Maya trying to be "attractive to boys," as Maya trying to be mysterious and different, and now, apparently, as just the way kids talk nowadays.

"Mom," I say, "we've been over this before. Maya is a lesbian. That means she's a girl who's attracted to girls. And she's dating a girl who's a counselor at the camp she's working at this summer. It's not a phase. She's always felt this way."

Mom shakes her head. "She must be confused. Her poor family."

I feel anger flare up in me. "She's not confused, nor is her family poor. Why do you always act like she can't really feel the way she feels? What's wrong with being gay?"

"It just makes things so much harder," she says, shaking her head sadly. And then she narrows her eyes at me. "Are you sure you're not gay, too?"

"Mother," I tell her. "Stop. I have a gay friend. I am not gay myself. Even if I don't date anyone, because the boys in this town are abysmal. But if I *was* gay, for the record: There would be nothing wrong with that."

She looks at me doubtfully, and I know she's thinking

about how I'm always hanging out with Nell now, and Grant sometimes, and how she wishes I were *always* hanging out with Grant. Since I hired him, she's made several references to how good-looking he is, how nice his family is, and what a cute couple we'd make. I know she dreams that the captain of the football team and I will date and fall in love and marry and have babies and live in this town forever, just like she did with my dad. (How little she knows about the truth of Grant Collins! Or how little I am head-cheerleader material.)

But I see this as a strategic moment, and I'm going to use it.

Mom is not a fan of the balloon festival. This is because it's loud and crowded, and because a lot of times teenagers get drunk in the woods and "wreak havoc," as she says. (That means break things and spray paint things and possibly have sex.) Every year I get a lengthy lecture about it before she finally lets me go.

But if she knows Grant is going, there's a chance she'll be on board a little bit faster than usual.

"If you're really going to that balloon thing"—she rolls her eyes—"you need to have something in your stomach." She fills a bowl with oatmeal and slides it across the island at me, and I grab a spoon.

"So, tell me the plan," she says, putting a lid on the oatmeal and leaning across the counter on her elbows, her eyebrows lifted.

"I'm going to go pick up Grant and Nell," I explain calmly, because calm is always the best practice when dealing with parents, "and then we're going to drive out to the campgrounds and pick a *safe spot* to set up camp, and then we're going to see the balloons and walk around and maybe play some card games. I promise if anything seems off, I will come home immediately, and otherwise, I will probably be asleep by ten and then you will see me the next day."

"I don't like the idea of you sleeping in the woods with a boy," she says.

"He'll have his own tent!" I say. "And Nell and I will be together in hers. And there are literally hundreds—thousands!—of people around, including a ton of adults, including Nell's parents."

My mom is utterly conflicted. If I'm sleeping in the woods with Grant, that eases some of her worries about how I might be gay. It sounds romantic. Maybe we really will fall in love, watching the sunset from the giddy heights of a balloon ride. But she also lives in fear that I might do something "untoward." I'm still not totally sure she doesn't in some way blame me for what happened at the water park, just like Mrs. Stokes did. And if her dear daughter were ever to be caught with her top down around a boy again—or worse—I think she would very nearly expire from shame.

Anyway, what I've told her isn't completely a lie. But I don't say that Nell's plan is to pitch our tent as far from her parents as we possibly can. And I definitely don't go into how I'm not sure Grant has his own tent (we might all be in Nell's), though I do know he has his own sleeping bag. He bought one at Unclaimed the other week.

She sighs. I eat my oatmeal slowly. The most important part

of parent-child negotiations is the pacing. Come on too strong, you lose because you seem to want it too much; wait it out, it's probably yours. Time's ticking, though: I glance at the clock. I need to be at Nell's in twenty minutes.

"Don't worry, Mom. I'm not going to get pregnant just because I'm sleeping in the woods near a boy," I say. Bringing up the p-word might backfire entirely, but I can't wait anymore.

"Doris, don't you dare even say that!" she says, swatting me with her spoon and frowning. "That is not something to joke about! Girls have lost their reputations and ruined their lives! And the lives of their families!"

"You know it takes more than just a woman to make a baby, Mom," I say, but she gives me a death stare, so I try to reel it back in. "You have to trust me. I'm your daughter. You've taught me well." I give her a hopeful smile, and she relents.

"I know. You would never . . . but I worry. I can't help it," she says. "In two years you'll be off living on your own at college . . . and who knows where you'll go after that. You're so much like your aunt; it scares me sometimes."

We're quiet for a minute, remembering Stel. I feel sad, but with a twinge of happy. I can tell she's going to let me go.

"Aw, Mom!" I get up and give her an awkward hug, since she's back at frenetically stirring her oatmeal, and kiss her on the cheek. "I'm not leaving the country. I just need to be me. What are you doing today?"

"We have a huge order for a family reunion: two hundred chicken wings, with Buffalo sauce! Plus my famous chess pie." She grins. "Money for Samford!"

My heart hurts a little because, while I appreciate that she wants me to go to college, she knows my heart is set on Brown, not on the Alabama Baptist college she and my dad went to *together*. High school sweethearts who never left each other's side, they might be one in a million.

But I don't want to start talking about college. "Don't forget the celery sticks," I tell her, because she always does when she stores something at home instead of in her catering company's kitchen. "Remember, they're in the bottom drawer of the fridge, under the onions."

"Thank you, honey bun," she tells me. "Have fun and be good!" She kisses the top of my head good-bye.

Then I'm on my way to Nell's house. This is my first campout. At the back of my mind, I can't help wondering about what my mom said. . . . Does Grant actually have his own tent? And, more to the point, do I want him to?

27
Grant

There used to be plenty of fanfare when I was leaving for a big game, or even a small one, because in my town even the tiniest games are still pretty big. Mom would hug me and kiss me on the cheek, and maybe tousle my hair if there wasn't a bunch of other dudes around. Brian would high-five me, or pat me on the back in a fatherly way. I haven't seen that in a while. But this morning, as I'm lugging my gear to the foyer so I'm ready when Doris picks me up, my mom is positively beaming like in the old days, and Brian has given me a high five twice. Which is kind of funny, especially since I'm about to go camp out with two girls, but like I've said before, these girls are different.

Even better, ever since the playhouse confession, I'm starting to feel like I'm different, too. I haven't had a drop of alcohol. I'm daring to hope I might be moving in the right direction. Maybe it shows.

"Doris is such a good influence!" I've heard my mom gushing into the phone when she talks to her friends. "She may not go to church, but she's a real sweetie pie. And Nell is new in town—have you met her family yet? Her mother is an actual rocket scientist!"

I survey my stuff in the hallway: duffel bag (I wonder what Nell would name this one) packed with a clean T-shirt and shorts and boxers and a hoodie in case it gets cold at night. Mom's stuffed a load of fresh-baked cookies in there, too, so my clothes are going to smell like chocolate. Could be worse. There's my flashlight and spare batteries, a first aid kit, bug spray, water, and some ropes and other camping stuff that I'm sure I'm not going to use. I've got my new sleeping bag tightly rolled next to the duffel, and that's when I realize I don't have a tent. Whoops. Probably should have thought about that before now.

I hear Mom and Brian chatting in the kitchen, and go in to find them. "Hey, um," I say, standing there and feeling kind of silly. "I'm a little late to this, but: Do we have a tent?"

Mom looks at Brian, and Brian looks at Mom. "That would be helpful, huh?" he says. I nod. "Yeah, follow me!" We head to the garage, and he starts digging through the boxes piled up high on shelves in front of the family cars. It's almost like I'm back at Unclaimed. I'm never going to look at a container the same way again after this summer. "Hold this, will you?" he asks, handing me a cardboard box that says G, FOOTBALL.

It's got no top, so right away I see the first football I ever owned and my tiny helmet from the peewee games I played in elementary school. It's like a slap in the face to the former me.

"Oh, sorry, man," Brian says, noticing my expression. He reaches for the box, but I hold on to it. That's when he notices my fingernails. "Is that . . . nail polish?" he asks.

"Yeah, it's for a joke," I say, which is the first explanation I think of. I'm certainly not going to tell him that Fireworks now lives in my bathroom, and sometimes my pocket, or that Doris and Nell have taught me the phrase "touch-ups." I'm also not going to reveal that so far the nail polish trick is working better than anything else I've tried to get me to stop drinking.

He doesn't press, though the expression on his face makes it clear he thinks I might have gone off the deep end.

"Can you believe I ever fit into this stuff?" I say to change the subject, digging into the box. I pull out the miniature pants and shirt styled just like a professional uniform to reveal a bunch of gilded trophies. Even then, I won. I always won, until I lost.

"Maybe someday the twins will want to use that stuff," he says, and looks at me carefully. "Maybe you'd want to teach them. I bet they'd like that."

"Maybe," I say. I think about how my dad taught me to play, back before any of the other stuff happened. I remember throwing footballs in the yard for hours. He'd never get bored, and neither would I.

"Here we go!" says Brian, pulling down a large backpack-tent contraption. "All the components are in here. You can carry it around on your back. Do you know how to put it together?"

"Um," I say. He glances at his watch.

"I'd show you now, but I have an appointment about the Dorsets' yard in ten minutes."

"That's OK," I say. "The Dorsets need more help than I do. I've never seen their lawn any color but brown. Can anything actually grow there?"

"We're going to try." He pats me on the back. "Have fun camping, Grant. Drink plenty of water; it's going to be a hot one. Call me if you need troubleshooting on the tent—or anything."

"How hard can it be?" I ask.

28
Nell

The balloon festival really is epic. I've seen hot-air balloons before, but never a whole field of them in different stages of life. Some are still half bubbles on the ground, tethered and attached to hot-air pumps. They look like living, breathing creatures as they slowly fill with air. Some are still flat little balloon worms clinging to the grass. And some are floating above us gently, hovering and bobbing like weird jellyfish of the sky.

We lug our backpacks and sleeping bags and tent equipment and Doris's mom's cooler packed with homemade treats from our parking spot to the entrance to the festival grounds. From there, we'll have to walk to the campsite, Doris explains. She quickly lapses into narrator mode as we go.

"The balloon fest is an annual tradition in town and has been going on since the seventies, when the mayor instituted an annual Fourth of July balloonfest hoedown. Luckily, they've since dropped the 'ho' part." She laughs. "No one really wanted to square dance, or at least, once the nineties got here, it was kind of a lost cause. But at night when the balloons are all tethered, bands still play on the stage over in the south field, and there's a pretty awesome fireworks display. The Allman Brothers used to show up. One year Willie Nelson came, and all the parents were so excited."

"Hey, should we find a spot to camp and drop off our stuff?" asks Grant. "This backpack tent thing is heavier than it looks." He wipes some sweat from his face.

Doris points at a wooded area in the distance, beyond all the balloons and vendors selling T-shirts and souvenirs and ice cream. "We just need to navigate through the crowds to get to the campground end of things."

We forge ahead, listening as we go. Doris is explaining how they schedule the balloons with different takeoff times throughout the day to keep them from hitting one another as they rise—before the staggered start times, that actually happened, but luckily no one was hurt. Farther off on the horizon I see balloons that look like tiny little dots, the way houses or cars appear from the air when you're up in a plane. "People come from everywhere for this!" she says. "There's a circuit of balloon festivals happening in places from New Mexico and Mississippi to Quebec, and some of the participants fly around all year, going to all of them."

"I guess once you own a hot-air balloon, you really want to take advantage of it," I say. "Where do you even keep it when you're not using it?"

"A giant suitcase?" quips Grant.

We pass a crowd of people waiting to go on balloon rides. I'm all set to jump in line, but Doris and Grant guide me back.

"Waiting can take forever," Doris warns me. "It's the old-people version of camping out to get the new iPhone. My favorite time to go is right at dusk. All the crabby kids have generally been taken home by their parents at that point. Sometimes you get on board with a newly married couple wanting to see the sunset, though, and that can be upsetting." She wrinkles her nose, remembering. "PDA-wise."

I imagine myself floating up above, getting to see everything from a new perspective.

"I haven't been since I was a little kid," Grant says. "Let's do it!"

But first we have to drop off our stuff, so we continue to trudge through the crowds as Doris points out the best funnel cake vendor and lemonade stand and the hot dogs to avoid at all costs—"The whole town had food poisoning one year!"—and throws out tips like "Never get stopped by a person with a clipboard. They're opinion surveyors, and you'll be stuck there for hours."

A few balloons have ads across their middles: There's one with a big logo stamped across it for the local bank, and another for a lawyer named William Hastings Manning III. His picture stretches across the balloon. He's giving an enthusiastic thumbs-up to the sky; hilariously, his thumb looks exactly like his bald head. There's a balloon shaped like a giant pie, which is totally making me crave a slice. Others incorporate patches of color, like quilts. Some are solid bursts, some are like rainbows, and the whole effect is larger-than-life artwork, spread across the sky.

Some people have trucks parked right next to their balloons and tents set up; others have full-blown giant motorhomes. There's everything from those fancy silver Airstreams to little pop-up trailers, and the people, too, vary: couples walking around holding hands; parents toting little kids on their shoulders; baseball-capped, beer-bellied Southern guys playing cards while casually tending to their balloons. There are visitors who've come for the day to watch, setting out chairs and picnic blankets and sandwiches. There are black people and white people and brown people, Southern accents and Northern accents and even a few languages I don't understand. And there are teenagers like us all over the place.

"Didn't we say the balloon festival is a must-see?" Doris asks.

"Yes! It really is," I say. I keep stopping to snap pictures to send to Ashton and my friends back in Illinois. "Let's take a selfie!" I insist, so Doris and Grant huddle up next to me, and we all smile in front of the balloons we've come to see, which look like brightly colored spots in the distance. **Baby's first balloon festival!** I write. **Wish you were here!**

We reach a big white tent full of women selling baked goods. There's a banner hanging across the front table that says MERCY

CHURCH, a name I recognize because it's the one Doris told me she and Grant both used to go to. The one with the awful youth-group director. Doris nudges me in the ribs as we get closer, and I follow her eyes to an imposing woman with a sharp nose and thin lips standing next to a giant pile of banana bread.

"That's her," whispers Doris. "My waterslide shamer. Priscilla Stokes."

"May I help you?" says Mrs. Stokes. It's exactly the way you ask that question when you don't really want to help anyone but instead you want someone to feel bad for needing your help. The woman's eyes widen, and there's a hint of recognition. "Doris Dailey?" she asks. "My goodness, I haven't seen you in ages! You're so much . . . bigger now."

"Yeah, puberty will do that to you," Doris whispers to me. "I'm no longer under five feet tall and ninety pounds and being sexually assaulted."

"Last I saw you, you were making a scene with that Scruggs boy. I presume by now you've learned how to behave in mixed company?" Mrs. Stokes eyes Grant before she turns her gaze back to Doris. "I hope you haven't forgotten about us. Your soul must be starving for the good food of Jesus!"

I take a moment to consider what "Jesus food" must taste like. Fishes and loaves, maybe, like in the Bible? Grape juice and wafers, like at Communion? Do puff pastries also count? Because I see a lot of those here.

"My soul is doing fine," says Doris. "And my mom's a really good cook."

Mrs. Stokes smiles, but there's an edge to it. "It's a shame how busy she always is with that catering business," she says. "Bless her heart." The words sound nice, but they aren't.

Doris stiffens but doesn't say anything.

"I heard your aunt passed last summer," adds Mrs. Stokes. "It's such a sadness she couldn't receive the blessings of the church, since she turned her back on Jesus as Lord and savior."

Grant makes a funny sound with his mouth, and that gets her attention.

"Well, Grant Collins, I didn't recognize you at first," she tells him. "I've been praying for your family. I heard about your little accident back in the spring."

"Hi, I'm Nell Wachowski," I say, and give a little wave with my hand, trying to divert her from my friends. "Wow, uh. That banana bread looks good."

"Wachowski," says the woman. "You're the new family in the Edwards' old house. From somewhere up North, I hear?"

"Yes," I say.

"Ma'am," she says.

"Excuse me?" I ask. I can't figure out why she's calling me ma'am.

"Yes, *ma'am*," she says. "I don't know how you Yankees are raised, but down here, when you speak to your elders, you say 'ma'am.'"

A group of other women have started to gather. "Oh, hello, Grant!" one of them says, doing a double take at who he's with. "How nice to see you out and about!" Another murmurs, "Well, bless his heart," and I'm even more sure that's not a compliment.

"We've had you on the prayer list every Sunday," Mrs. Stokes tells him.

Grant looks almost as uncomfortable as Doris. "No, thank you," he says.

"What?" asks Mrs. Stokes.

"No, thank you," he repeats. "I don't want to be on your prayer list. Please take me off your prayer list."

"Excuse me?" she says.

"You heard what I said," says Grant. "Ma'am. My problems aren't for you to discuss at church." I'm worried he's about to punch a loaf of banana bread. "I didn't ask for that. I don't want it."

Mrs. Stokes frowns so hard her face might stay that way.

"Hey," says Doris softly. "You OK?" She takes Grant's hand.

He nods, and I take his other hand.

"We have to go," says Doris tightly. She pulls a ten-dollar bill out of her pocket and leaves it on the table. "Please consider this a donation. You may think you're doing the Lord's work, but you're really just using the church to be judgmental and nasty. Religion deserves better than you."

And then we run.

29
Grant

The questions start once we're in the woods, away from the crowds. "What just happened, exactly?" asks Nell.

"You met the town busybody, defender of 'ma'am,' and, lest it be forgotten, the woman who yelled at me for being a brazen temptress on the waterslide when I was twelve years old," explains Doris. "I'd say she was in rare form, but she was just in her usual form."

"Her name is *Stokes*?" says Nell. "As in, verb related to making things burn?"

"Also 'to encourage emotion,' especially anger," answers Doris. "Which is appropriate. How can you feel anything but mad about someone who thinks women should be delicate and timid and obedient and also, never, ever wear Minnie Mouse swimsuits since men can't handle any sort of temptation whatsoever, even temptation brought to you by a cartoon character."

"Wait. Did you just say waterslide?" There's a memory, all of a sudden, of Doris crying after her swimsuit was yanked down by that kid I used to hang out with sometimes—what was his name?

Doris nods slowly. "So you remember?"

It's something I haven't thought about in years. Teddy Scruggs, he was the kind of kid who liked pulling cats' tails and stomping on ants. *Let's embarrass her*, Chassie had said—why was she so mean, even then? Why hurt Doris, who had never done anything to anyone? I remember being angry about it when it happened. I told Scruggs to stay away from Doris after that.

"I felt bad about that," I say quietly.

"You should have," she says. "And you shouldn't have looked at me like I was dirt. You should have treated me like a person."

"I remember not knowing what to do when everyone was teasing you," I say slowly. "I was disgusted by them, not you. And I was so scared Chassie was going to be mad at me. She hated when I talked about you, or defended you." I've said sorry so many times to so many people. But this time I really mean it. "I'm really sorry."

"It's OK," she says eventually, patting my arm. "You were a different person then. And so was I. I forgive you." She gives me a hard look. "As long as you never, ever, ever, *ever* do anything like that again."

"I won't," I promise. "I couldn't. I wouldn't."

"Good," she says, and smiles, throwing her arms up at the sky. "Y'all! I'm actually just so happy we're here!" All the rage from that conversation with Mrs. Stokes comes pouring out of her, but the anger has somehow turned to joy. "AH-OOOOOOOO! I don't even care that I just told off Mrs. Stokes! You know what? I'm thrilled that I did! Even if my mom finds out and grounds me!"

Nell throws her fists up to the sky, too, and yells, "WHOOOOOOOOOOO," releasing a whole party keg of emotions. I start to yell, too, except out of me comes words: "HELLLLLLLLLL YESSSSSSSSS!" I shout. We're all spinning around and screaming and laughing, and we eventually collapse on the ground, giggling at each other and our general ridiculousness. We're sweating bullets. Brian was right; it's a scorcher already. But no one says a word to complain.

· · · · ·

We find a patch of grass that Doris deems acceptable for setting up camp according to her list of priorities: (1) no traces of animal droppings; (2) dry, firm, even earth underneath us; (3) other campers in the distance but nobody close enough to hear us breathe—or talk. Even though the plan was to have the girls in one tent and me in the other, Doris suggests we just use my larger tent and bunk up together. "That way we can tell ghost stories," she says, looking mischievous.

"And we only have to put together one tent," says Nell. If they're cool with it, I don't see any reason to say no.

I turn to the contraption I've been lugging around and get ready to make it bend to my will and—presto, change-o—become a tent. I'm a big strong dude, I've got this covered, right? But it's got long pieces and short pieces and metal poles and big partitions of cloth in different sizes, and I have no idea what goes where. When Nell pulls up instructions on her cell phone, it's as if the words were written in another language. I regret my flippant last remark to Brian.

"What the hell is a 'fly sheet'?" I ask, expecting no answer, but Doris, who has been quietly watching me fiddle with the equipment, pipes up.

"That's the outer tent, the waterproof part," she explains, pointing. Then she takes the poles and lays them out on the ground along with the different pieces of fabric. "Where's the ground cloth?" she asks. When Nell and I simply stare back, she takes the ground cloth from me and shakes her head slightly, with a hint of a smile. She pitches the goddamn tent pretty much all on her own, except for occasionally telling me to hold a pole upright or to use a hammer to pound in the stakes. All of a sudden, there's a functional, standing, real-as-day tent out of what might as well have been a pile of garbage in my hands.

"Wow" is all I can say, wiping sweat off my face.

Nell gives Doris a hug. "How did you *do* that?" she asks.

"I watched a video on YouTube this morning," Doris says, lifting the entrance flap and crawling inside. Nell creeps in after her, and I follow. I like the space of this tent, the air contained inside of it. It's big enough that we can sleep side by side with some room between us, and the low ceiling feels safe, protective. It's quiet in here; the thrum of the crowds that aren't that far away can't penetrate the woods. This, like the stockroom at Unclaimed, like the pink playhouse, is a space just for us. Doris unclips the sleeping bag attached to the bottom of her backpack and unrolls the bag neatly in the far corner of the tent.

"Voilà!" she says. "Instant sleeping arrangements." She steps outside to pull the cooler her mom has packed with food up close to the tent so we can reach it but won't trip over it, and I internally punch myself again for being such a failure at doing things.

"Doris," says Nell, who's still stuck on the tent accomplishment, "you're a genius." Doris kind of blushes. "Well, I did just watch the video today, and there was a really cute guy in it, so maybe I paid extra attention. But, Grant, remember Camp Shining Sumac?"

"A cute guy?" I say, wondering for a second what Doris considers cute in a dude. "And yeah, the name sounds familiar."

"Church camp," Doris tells Nell, ignoring my other question. "About two hours south of here. Sometimes the Mercy Church families would go on these retreats. There was a father/daughter-father/son one and we all slept in tents in the woods."

"Oh, you know, I *do* remember," I say. "My dad took me there the summer I turned eight so we could bond 'man-to-man' with God. Whatever that means. He cheated on my mom not too long after that and left town." The girls are quiet, so I press on. "Mostly I remember playing football with him and a bunch of other guys in the big field. And pretending to pray when we had those moments of silence, but really watching to see what everyone's faces looked like with their eyes closed. And drinking bug juice."

"Ugh, why is that even a thing?" says Nell.

"It's surprisingly delicious," I offer. "Sweet and refreshing! I could use some right now."

"How about regular water?" she asks. She pulls a bottle out of the cooler and hands it to me, and I chug it down. I'm so thirsty, I realize. Must be the long trek across the field in this heat. My head is kind of pounding, too. I try to ignore it.

"Do you remember singing 'Michael, Row the Boat Ashore' in rounds at the fire pit?" asks Doris. "That song still just pops out of nowhere into my head. I'll start humming it at work completely involuntarily." She hums it again, and the sound seems to insulate the thudding in my skull a little bit.

"There was a workshop on how to set up a tent back then," she says. "My dad loves that stuff, putting things together and taking them apart. I guess the information stuck, or maybe I have some of those genes, too."

I can't remember that workshop (I'm sure Dad and I skipped it in favor of something pigskin-related), but I also haven't thought about Camp Shining Sumac in years.

And that's when I get this spinny sensation, like I'm drunk, even though I haven't had a drink in days.

"Whoa," I say. "That was—whoa."

"Are you OK? Grant? Hey?" I hear voices and feel something cold on my forehead. I open my eyes, and Nell, who is at my feet—I'm lying down now—says, "Thank God, you're alive!"

"What happened?" I ask.

Doris speaks from behind me; she's holding a towel full of ice to my head. "You were sitting there, saying you were dizzy. And all of a sudden, your eyes kind of went back in your head and then you were just blank."

"You were really pale," says Nell. "And you felt kind of clammy. We tried to talk to you, but you didn't answer, and then we got scared, so we laid you down here."

"Have you been drinking?" asks Doris. "Please tell us the truth; this is important."

"I haven't!" I say. "I haven't had a drink since before that night in the playhouse. The nail polish trick is working." I show them my hands, as if that's proof of anything. In this case, it really is.

"Maybe it's some kind of withdrawal symptom," says Nell. "Can that happen?"

"Maybe," says Doris, though she doesn't sound too sure. "Grant, was it a seizure? Do you have epilepsy or something? You can tell us. We're your friends."

"I don't have anything that I know of," I say. "But I know that sometimes when I'm drinking, I black out. Sometimes I don't remember what's happened. Could that happen when I'm sober, too?" I feel scared all of a sudden.

Nell looks at me solemnly. I try to get up, but Doris presses my shoulders back down. "Just lie there for a minute or two," she says. "I'm Googling to figure out what to do, but I'm pretty sure you shouldn't make any sudden movements." She reads her phone. "They say that 'vasovagal syncope'—that's a 'common faint'—can happen in moments of fear or distress. Are you upset about something? I don't think that our walk across the field counts as extreme exercise. I mean, it's hot, but is it heat-stroke hot?"

"How long was I out?" I ask.

"Just a few seconds," says Nell.

Even though I'm freaked out, part of me is kind of enjoying their attention. But my head throbs angrily back at my voice. "Ow. Do you have any Advil?" I ask, and Nell starts to rummage through her stuff to find me some medicine, which she passes over to Doris, who puts the pills into my mouth from above along with a swig of water from a bottle she's got next to her. I swallow and then laugh and say exactly what comes to my head, which is "This must be what a threesome is like." And then I feel mortified, except they both start laughing.

"Yeah, right," says Doris. "If you want things to get really sexy, maybe you'll fall down and break your nose."

"Hot," says Nell. "So hot."

"I really do think I can sit up, though," I say a few minutes later, because it's hard to think with two girls staring down at me in concern, not to mention I'm afraid the situation really could get a little "sexy," if you know what I mean, or at least, my body might think so and do something inappropriate. "You know, maybe I've been having these little blackouts for a while," I say, thinking. "But what if I've been too drunk to know?

Sometimes there are moments I've forgotten that pop up from the middle of nowhere, like when you suddenly remember a dream."

Doris shakes her head. "Grant, you probably had a concussion that night you got hurt. Probably you've had a lot of concussions. And that paired with the drinking . . . Look, a healthy teenage boy does not pass out in the middle of the day just because. What about all those football players with brain injuries? Have you read about that?"

I shake my head. I don't tell her I've specifically avoided reading about any of that.

"My uncle had a concussion from skiing," says Nell. "He ended up in the hospital for days. And he still has weird amnesia from the time of his accident."

"I think you should see a doctor," says Doris. "How do you feel now?"

"Better," I say.

"Drink more water," Nell tells me, handing me another bottle.

"We should take you to the nurse," says Doris. "I saw the medical tent on our way to the campsite. Do you think you can walk?"

Oh man, the last thing I'm going to do is go to the nurse and get checked and have someone who reminds me of my dad's girlfriend-who-became-his-wife tell me I've got something wrong with me; there is no way in hell that's going to happen. But because I appreciate what Doris has done and I don't want to make her mad and also it seems like I'm still a pretty good liar, I say, "Oh, definitely, I can walk over there. But let me go by myself. I'll be fine."

The girls look at me uncertainly. "Are you sure? We can go with you!"

"No," I say. "Come on, I'm a grown dude. I need some privacy! Why don't you two stay here and chill. I'll be back in less than an hour."

They don't want to let me go, I can see that, but they also can't tell me what to do.

"OK," says Nell.

"Fine," says Doris. "But you better text us if you feel weird or need anything at all. OK?"

"Yes, *ma'am*," I say, slowly rising to my feet. I walk, hobbling a little, out of the tent, and look back to see their concerned faces. "Everything will be fine. This is a small town. Nothing bad ever happens here," I tell them.

I don't know where I'm going, but it's not to the nurse.

30
Doris & Nell

As soon as he's out of the clearing, we start asking questions.
They're the kind that don't have any answers—not yet—but
you have to say anyway, just to get them out of your own head.
After all, a lot of things are better figured out when you can say
them out loud to a friend. And even if you don't get to any so-
lutions, talking makes you feel better, especially when you have
no idea what else to do.

"Do you think he's OK?"

"I don't know."

"I'm worried."

"Me too."

"Should we tell his mom? Someone?"

"We can't! He'll never trust us again."

"Should we have gone with him?"

"He wouldn't let us!"

"Should we follow him?"

"We could. But I'm sure he'll see, and then what . . ."

"What *should* we do?"

"I think we have to trust him. We have to be his friend. We told him we'd keep his secret if he wasn't drinking, and he's not drinking."

"You're right. I guess we need to be patient."

We try our best to do that, and we wait.

Patience is hard.

31
Grant

I walk and walk, and I keep walking. I pass balloonists setting up, vendors selling ice cream and fried dough, and the Mercy Church tent, where I avert my eyes. Mrs. Stokes will only make me feel worse. I pass the medical station and think for a minute about going in because I, too, am pretty sure it's not normal for a healthy seventeen-year-old boy to faint after setting up a tent, even if it was just for a few seconds. But I'm scared I know the answer already: There's something wrong with me. I've drunk too much, blacked out too many times. I've fallen on my head too many times. The car accident, what might that have done to me? I ran away from it, somehow, but I didn't get off scot-free, maybe in more ways than I even know.

And because I'm truly afraid of what the nurse might find in me—and what that would mean for me next—I keep walking.

On my way across the field, I bump into Nell's family, toting a tent and a bunch of other camping gear. Jack runs out ahead of his mom and dad, shouting when he sees me.

"Grant! Hi! Hi! Grant!" He stands there and looks up at me expectantly.

"Hey, dude," I say. "Cool outfit." My head's feeling a little better now—the walking and the air have helped. Something about the sight of Jack cheers me up further. He's got on shorts and a T-shirt, regular little-kid clothes, but around his waist he's wrapped about seven bungee cords in different colors.

"This is my utility belt," he tells me. "I'm Bungee Man."

"Wow," I say. "What are your superpowers?"

"Bungeeing, duh," says Jack. "Bungee Man can bungee anywhere he wants to go, in a split second. Also he can make Kool-Aid appear before his very eyes, but only the red kind."

"Can he make chicken fingers appear, too?" I ask.

Jack looks at me, considering. "Yes. And chocolate bars. And pizza on Wednesdays."

"Man, Bungee Man has it made," I say.

"Hey, Grant!" says Mr. Wachowski as he and Nell's mom catch up to us. "How goes it? Did you get the tent put up?"

"Hi, Grant!" says Mrs. Wachowski, and I see the resemblance yet again—it's in their eyes, their mouths, and the curves of their bodies. Not that I'm being a creeper or anything. Gah. "Where are the girls?"

"Hi," I say. "Turns out I'm sort of a loss with tents, but

Doris managed to put ours up in about ten minutes flat. She and Nell are back there doing the finishing touches as I . . ." I look out into the crowd for some reason I'm here on my own. "Buy ice."

"Just one tent for all three of you?" Nell's mom asks. I see her glance at Nell's dad. "I hope it's roomy."

"Doris is phenomenal," he says, seemingly oblivious to his wife's pointed look. "Where did you guys set up?"

I point in the direction I came from. "Maybe half a mile that way, in the first clearing past the tree growth. Not too far from the public restrooms."

"We'll pitch our tent over there, too," says Mr. Wachowski. "Not too close, but near enough that you can join us for breakfast in the morning. How's that?"

Mrs. Wachowski gives him another look. I feel the need to escape before a serious parenting discussion goes down.

"We have doughnuts!" says Jack. "Krispy Kreme!"

"Oh, yum," I say. "Hey, wanna come with me? Get some ice, see some balloons?" I try to make this offer sound as enticing as possible because I really do want Jack to come with me, not to mention, this will give me a chance to beat a hasty retreat.

"Yes!" Jack says.

"Oh no, Jack," says Nell's mom. "There will be plenty of time later to bug Grant."

"I don't mind," I say. "He can help me carry the ice. Bungee Man looks very strong."

"As long as you're sure," says Mrs. Wachowski.

"Jack, stay with Grant," says Mr. Wachowski. "We'll expect

you back at the campsite in twenty minutes. No going off on your own this time!"

"OK!" says Jack, pulling one of the cords from his waist and stretching it out as far as it goes. I'm afraid he's going to snap it back and give himself a monster bruise, but he gently places it back against his shirt as he says, "Bungafralacagelistica, Bungee!"

His parents and I stare at him.

"Chill out, dudes," he says. "It's a fake magic spell, but you can at least act like it's real. It's *fun*! And, no, I'm not going to hurt myself with a bungee cord. I am seven years old, not a toddler."

His mom and dad start laughing, and I give Jack a high five. My brothers love those.

"We never thought that, even when you *were* a toddler," Mrs. Wachowski tells him.

I point in the direction of the ice hut, which sells not only bags of ice but also sticky sweet liquid sugar poured onto shaved ice in different neon colors. Jack reaches out and plants his sweaty hand in mine as we traipse across the field.

"Don't let Grant out of your sight!" Nell's mom and dad call. "And, Grant, don't let Jack out of yours!"

"Yes, sir and ma'am!" I say, and Jack waves. "Bungafralacage-listica, Bungee!"

Being with Jack reminds me of being with the twins. They notice everything; they have so many questions! He's pointing and shouting in glee at balloons and cloud shapes in the sky and old ladies' purple hair and funnel cakes. It makes me remember the first time I was here, with my mom and my real dad. I was probably around Jack's age. I loved it: all those colors, and the two people I cared about most in the world with me to see it all. We went up in a balloon. We could see our house from the sky.

On the way back down, my mom and dad got in a fight. He was working too much. She was nagging too much. In hindsight, I guess that was kind of the story of their split, with a few important details missing about why exactly he was working so much, and why she was nagging. Now here I am a decade later, and everything's different but the balloons. I try to hang on to those few moments we had up in the air, when it felt like everything was perfect.

32
Nell

It is, in a word, *mortifying* that my parents are camping so close to us. On the plus side, Grant came back with Jack and said the nurses had pronounced him perfectly fine, if a little bit dehydrated. "Are you sure that's it?" asked Doris. "I swear on the dildo's grave," he said, holding his hand over his heart. She made him promise to tell Dr. Laura, and then we let it go, at least for the moment. We roamed around the festival for hours afterward, and there was no trace of another blackout, though Grant's been chugging water like it's going out of style. And now my dad is grilling and Mom has set out a spread of delicious stuff—homemade coleslaw and potato salad and ingredients for s'mores for dessert.

There's a fire pit where we sit and eat our dinner, Grant and Doris and Jack and Mom and Dad and me, and some people camping nearby join us, too—twentysomething Australians named Jamie and Beatrice who are traveling through the US "on holiday," and an older couple who've brought their balloon down from Tennessee, which they tell us they do every year. Dad and Grant build a fire, and Doris and I tease them for being stereotypical "manly men." But the fire is nice: Even though it's been a roasty summer day, it's cool in the woods, and the heat feels like sunshine on my bare arms. Mom keeps trying to make me put on a sweatshirt, but other than that, she and my dad are being pretty chill.

I've got a second helping of potato salad on a paper plate on my knee when Grant, who's gotten up to replenish his own plate, sits down next to me, grabs my fork, and helps himself to a scoop.

"Rude!" I say. Doris comes in on the other side with her own fork and eats another bite. "Can a person not have her own plate of food here?" I ask.

"This is so good," says Doris. "I need the recipe for my mom."

"Mrs. Wachowski, we love your potato salad!" shouts Grant across the fire. My mom is on the other side talking to the people from Tennessee.

"What?" she calls.

We yell, "Potatoes!" and Grant gives her the A-OK symbol while Doris and I make finger hearts.

She smiles and yells, "Eat more! I don't want to have to take it home!"

"OK, so what's our plan?" says Doris. "Do we walk among the masses? Check out the band, and maybe the fireworks? Investigate how long the lines currently are for balloon rides? Stay here and consume the rest of your mom's outer-space-worthy potato salad?"

"I dunno, what do you guys want to do?" I ask. "You're the locals. Grant, how do you feel?"

"I feel fine," he says. "Except I'm tired of answering that question! Hey, how about an after-dinner stroll through the festival, and we take it from there? I think National Velour is opening."

"National Velour? Like . . . National Velvet but . . . velour?"

"Yes," says Doris. "You didn't know? It's Cat's band! They wear horse heads while they play. They used to pair them with these shaggy velour capes, but one caught on fire at a concert, so they switched to wearing spandex jumpsuits. I saw them here last year with Maya. They rock. It's Cat and these two guys who used to go to our high school."

"Toby Marcus and Beau Bonner," says Grant. "I knew 'em from football. Neither were very good, which is why they have a band." He frowns. "Maybe I should have been worse at football."

. . . . .

The field is different at night. It's not only that it's dark, with just the light of the stage and flashlights and the stars above to keep us all from bumping into each other. The energy is also different. Some people seem a little drunk, swaying to the music, and others, including a guy I see puking miserably into a trash bin, are definitely drunk. Doris and I keep glancing over at Grant to make sure he's (1) OK and (2) not tempted.

"Let's stop here," says Doris, when we're close enough to see the band without binoculars but not so close we can't hear each other talk. Grant spreads the blanket he's been toting, and we all flop down on it, lying on our backs and looking up. You can see each star so clearly here, distinct pinpricks in a dark carpet of night. It reminds me of my bedroom, but a thousand times better. For one thing, it's real.

"It never looked like this in Illinois," I say. They both look at me and grin.

"Welcome to Alabama. Our night skies are unforgettable," says Doris.

"As for the other stuff, enjoy at your own risk," jokes Grant. National Velour starts playing, a low hum that swells into a poppy, dance-y riff, and Doris gets up and starts spinning circles on her own.

"I love this song; I can't help it," she says, and Grant and I lie back and watch her cycle through a range of standard dance moves until she starts to goof off and present every ridiculous motion she can think of, pretending to write a paper, mow a lawn, drink a milkshake, and make and deliver and eat a pizza. The song ends, and she flops back down on the blanket with us. "I'm exhausted," she says. "They better play a slow one next."

She gets her wish: It's a sweet ballad. We're all nodding along, side by side on the blanket. "Into it?" Grant asks me.

"Yeah. Though I still question their name," I say.

"In the history of music has there ever been a truly great band name?" asks Doris.

"So many artists sound like they were named in some musty garage after a bong hit," says Grant. "When whatever you'd come up with would be a fantastic, hilarious, brilliant idea. Think about it. Odd Future Wolf Gang Kill Them All. Imagine Dragons. Arctic Monkeys. Lady Gaga. Eminem. Greeeen (with four *e*'s, naturally). One Direction—that one kinda sounds like a halfway house, actually."

"The String Cheese Incident! Butthole Surfers! Vampire Weekend!" adds Doris. "By the way, Eminem is Eminem because it's '*M* and *M*'—his real name is Marshall Mathers. Get it?"

"That's exactly what I'm talking about," says Grant.

"I like The String Cheese Incident. Probably because it's got cheese in it. What would your band name be, if you had one?" I ask.

Grant doesn't hesitate. "Necrotic Flesh!"

"Ew," we say.

"Or . . . Dogs of Pyrex," he amends. "That was a band name Brod and I came up with last summer. I was going to be the lead singer, but we never did anything other than talk about it. I don't even think he plays an instrument. Neither do I, for that matter."

"I always wanted to have a band called Purple Violet Squish. I have a trombone in my closet. . . ." Doris trails off.

"The Ramen Doodles," I say.

"What?" they ask.

"That was the band I was in in kindergarten. It was a bunch of the neighborhood kids. We did one—and only one—performance for our parents. I drummed on a pot and sang, and my friend Jackie had a keyboard she could play 'Chopsticks' on, and this kid, Ramesh, was like a saxophone prodigy. I think he got into Juilliard."

"Did I just feel a raindrop?" asks Grant.

"Uh-oh!" says Doris. "Did we zip the tent?"

We all jump up, because it's not just rain—it's a sudden, torrential downpour. Water is falling from the sky in sheets.

"Run!" I shout, as droplets cascade down my face. I didn't even hear thunder. Maybe the music covered it up.

Doris is already on the move with our blanket under her arm. We trace our path through the field in half the time it took us to get there, passing crowds of people choosing their strategy: hunker down in place (I see some umbrellas being raised against the sky, and ponchos being ripped from bags and donned with haste), evacuate like you're being chased by a demon (us), or dance and revel in the magical drops coming from the sky, a decision, I think, made based on how drunk (or otherwise influenced) each person happens to be. We weave through the people waiting it out, and I hear Cat say, "We're going to take a break to see if this blows over. Stay dry, y'all!"

"God, I love a summer storm," says Doris when we get back to the clearing where our tent sits waiting for us. We breathe in the air, which smells fresh and damp and alive. The campfire is still glowing from some well-covered embers, and even though the rain is falling, our new Australian friends, Jamie and Beatrice, are cozied up next to each other on logs overlooking the fire pit, his arm around her shoulders. Grant unzips our tent and we pile inside, laughing and falling all over each other.

"Here, use my towel," says Doris. "Take your shoes off and wipe your feet if they're wet!" Grant and I comply.

There's a little knock-knock at the tent, or a rustling of the flap, anyway, because you can't really knock at the door of a tent. Doris reaches over and unzips it, and there's Jack, his face peering in over the zipper.

"Hi!" he says.

Doris unzips the door, and my little brother piles in, his child-size sleeping bag under his arm and a giant waterproof poncho on top of that to keep him dry.

"What are you doing?" I ask.

"Mom sent me to spend the night with you guys," he says cheerfully, unrolling his bag right between me and Grant.

"Oh, did she?" I say.

"She called me a secret weapon," he says, and gives me the most angelic smile in his arsenal.

"You're a weapon, all right. That's not so secret," says Grant. "I see you took off the bungees?"

Jack nods seriously. "I was over it. My dad says every shtick has a use-by date."

"You're just in time," says Doris. "We were about to start telling ghost stories."

I raise my eyebrows at her, but then my brother cuddles up next to me in his sleeping bag, his soft brown hair against my shoulder, and I remember the water park and hug him.

"I'll go first," I say. "Once upon a time, there was a boy who was seven years old, and his name was Jack Wachowski, and he loved peanut butter cookies and video games. And one day a voice on his favorite video game asked him a question."

"What did it ask?" says Jack.

"Can you stop getting so many crumbs on me, please?" I answer.

Jack starts giggling, and Doris and Grant groan.

"No judgments, please," I say. "Unless you want *your* story to be judged, which, you're next, Doris."

We take turns telling tales that are increasingly ridiculous. Doris's is about a ghost in a department store who likes trying on furs. Grant's is about a football ghost that's always kicking the football when no one else on the team expects it. Jack tells a story that's not about a ghost at all but about an all-white hamster named Ghost, and then he asks Doris to tell him about her aunt Stella and all the things she and her lifeguard friends found in the wave pool, which Doris does. The rain is now falling lightly on the top of the tent, making a soothing *pitter-patter*. We hear fireworks going off in the distance, but no one feels like going back outside.

I look at my phone, and there's a text from Mom; it says **Love you!** ☺ And the thing is, even if it was probably the least cool move in the world to send my little brother over to camp out with us, at the moment, I really don't mind at all that she did. Pretty soon Jack has fallen asleep on my shoulder, and Grant's conked out on top of his sleeping bag. I hear faint strains of music, so I guess National Velour has gone back on, but I don't think we're missing anything. I settle Jack back on his pillow and turn to see what Doris is up to.

"Whatcha doing?" I ask quietly.

"I'm just drawing," she says, and passes her notebook over. It's a sketch of the stockroom at Unclaimed, with the manatee sitting on top of the table, surveying everything. It's so detailed, you can see items on the shelves. You can even see the different types of doughnuts in the box, and the purple leopard suitcase we found with nothing in it in the corner. Seated at the table, there's Red and Heather and me and Grant and Byron and Cat and Nadine and Freddie.

"You are really talented," I say.

"Putting stuff down in different ways—lists, pictures, whatever—helps me figure things out sometimes," she says. "It's a way to see things from above ground level."

"Like you're in a hot-air balloon," I offer.

"Kind of! It's a matter of perspective." Doris looks over at Grant. "Do you think he's OK?" she whispers. "Like, really OK?"

"I don't know," I say. "He seemed fine all night."

"He seemed fine before he fainted, too," she says. "I'm just worried there's something more going on. He's probably hit his head more times than he knows, playing football."

"Not to mention the car accident."

"We need to watch out for him. Make sure nothing more happens . . . and if it does, we should tell someone," she says.

I nod, and she shakes her head. "Who would have ever thought I'd care so much about the well-being of Grant Collins?"

"Well, he's our friend now," I say. "For better or worse."

"Speaking of friends," says Doris, "I'm so glad I got to share your first balloon festival with you."

"Me too," I say.

"And there's more fun tomorrow!" she says. "'Night, Nell." She turns over in her sleeping bag and quickly falls asleep, but I stay up for a little bit longer, looking at her drawings by the light of my flashlight. I turn the pages of the notebook and find more pictures of the store. Grant Collins, toting a football across a green field, his eyes the color of the grass. A sea of hot-air balloons across the sky. A girl wearing a name tag that says MAYA, holding hands with a girl with a name tag that says HANNAH, a heart floating between them. A picture of a woman with her hands around a giant mason jar with a straw in it, her expression bright and expectant, as if she's right in the middle of hearing a really good story from someone she loves. Underneath the picture it says STELLA. I stare at that one for a long time.

.

234

33
Doris

I bolt upright in my sleeping bag like I've heard a gunshot. It takes me a second to remember where I am, and then I wonder if I was just dreaming about fireworks. I look around. There's Nell, snoring quietly, and Jack, who moved from his sleeping bag to hers at some point in the night and is cuddled up inside with her. We're missing someone. Grant. Has he gone somewhere and gotten drunk again? Is he hanging out with his bad influences? The sun is barely peeping over the horizon, and the tent is full of the kind of pale light that comes after dawn. I check my phone. It's only six a.m. Then I hear the noise, whatever it was that must have woken me up, again: a rattling, clunky noise, like the sound of someone shaking rocks in a box. I'm slightly reassured by the fact that Nell's parents are close enough that they could definitely hear me scream—and scream I most definitely would. That's one thing the waterslide incident has taught me: not to be silent.

I gather my courage and creep to the opening flap of the tent and zip it down a tiny bit, preparing to face off with who or whatever is outside. And there at the nearest picnic table eating a bowl of cereal from our rations, just as happy as can be, is Grant Collins.

I start to crawl out of the tent in my pajamas and bare feet; then I think better of it and put my shoes on. He doesn't seem to notice me at all, so when I get close, I whisper, "Boo."

Grant jumps out of his seat, yelps, and drops his metal camping bowl to the forest floor, hitting his toe with it. "DORIS."

"Why are you awake?" I ask.

"Why does it always hurt *so freaking bad* when you drop something on your toe?" he answers, which isn't an answer, but I empathize. "They're so small, toes. Yet so FULL OF PAIN."

"I didn't mean to scare you," I say. "Well, I did mean to scare you, but I didn't mean to foot-scare you. It was meant to be more of a fun scare."

He grimaces and inspects the pile of cereal that's fallen.

"Oops," I say.

"Eh, that was just my first course," he says. "I woke up starving. Do you think there's any leftover potato salad?"

"Maybe," I say. "Should we go creep around Nell's parents' tent and terrify them, too?"

"How about we go for a walk?" he suggests. "They'll be awake when we get back, and they can feed us!"

"OK," I say. "I'll bring some of my mom's brownies for the road."

"Yum." Grant reaches for my hand, and I take his and pretend to help him up. As he rises, he squeezes gently, which for some reason gives me chills that run up and down my back.

"Shall we?" he says, pointing to the trail off to the side of our campsite.

He's got on shorts and a T-shirt, but I'm still in my pink shortie pajamas, which has me flashing back to that other babyish outfit, the Minnie Mouse swimsuit, and what happened next. I'm tempted to change, but it's just Grant. Who do I need to impress? Plus, I want to get out of here before we wake anyone up. I grab a couple of brownies from Mom's cooler while he slips on his shoes, and we walk quietly to the trail, eating and leaving crumbs behind like a teenage Hansel and Gretel.

"Why'd you get up so early?" I ask. "You didn't go back out last night, did you? Do you feel OK?"

"Stop!" he says. "Seriously, don't worry. I slept clean and pure and woke up when my stomach started growling. All that fresh air! I feel great."

"Good," I say.

"And . . . I couldn't stop thinking about my dad," he admits. "The balloon festival reminds me of when we used to come here, when I was little."

"What *did* happen with your dad?" I ask. "If you want to talk about it?" I know his parents split when we were in elementary school and his father moved away, but I've never heard the whole story.

"Your typical midlife tragedy," he says. "Dad fell for the nurse he worked with, Mom kicked him out, he got a better job at a hospital in South Carolina. Now they both have new lives, and their teenage son is left to figure himself out on his own. Badly, in my case."

"I'm sorry," I say. "If it's any consolation, I'm pretty sure my parents wish they could trade me in for, like, a Chassie. They don't get me at all. But I do know that they love me. I'm sure your dad loves you, too."

"I don't know," says Grant. "If you leave people, do you love them?"

"Sometimes," I tell him. "Sometimes you can't help leaving." I think about Aunt Stella. "You could call him, you know. Maybe talking about it would help. You should tell him how you feel."

He makes a face. "Then I'd actually have to speak to him. Let's not go too far."

As we reach the road that leads to town, a strange sweeping noise comes from above. I think it's a small, low-flying plane at first, or maybe some kind of kite. But no: A partially deflated hot-air balloon has come undone from its tether, and it's been picked up by the wind and is bobbing along the treetops.

No one comes running after it. No one must know it's gone. Except us.

"Quick!" I yell, pointing forward. "Follow that balloon!"

For a few hundred yards, we jog after the floating bit of cloth, which can't possibly go too far; it's not even fully inflated. But it's a pretty windy day, and the gusts keep pushing it farther away from us. Its wicker basket eventually gets caught on some tall tree branches and the balloon is stuck, trailing out across the sky like a planted flag. I can make out some letters on it, a *P* and maybe an *L*.

Grant looks at me. "Have you ever found a hot-air balloon before?"

"Nope," I say. "I guess there's a first time for everything."

"How does someone lose an entire balloon?" he asks.

"People lose everything!" I tell him. "The more relevant question is, who do you think lost it? PL might be for Planned Parenthood. They had a balloon here last year, even though some folks in town tried to block them from attending."

"We should tell someone we saw it," says Grant. "Whoever's it is, they'll be wanting it back."

I agree, and we turn back to the trail that will take us to where all the balloonists, and park security, are located.

On the way, we fall into comfortable silence. I'm wondering if we've ever sold a hot-air balloon at the store, and what we'd charge for one if we did. But Grant's mind has traveled further.

"Do you remember hanging out in these woods when we were kids? All the exploring we did? Everything felt like such an adventure," he says.

He's right, when we were little—before the waterslide, way back in elementary school, we'd play here sometimes. That was when Chassie and I were still friends, kind of. Before Grant was a football star. I was always sandwiched between the two of them in Sunday school, our names an alphabetic chronicle that never changed: Collins, Dailey, Dunkirk. And even though they were a year older than I was, we were together a lot more than we were apart. Small towns are like that, at least before people grow up.

"I used to collect rocks that looked like they had faces," I say. "And one time I found a puddle full of tiny baby frogs. They were smaller than my pinky finger."

"I used to hunt for crawdads!" says Grant. "With the Benson brothers. We'd bring a pile of 'em back home, and our parents would pretend to cook them up. They'd really let them go in the creek and serve us hamburgers instead."

"Sometimes I can't wait to get out of here," I say. "And sometimes I love this town so much. I mean, it's a part of me. No matter what."

"I don't know if I'll ever leave," says Grant. "Like, really leave. I don't even know if I'll go away for college at this point."

"Do you want to?" I ask. "Leave?"

"I think so," he says. "But wanting doesn't change anything."

"Wanting is the only way to change something!" I say. "If you want to, you will."

We pass a tree that's got a heart carved into it. Inside the heart, someone's spray painted the initials GC and DD, which makes us laugh.

"Is that what you were doing while we were all sleeping?" I ask. "Ahem. You know you can tell me if you're secretly in love with me."

"I bet that stands for Garrett Carey and Daisy Duvall," says Grant. "They were hot and heavy last year, until he went to Auburn and she went to Alabama. Now their families won't speak to each another."

He's surely right, yet part of me longs for it to be my DD carved into that tree. Along with a GC for Grant Collins? Ugh, I think I've been listening to Nell talk about boyfriends and love too much. I pinch myself and remember what happened on the waterslide, and how Stella said never to get too attached. Falling for a guy in this town would derail all my plans. Falling for Grant Collins would be a downright disaster, for all sorts of reasons.

There's a tent up ahead of us, and as we get closer, we see figures outside of it. It's exactly who I don't want to run into, right after Mrs. Stokes. It's Chassie and Mac Ebling.

I glance at Grant, hoping this isn't going to set him off. He looks calm. "Hey there," he tells them. "You're up early."

"We still haven't gone to sleep," says Mac. "The party went all night. You know how it goes."

"I do," says Grant. "Or I used to, anyway."

I look at Chassie. Her red lips and wavy hair and cheerleader physique are the same as always, but she's holding one arm stiffly, like it hurts.

Grant notices. His face gets pinched.

Chassie looks from him to me, and back again. With her good arm she reaches around Mac's waist and pulls him toward her, giving him a kiss on the cheek.

Without thinking, I grab Grant's hand, and he squeezes mine. Again, shivers go up and down my spine. I think about how Nell kissed the Magic 8 Ball. Part of me suddenly, desperately wants to do the same thing, to Grant Collins.

Chassie frowns. "I'm going to sleep." She glares at Mac and flounces into their tent. She reopens the entrance flap and shouts out, "Stop calling me, Grant. I don't want to see you, and I don't want to hear your voice on my voice mail, either!"

Grant looks pained, and Mac shrugs.

"Women," he says. "Can't live with 'em, can't live without—"

"You should really get that written on a pillow," I say, interrupting the inevitable cliché.

"You think?" He looks confused.

"Oh, definitely. Big money maker, pillows with aphorisms," I say. "You could have an Etsy store."

"Huh?"

"We better go," says Grant.

I think I see Chassie watching us from the narrow open sliver of the tent.

"Report that balloon missing," Grant adds, nudging me to move, and so I do.

· · · · ·

After we alert a surprised group of rangers that a balloon has gone rogue, we head back to camp. Grant doesn't seem to want to talk about what happened with Chassie, but he holds on to my hand the whole time, until we reach our tent. And there, right before we unzip the flap to crawl inside, he takes my hand to his mouth and he kisses it.

"Thanks," he whispers. I don't know what to say back, so I just nod. My heart is going ninety miles an hour.

As soon as we're inside—there's really no way to quietly enter a tent—Jack's eyes pop open in excitement and Nell squints at us. "Morning," she says sleepily. Pretty soon Nell's dad is banging around making blueberry pancakes on the kerosene stove. We're heating up the casserole my mom sent with me, and we're devouring everything like we haven't eaten in days.

"It's the perfect morning for a balloon ride," says Mrs. Wachowski, remarking on the blue sky. The wind from earlier has died down, and last night's storm has left us a gorgeous, sunny day. Grant and I tell everyone about the renegade balloon sighting we had that morning, and how park security is now trying to find its owners. We keep our other sighting, of Mac and Chassie, to ourselves—at least for now. As for the hand kissing, I need to think about that for a while before I share it with anyone else. Even Nell.

34
Grant

The balloon festival is already thronged with people when we arrive, Jack and Nell's parents in tow. They're looking around in wonder. It's hard not to feel overwhelmed by the sight, no matter how times you witness it. Doris has taken it upon herself to try to find the balloon's owners; she's asking everyone we see if they know anything about it and whether there's a Planned Parenthood tent this year. All she gets are blank stares and shaking heads.

"Sorry, hon," says one woman who sells sand you can swirl into glass bottles in different patterns. "But come back if you want to make your own keepsake of the festival; our beautiful sandcrafts will help you remember this moment forever!"

"You know what I'm going to have to remember forever is the word *sandcrafts*," Doris tells us.

We pass the funnel cake vendor again, which elicits an involuntary mouthwatering reaction in me. We turn our heads to avoid the Mercy Church tent, and all of a sudden, there's a voice coming at us, an old-fashioned country drawl. It belongs to an old guy wearing a gray uniform that looks like something out of the Civil War. He's also sporting a military cap and a grizzled beard.

The Wachowskis do a double take. I don't blame them for turning in the opposite direction, toward the souvenir stands. But Doris has plowed ahead to talk to the old guy for some reason. Nell and I wait as Jack begs his parents to let him stay with us.

"OK, but stick with the big kids," they tell him. "Absolutely no running off this time. Do you understand?" They look at me and Nell. "Keep an eye on him, OK?"

We nod, and so does Jack. "I won't even *walk* off, either," he says.

We join Doris, who's chatting to the guy dressed up like a Confederate soldier about the stray balloon sighting we had over by the woods this morning. I want to ask him about his outfit, and why he's wearing it in the twenty-first century, but I can't get a word in. "Not mine!" he says of the missing balloon. "We tie her down real good every night."

"I think it really was the Planned Parenthood balloon!" I say, but no one pays any attention because this guy, who introduces himself as Earl, has offered to take the four of us for a ride in his balloon "for the low, low price of five dollars for teens, and the kid rides for free." Doris whispers that we should do it, to show Nell another side of the South.

"Plus, information gathering!" she says.

Nell is unsure. "What's up with the whole Civil War thing?" she asks.

Earl hears her and launches into his spiel. "You gotta have a shtick, you know? Everybody wants more than just the standard balloon ride. The deal is, I'm a Confederate soldier, and we're going up for surveillance, just like they did in the old days, except now we've got a bit more power and, luckily, less war," he says. "Get ready to take a peek over yonder at enemy lines." He eyes Jack. "Kid, can you behave yourself up there in the air? You'll do what I say? No funny business, like trying to climb over the edge or throw stuff over? Don't tell me how old you are. I don't want to know."

"He's very small for his age," I say. "He's actually in college. Pre-med."

Jack nods vigorously. "I promise I'll be good." He holds up his pinky.

"Ah, ye olde pinky swear. Yer speakin' my language. Hop in, then, quick," says Earl, and helps Doris and Nell and Jack and finally me into the basket.

He points to a woman down on the field who's waving sweetly as she releases the remaining ties keeping the balloon on the ground. "Betty Lou. Love of my durn life." He blows her a kiss, which she catches and pretends to put in the pocket of her old-timey petticoat.

"Hey, buddy, watch this," I tell Jack, pointing to Earl's deft management of the balloon's internal components. The guy may look like the ghost of a Confederate soldier, but he knows what he's doing. Jack shouts in glee as fire shoots from little burners into the opening of the balloon, and pretty soon we're sweeping through the field, lifting gently as we go. The surge of power comes with a rush of sound that makes it hard to talk, so we grow quiet, mesmerized by objects below getting smaller and smaller.

"We're flying!" shouts Nell, pointing out her parents, shrinking in our view, on the ground: "Look, Jack, there's Mom and Dad!" We yell and scream, and they probably can't hear us, but they're watching, so they wave as we swing higher into the air.

Then we're simply floating, suspended in time, the quiet punctuated by Earl letting off occasional bursts of heat to keep the balloon steady. I'm more at peace than I've felt in a long time, happy to watch everything go by and listen to Earl's talk about how it works.

"I pull the cord here, see," he says, "and that makes us go lower. But if I punch the gas on the burners, we'll lift up again. Hot-air balloons were used in the Civil War for aerial reconnaissance and artillery spotting. That's a fancy way of sayin' it let people see who was comin', and how best to fight 'em. Spies flew some of these, and information was transported this way, too."

Doris and Nell are pointing out various town sites, living in real time instead of the past.

"There's the wave pool," Nell says. "And the waterslide!" We move out over the river for a few minutes, gazing down at the brown water, and Doris claims she sees a water moccasin, which makes Nell scream.

"Look, Grant!" Doris says, pointing to a rescue crew with a cherry picker trying to free the balloon we saw earlier from the tree it got snagged on.

On the way back, we take a spin over town, getting close enough to see the sloping tops of our houses.

"There's Unclaimed," says Doris, pointing to the gray metal roof of the store. We all gaze at it, thinking about how, if it were another day, we might be inside that building working. Either way, I realize, we'd be finding things.

All too soon, it's done; we're heading back down again. Jack peers eagerly over the edge of the basket, the tip of his nose barely clearing it.

We land with a light bump, and quickly Betty Lou and a younger man with a beard and his own gray suit are securing the basket and Earl is helping us out. We each accept his hand and jump lightly onto the grass, then thank him and walk away in a daze. People are clamoring to get on board next.

"That was awesome," I say.

"It was pretty cool," agrees Doris. "I love that you can see so much from up there! Stuff you'd never see from any other vantage point."

"Totally," says Nell, but she looks concerned. "I still don't get it, though. Why is he a Confederate balloonist? Are there Union balloonists, too?"

"Not in Alabama!" says Doris.

"Some people around here are really into Civil War history,"

I explain. "And some of those people say the South will rise again, or whatever. I had one teacher call it 'the War of Northern Aggression.' And a lot of Civil War battle reenactments really do have the South winning."

"Isn't that kind of racist?" asks Nell.

"Yes," says Doris.

"Well, it's heritage," I say. "It's our history. It's a way of teaching people about what happened—"

"The thing is, Earl is harmless, and he's doing it for business, not because he actually believes 'the South should rise again,'" interrupts Doris. "If he'd been spouting off nonsense like that, I never would have agreed to get in his balloon. But if you're wearing a Civil War uniform, you're still pretending to be someone who fought to keep slavery legal in America. You may not 'mean' to support it, but you are. And how do you think people who aren't white feel when they see that guy in that uniform? Aren't there ways of teaching—and, for that matter, running a business—that don't include that?"

Nell is nodding. "Ashton would definitely feel weird going up in that balloon. And so should we."

"You have a point," I say. "I didn't think about it like that. Hey, did you know that a bunch of people protested the Confederate flag hanging outside the courthouse this spring, and a couple months ago, they actually took it down?"

Doris smiles at him. "I was part of that protest."

"Why does that not surprise me?" I ask. We share a look, and the odd thing is, I kind of want to kiss her again, and maybe not just her hand.

"Then shouldn't we have said something to him?" asks Nell. "Like, told him what he was doing was wrong?"

Doris smiles. "Probably. But sometimes it's good to get organized first. And I have an idea for a new protest now."

"Hell yeah," I say. "I've never been part of a protest."

"I'm so in," says Nell.

Our next stop is the funnel cake truck.

"Now, this is a tradition I can get behind," says Doris.

"Me too," says Nell.

"Me three," says Jack.

I order two with extra powdered sugar and chocolate syrup—they're big enough to share. The woman taking the order gives me a wink.

"You got it, hon," she says, and throws in a bag of powdered-sugar-covered fried cast-off dough for free. "A man has to eat! All that football!" We walk away carrying our load of goodies, which we split four ways between us. As we lie on the grass licking powdered sugar off our fingertips, I think about how some traditions are worth keeping, while others need to end immediately so new, better ones can start. Or as Jack said yesterday, *Every shtick has a use-by date.*

35
Nell

None of us wants to leave the balloon festival, but Grant and Doris promise we'll all come back together next year. Meanwhile, a tent has been set up in the middle of the field to help crowdfund for repairs to what really does turn out to be the Planned Parenthood balloon. We head over to make our donations, and Doris tells a woman named Alanna about how she and Grant saw the wayward balloon this morning and reported it. "Finding things, it's kind of a talent of hers," says Grant, and Doris blushes. By the time we leave, we've told them all about Unclaimed Baggage. They're planning a trip to the store before they head back to New York City, where they're from.

"Where do you even keep a hot-air balloon in New York City?" asks Grant.

"Manhattan Mini Storage," says Alanna. "None of us have an apartment big enough to fit this baby!" She pats the side of the balloon. We sit for a while and listen to the group tell stories about their adventures: They travel to different festivals around the country to help educate people about sexual health, she says. After New York, their next stop is Taos, New Mexico. "It's fun, but it's also genuinely useful," Alanna explains. "Meeting people face-to-face and having real conversations is the best way to share what we do, and to really help those who need us. Otherwise everyone has these preconceived ideas. And the internet gets in the way as much as it connects sometimes!" I nod. I've seen how things can get ugly in the comments, even on the store Instagram.

Alanna is giving her business card to Doris. "Let's stay in touch," she says. "I'd love to repay you for the favor somehow!"

"Aw, it was nothing," says Doris, smiling.

Grant's gazing longingly at the balloon. "Part of me wishes we could come with you," he says quietly, and Doris gives him this look, almost like she's seeing him for the first time.

I imagine the roving balloonist life, the literal highs and lows, the fresh air that never stops. But I'd miss Ashton, and my friends—old and new. For me, well, I think I like to keep my feet firmly planted on the earth. With occasional perspective-shifting trips to see things from above ground level, that is.

As we're packing stuff in the trunk of Doris's car to head

back to our houses, my phone emits a special ring. There's that picture I love, and the emoji with the heart eyes.

"Ashton's back from camp!" I yell, and answer. "Hi! Oh my God, I missed you! How are you? It's been *FOREVER*!"

Doris and Grant roll their eyes and smile. I know I'm being a total cheeseball, but Ashton's voice is all that matters for the moment. The whole way back to my house, I talk to him nonstop about the balloon festival and our adventures, including going up in the air with a guy wearing a Confederate uniform.

"Yikes," he says. "So that stuff you hear about the South is true, huh? You sure it's safe for me to come visit?"

"Yes!" I say. "It's not all like that. A lot of things are great. You'll see."

He tells me how he got the MVP award at camp, and that his coaches think he has a shot at playing for a Division I team in college.

"It was awesome," he says. "But I missed hearing your voice. Hey, what do your parents say about my trip? Is Jack ready to try to beat me at *Lego Star Wars*?"

"Totally," I tell him, which is a lie because I haven't told them yet. But I will. I change the subject. "What do you want to do while you're here?" I ask.

"Maybe we can go to that water park you told me about," he says. "The wave pool sounds fun. And I want to see the store! And meet your friends."

"They want to meet you, too," I say, and Doris and Grant smile and nod.

"And I want to just hang out with *you*," he says, his voice getting softer.

"I want to just hang out with *you*," I croon back. I close my eyes and imagine his face, and we murmur back and forth to each other until I realize the car has stopped moving. I open my eyes. We're at my house, and Doris and Grant are peering over the front seats at me in the back, my phone cuddled up to my face.

"Oops," I say.

"I really can't wait to be properly introduced to this guy," says Grant. "He seems very compelling."

"Should we tell him she's having a secret, passionate affair with her phone?" Doris asks.

"Hey, Ash, I gotta go," I say. "I'm being mocked mercilessly for *being happy*."

"OK, Pony," he says. "Counting the days till I see you!"

I hang up. "So, do you two monsters want to come over?" I ask my friends. "We can hang out in the playhouse and eat the rest of my mom's potato salad. She ended up bringing a tub of it home after all. She'll be thrilled if she doesn't have to look at it in the fridge anymore."

"Signs point to yes," says Doris.

36
Doris

The next day, I'm back in my car, listening to this awesome crashy-yelly song called "Debaser" by the Pixies, an indie group that was popular in the '90s. Cat got me hooked on the band when a shipment came in that included a whole stack of their records and she started playing them in the store. It's kind of weird, but I love it. Even though I don't really sing, I sing to this one, because it's just about saying the words as loud as you can.

I crank it up and shout along, and even though it's Alabama-July hot outside, I open up the windows because I want to feel the air around me, warm as it is, to let the air in and the music out and feel *alive*. I'm on my way to Unclaimed Baggage. Red has asked me to come in to move some fresh merchandise out to the front. With the balloon folks in town, we've been selling more than usual—T-shirts and camping equipment and a ton of rope, but also toiletries and books and even some cooking stuff. I stop at a red light, and the woman in the car next to me looks at me in surprise, like I'm some ridiculous kid blasting my obnoxious tunes, and I realize it's Grant's mother. She waves at me, and I think she wants me to stop so she can say something, but I don't—I can't, I shake my head, I have to keep going. I know too much about her son to be caught in conversation with her; I'm a girl with the gift of gab, and I'm afraid I might spill. She slows down and, uh-oh, she's getting in a lane behind me, following me.

I divert my route, hoping to lose her. I turn left at the church instead of right, and by the time I'm at the Family Mart, I think she's gone. But as I reach the Unclaimed parking lot, there she is, Mrs. Collins in her shiny minivan. She's a smart lady. Of course she could have guessed that was where I was going.

"Hey, Doris," she says, rolling down the passenger side window and leaning across the seat to talk to me. It looks like she's not going to get out, which I take as a good sign. "Where's the fire? I coulda sworn you were trying to lose me back there."

"Oh, hi, Mrs. Collins," I say, pushing my sunglasses onto the top of my head. "I had to make a quick stop before getting to the store! There's an . . . inventory emergency."

"The store is closed today, isn't it? That's what Grant told me." She raises her eyebrows like she's scared she's going to catch him in a lie.

"That's right. Red asked me to swing by specially, so I could replenish the floor for tomorrow. The balloon people are buying everything!"

She looks relieved. "Ah, don't let me stop you," she says, and waves a manicured hand.

I roll up my windows and grab my bag from the passenger seat and am locking the doors to my car when I notice Mrs. Collins hasn't moved. She's staring straight out at the pavement in front of her. I hope Grant's fainting spells aren't some kind of hereditary thing. I wave "bye" at her, but when she doesn't respond, I get a little concerned. I go over to the driver's side window and knock on it, doing that universal sign for "roll down the window, please?" She does.

"Oh, Doris," she says, and I can see her eyes are red and puffy, like she's been crying. "I'm just so worried. Tell me Grant's OK? I feel like you're one of the only people who really knows him. I wish I'd had girls. Girls are so much easier to understand. How is he doing? What does he talk about? Does he seem happy?"

I want to tell her that Grant *does* seem happier. And better. Of course, there was the weird incident at the campground, and part of me thinks I should talk to his mom about that. What if he's really sick? But the nurse said he was fine. And the truth is, maybe I don't want Grant's mom to suspect anything's wrong with him because that would mean he'd be able to spend less time with me. At work or out of it.

"Oh, he's doing great!" I say. "He's so much fun to have

around. He's a hard worker, too. You should see how many boxes he can carry at a time. . . ." I'm burbling a bunch of meaningless nonsense, but she's smiling, so maybe it's helping.

"That's so nice to hear. You and . . . what's your other friend's name? The one who works with you and Grant?"

"Nell."

"You and Nell should come over for dinner. I'd like to meet her! We need to spend more time with Grant's friends," she says. "He talks about you."

"That would be nice," I answer, wondering what Grant Collins is telling his mother about us, and whether she means "you" in the plural or the singular sense. Does Grant Collins talk about me, Doris Dailey? I can't ask that any more than I can tell his mom he blacked out at the campsite. Or about his playhouse confession.

So even though I don't know if I believe this, I say, "Mrs. Collins. Everything will work out OK. It will." I want this to be true so badly, I can feel myself trying to will it into being. I want it to be more than OK. I want it to be good. For me *and* Grant. And wanting matters. It has to.

She nods. "Don't tell anyone you found me like this, if you don't mind? It's just, sometimes acting like everything's fine is so . . ."

"Exhausting?" I think about how it was right after Aunt Stella died. I didn't know how to talk to my parents, to anyone. Maybe that's how Mrs. Collins feels, too: alone, and unable to express how she feels to anyone who gets it.

She nods again. "I love my boys. I love Grant. But . . . there's just this wall between us sometimes."

"You're his mother," I say. "He's a teenage boy. I think that's maybe normal? Not that I know anything."

"I think you know quite a bit," she says. "You've got a good head on your shoulders. You know, I really liked your aunt. I'm so sorry about what happened to her. That must have been incredibly painful."

"It was," I say. "It still is."

"Losing people is so hard," she says. "Sweetie, can you do me a favor?"

"Yes, ma'am."

"Please keep looking out for Grant."

"I will," I tell her.

"Thank you, Doris," she says. She puts her sunglasses on to shield her puffy eyes and drives out of the parking lot, leaving me alone to sort through the latest of what's at Unclaimed at the same time that I mentally sort through whether I should have told her the truth. One of those tasks, by the way, is a whole lot easier than the other.

. . . . .

Before I get off work, I call Nell from the stockroom to tell her about seeing Mrs. Collins.

"Whoa, what happened?" she asks. "What did she say?"

"She was worried. But she doesn't seem to know anything."

"Did you tell her what he told us?" asks Nell. "Or what happened at the balloon festival?"

"I was afraid to," I say. "Wouldn't that betray his trust completely?"

"Yes," says Nell. "But I also worry, what if there's something really wrong with him? And what if he's not getting better, he's getting worse?"

"Let's keep an eye on him," I tell her. "He's doing so well! I think it's better if we can help him for now. So he doesn't cut us off. Or his parents don't."

Nell laughs. "Maybe, just maybe, you like Grant Collins."

"I might," I admit. "I never thought I would be saying this, but I might." I decide to unload everything I've kept to myself since our campout. "He kissed my hand that morning at the balloon festival. After we ran into Chassie and Mac. I think it was just to thank me for being there, but . . ."

"You got chills, didn't you."

"I did."

"Oh my God, Doris. You might love Grant Collins!"

"No," I say. "I know you love love, but . . . we have to take this slow. He's my friend. And I don't entirely know if I can trust him. Much less date him. Not to mention all the other issues."

"Even so. He's kind of hard not to have a crush on, isn't he?" asks Nell. "Never tell him I said that. And definitely never tell Ashton! But we could double-date! How fun would that be?"

"Until it all went wrong," I tell her. "Even if he did want to date me, we should probably stick with how we are now.

Romances have a way of getting complicated. Especially when you start as friends. Especially when he's trying to get better."

"You're right," says Nell. "Getting romantically involved could open up a whole can of worms. And our entire dynamic would change, the three of us."

"Ew, a can of worms. Why are we even talking about this? There's, like, zero chance Grant likes me."

"I don't know about that," says Nell. "Hey, want to come over? It's time I tell my parents about Ashton's visit. And if you're here, they can't go ballistic."

"Be right there," I say.

37
Nell

We're all hanging out in the kitchen, which is where pretty much everything important in my family goes down—Mom told me she was pregnant with Jack three kitchens ago; the kitchen after that was where Dad broke the news that Grandpa had died; Mom announced her new job and our impending monumental move in our last kitchen. So today I might as well add to the kitchen tradition. It's about time I had some say about what happens in this family.

"Mom," I begin. "Dad." They turn from their respective occupations—she's reading the paper, he's unloading the dishwasher—and Jack lifts his head and looks at me, too. He's been sitting at the table next to me coloring as I update the store's Instagram account while psyching myself up for this talk. My group text with Nisha and Morgan has helped, too: **JUST TELL THEM!!!!!** is the last message on my screen. I press forward. Doris isn't here yet but she's on her way, and it's now or never. "I have something to say." My parents raise their eyebrows at me, and I blurt it out. "Guess what! Ashton is coming to visit."

There's a reason I decided to tell, not ask. I did a lot of internet research, and the prevailing opinion seems to be if it's not clearly against the rules, go ahead and do something before you find out it's not allowed. A person can always plead ignorance, or apologize and say they won't do it again. However, in this case, a mom is involved, and from the reaction mine has, I would say the internet may have led me astray.

"Excuse me?" she says, putting her paper down and staring at me with all the fire she can muster.

"I like Ashton!" says Jack. "He's cool! And fun! And—"

My mom hushes him with a look.

My dad is clanking around with the dishwasher, not wanting to get involved. I don't exactly blame him.

"What do you mean, Ashton is coming to visit?" my mom asks.

"He bought a plane ticket. With his own money. He's coming in two weeks, for the whole weekend! Isn't that great?" I feign pure, unadulterated enthusiasm. How can she crush me if I'm this excited?

"Nell, my dear darling. You are sixteen years old. You are a minor. You do not own this house, or even rent a room in it. You are not an independent adult. Did you not think this was a matter that should be discussed with your family before you agreed to it? I can't believe Ashton's parents are just fine with this. Or haven't reached out to get the OK from us, first!" she gets up and starts pacing, which is how she "thinks."

"Jack is excited," I say, and he looks up from his coloring book and grins at me and nods.

"This is not about excitement," Mom says. "I'm sure we'd all be happy to see Ashton for a reasonable amount of time, and then see him go sleep at his own house at night. But this is something that you should have asked us about, not simply gone ahead and done."

"You mean like how you moved us here?"

My mom's mouth turns down, but I look at my dad and I think I see the hint of a something unexpected.

"You didn't ask," I point out. "You just told us this was how it was. We didn't have any choice in the matter."

She fumes. "I am the parent!" she says. "My job puts food on this table for you and Jack! What does Ashton coming to visit do for us?"

"It makes me happy," I say.

Dad pipes up, surprising me. "I think he should visit. Why not? If he's done the work to buy his own ticket, what's the harm? It's only a weekend. Oh, hi, Doris," he says. "FYI: Family discussion underway."

Doris has arrived, thank goodness. She slips her arm through mine and stands next to me. "I know this is a matter for y'all to decide, but I just wanted to say that Nell talks about Ashton every day and really loves and cares about him. I think it would

be a mistake not to let him visit. She needs to see him and figure out what might happen between them."

"That's what I'm afraid of," mutters my mom.

"Mom." I stand taller. "I don't know if I want to be with him
forever, but I want to see if what I feel is real. In two years, I'll
be off at college. Maybe we'll pick one to go to together. Maybe
not. But just the way you had to take this job, don't you see, I
need to do this?"

"She's right about the job," Dad says. "Diana, you did just
sort of say we were going to move, no debate. I mean, don't get
me wrong, I support you. I'm so proud of you. But this was a
big change coming here, and it hasn't been easy on any of us.
Including me."

"Where will he sleep?" asks my mom. That's when I sort of
know I've won.

"The couch folds out," says Dad.

"Or maybe the playhouse," I say. "We could put an air mattress in there."

"Ooh, I wanna sleep out there, too," says Jack.

My mom is pursing her lips; she's still a little bit angry. "I'm
going to have to have a call with his parents before he arrives,"
she tells me. "Can you set that up, find some times they can
talk? I really wish you'd given us more notice."

"Yes . . . ma'am," I say, and her eyes widen.

"Why don't you girls go dig out the old air mattress from
the garage? I want to make sure it works and that it fits in the
playhouse," she instructs. "But you have to promise me you
won't sneak out and sleep in there, too, Nell."

265

I nod solemnly.

"And don't call me ma'am," she says. "We may be living in the South, but we're still proud Yankees. Plus, it makes me feel like an old lady."

"You could never be an old lady," says my dad, who walks over and puts his arms around her waist and kisses her on the cheek.

"Thank you thank you thank you thank youuuuu," I say.

All of a sudden, the Ashton visit I've dreamed about the entire summer is starting to feel real.

38
Grant

I've had a realization that goes greater than any nail polish: If I'm not bored or lonely, I'm not tempted to text Brod, no matter how many taco emojis he sends me. And if I stay away from Brod and the old gang, I don't drink. I haven't had another blackout. I make sure to look down at my fingers, and I repaint them when they chip. I ignore the stares of people who judge me for being a boy with glittery black nail polish on my fingers. To tell the truth, I kind of like it. I feel different. More like me. I don't know if this can last forever, but for now it's working. Working is working.

Today, Nell and I are unpacking a shipment from Des Moines International Airport, which contains a lot of business casual apparel, plus a suitcase full of dream catchers, when Doris comes into the back. She's been working the register while Byron takes lunch—since she's got so much store experience, Red's been using her as backup cashier. She automatically looks down at the pile I've got in front of me, analyzing what's good and what's bad in the way that's second nature to her. She pulls out one of the dream catchers and holds it in the air, letting it sway slightly on her fingers.

"I always wanted one of these," she says. "A place to store my dreams, so every night before going to bed, I could pull out the one I wanted and lodge it back in my brain, like watching a movie or something. Why bother with new dreams when you can rely on those good, old ones?"

Nell nods like she totally gets it, but I can't think of the last time I remembered an actual dream at all. "What's been going on out front?" I ask.

"More of a nightmare," she says. "Ms. Bunce is shopping for swimsuits."

"Oh no," says Nell. Ms. Bunce lives down the street and is about ninety million years old. She never buys a thing, but she comes in for hours at a time. She likes to ask as many questions as possible and try on anything that might or might not fit her.

"Today she wanted me to grade how she looked in bikinis," says Doris, turning bright red. "She said she's really into water aerobics now that she's got a 'new man in the mix.'"

"You should get a raise for that," says Nell.

"So should you. Remember the dildo?" Doris asks.

"How could we forget?" I ask. "It's burned in my brain."

"Burned into my brain like Ms. Bunce in a bikini," says Doris. "Except, honestly, she's in shockingly good shape."

"Hey," says Nell, "not to change the subject, but look what else I found in the shipment from Des Moines." She hands Doris a set of vintage playing cards, each featuring a quirky animal illustration. "It's animal rummy," she says. "Next time we camp out we should play! Check out the 'Sassy Squirrel.' How adorable is he?"

Doris inspects the card. "He *is* pretty sassy in that red cap and striped shirt. You know, I love squirrels. They're so . . . human, in a way."

"Don't they lose like seventy-five percent of the nuts they bury?" I ask. "I heard that somewhere."

"Actually, no," she says, and Nell and I look at each other and smile because it's so *Doris* to know. "There's this misconception that gray squirrels only locate a small percentage of the nuts they've hidden, but scientists have found they have amazing spatial memory," she continues. "They also pretend to hide nuts when other squirrels are watching to throw them off the trail. How smart is that? But this is a red squirrel." She holds up the playing card. "Red squirrels don't actually bury their nuts, they pile them up in caches. And they defend them vigorously! No one wants to get in a fight with a red squirrel."

"How in God's name do you know so much about squirrels?" I ask.

"YouTube videos, obviously!" says Nell.

Doris shrugs. "The internet is a very interesting place," she tells us. "And there was a science project I did back in fifth grade that—let's just say—I was really into."

"If humans are like squirrels, which of us are the gray kind and which are the red?" I wonder.

"Gray squirrels are the type to check luggage, while red squirrels definitely carry on, and they're probably pretty pushy about overhead baggage space, too," Doris decides, laughing.

"Speaking of losing and finding nuts, we just connected someone to their own lost stuff through the Instagram account!" says Nell.

Doris claps. "Really! How?"

"Remember the Kermit the Frog puppet we found last month? It belonged to a set designer who lives in Malibu," explains Nell. "He was trying to fly it to a shoot in Memphis a year ago. I posted the picture, and it kind of went viral, and he saw it online. He DM'ed just a few minutes ago. Look!" she shows Doris her phone.

"We'll have to tell Red," says Doris. "He'll probably offer to give it back for free, knowing him."

Nell starts scrolling through our feed then. It's full of colorful product pictures and staged photos of us wearing different outfits. Each picture has a ton of likes and comments.

"You're so good at this," Doris tells her. "Maybe even better than Cat."

"It's not me; it's the products," Nell says. "People love looking at what someone else has lost. Every time I post a picture, there's a surge in interest. Sometimes it's people from here, but other times they're randoms who live far away. We get calls about whatever I've put online, Red told me." She aims her phone at me and Doris. "Smile!"

"Don't you dare post that," says Doris.

"I have so many ideas!" Nell continues. "We can show shipments from exotic places like London or Dubai and be like, *This just in, come and get it before it's gone!* People are motivated when they think something's going to sell out soon. But it doesn't have to be new at all, we can just pretend it's new to give it some momentum. Doris, how long have some of those boxes been here?"

"I don't really know!" she tells us. "There's stuff in the way back that we never seem to be able to get to. And the manatee came from a box that had been lost at an airport for eight years!"

I shudder thinking about a bag of Doritos waiting in a suitcase for nearly a decade. What a waste!

"Check out this one," Nell's saying. "A few days ago, I shot Grant pretending to play golf with those clubs that have been sitting in the store since I got here."

I look over her shoulder at the phone. "I look like an idiot in that picture. When have I ever worn a sweater over my shoulders? I'm like somebody's golfing grandpa."

"Did we or did we not sell the clubs?" asks Nell. "Plus there are fifteen comments asking if you're single and what your phone number is."

"Maybe I should start wearing a sweater over my shoulders more often," I say.

"The more pictures you post, the more followers you get, and the more followers, the more sales," explains Nell. "It's a win-win!"

"Wait!" says Doris. "Let's do one with that purple suitcase

you named the Daphne. Maybe we'll get a clue about why it's empty."

She heads to the corner of the room, where there are a bunch of suitcases we haven't yet put out for sale, and yanks the Daphne from its place in the row, dragging it over to us.

"Our MacGuffin!" says Nell. "Except we don't know why it's a MacGuffin."

I groan. "Y'all are gonna stay stuck on this, aren't you? The mystery that isn't a mystery at all?"

Doris sticks her tongue out at me. "Stop being such a party pooper." She opens zipped pockets and presses the edges with her fingers, feeling for anything that might be beyond the norm. "So weird," she says, looking crestfallen when she comes up empty yet again. "I think my powers are failing me. I still haven't found Red's master keys, either."

"Maybe it's that there's nothing to find," I say. "Maybe some things are just gone. Not everything has an answer."

"Nope. There's a story here, and it's driving me crazy that I can't figure it out," Doris says. "Wait, what's this?" She shakes the suitcase. "Doesn't it make a weird noise? I think it's more than the wheels turning."

We crane our necks to listen, and there's a faint rattle, or more like a metallic clinking. "Probably acorns," I joke, and Doris rolls her eyes at me. She inspects the inside again.

"Wait a minute," she says, pressing in different spots. We all hear it, then: There's a snap and a pop and maybe even a little bit of a crackle. "Y'all," she says. "There's a false back! I found a secret compartment!"

We rush over as she pulls out a cloth bag that clanks when she shakes it. Like money. Real money.

"That's not bitcoins I hear," I say.

"Um, we're definitely going to have to tell Red about this one," Doris says. She unties the bag, reaches in, and holds up what looks like a gold coin. We pass it around. On the front there's the head of a woman; she's wearing a crown that says LIBERTY. The back has the picture of an eagle and an embossed TWENTY D., but it's gotta be worth more. The date is 1859. There are more where that came from.

"You think this would pay for Brown?" asks Doris.

"At the very least you can get an essay out of it for your college applications," I say. "You should include some of that stuff about squirrels, too. I hear admissions boards really go nuts over a good metaphor."

"Grant," says Nell.

"You didn't," adds Doris.

"I did," I say, and I smile extra big, because when you're with your friends sometimes the coolest thing is being not even remotely cool.

· · · · ·

I've never been interviewed for anything other than football, but because I'm one of the kids who found the mysterious bag of old gold and silver coins in a piece of luggage at Unclaimed, local news is interested in Grant Collins in an entirely new way. After we tell Red, he places a call to a journalist friend, who sends over a cameraman and a reporter to investigate our find. Everyone at the store is really excited. It's almost how it feels after winning a game. There's a swirl of energy in the room, but without the spiraling feeling that makes me want to reach for some booze to help me calm down.

The store is busier than ever. The town's rumor mill has sprung into action, and there are a bunch of regulars and plenty of newbies wandering around, too, trying to get the scoop. Cat and Nell are taking pictures of the coins for Instagram, and Heather and Red are Googling, estimating what they think the money might be worth and debating what they should do with it. "We'll have to have it appraised," Heather says. Red goes to dig up his contract with the Tucson airport, where the Daphne was shipped from, to see if there's any information about what happens when you uncover buried treasure in a suitcase. The TV crew is setting up in the middle of the store.

Of course, Doris is the star of the show—she's the one who suspected there was something in the bag the whole time, even when I didn't believe her—and everyone is congratulating her on her greatest discovery yet.

"You were right," I tell her. "How does it feel?"

"It's funny," she says. "I've realized, it's not finding things that makes me feel good. It's when people and things—or people and people—come together. Since I don't know who lost this, I don't even know if it matters at all! What if it's smuggled coins? What if there's some terrible story to it, and someone wanted to just be rid of the money, but by finding it we've brought it back?"

"It's such a fascinating mystery, though," says Nell, joining us. "Don't you want answers, either way? Did someone lose the coins or try to hide them? Was this all an accident, or did someone do it on purpose? Why would there be a secret compartment in a suitcase?"

"Are the coins even real?" asks Doris. "I mean, sure, I'm intrigued. But in the end, it's still just money, you know? It's not . . . people."

"Hey, kids, Maria is ready for you now," the cameraman tells us, ushering us over to the velvet couch, where they'll film us chatting with Maria Lopez, host at the nearest local news channel. We settle into our places, Doris between me and Nell.

"OK, rolling!"

"I'm here now at Unclaimed Baggage with the three teens who found a mysterious bag of gold and silver coins dated from the 1800s," she begins breathlessly. "Tell us, what was it like to open that suitcase?"

"Well, you really never know what to expect when you open a bag," begins Doris, and we look at each other and try not to laugh. I know we're all thinking of the dildo, still buried out back. In its own very special way, it counts as treasure, too. After all, it was the start of something great for the three of us.

· · · · ·

Later that night, after the camera crew has gone home and so have we, I call Doris. We talk for two hours. About everything. She tells me about her aunt Stella, and how much she misses her, how she wishes Stella were here for the story of the gold coins. "She'd have so many theories!" Doris exclaims. I tell her about my dad. How it felt when he left us, how I missed him so much at first that it was physically painful. I cried night after night and told my mom she had to make him come back. *Why did you let him go?* I demanded. But when Dad eventually decided to return, by way of the occasional phone call or speculative summer vacation, I wasn't sure I wanted him anymore. The truth was, I was mad. I wanted him to feel the way I did: rejected and lonely; I wanted to punish him for not choosing us. And now he keeps calling me, and I'm not ready to answer.

She urges me to do it. "Talking helps," she says.

"I just feel like he's already gone," I tell her.

"But he's your dad," she says. "You don't want to give up on your dad. Even when I've been angriest at my parents, when they feel less like me than just about anyone, I still want them to be my parents."

I change the subject. "I can't believe school's starting so soon," I say, and she says, "Yeah," and kind of sighs. We don't mention what will happen with us. I'm not sure what "us" is, exactly—but I know whatever it is, I don't want it to end.

"You're a good person, Grant," she tells me.

"How do you know that?" I ask.

"I just do," she says. "I know you. Bad people don't help find little brothers at water parks or stand up for their friends. Bad people don't try to stop drinking. Bad people don't *care*."

"Bad people might accidentally do good things sometimes. Especially if it's in their own interest," I say.

"But the good people are the ones who know that."

"A bad person gets drunk and crashes the car with his girl-friend in it. And then runs," I say. She has no answer to that.

"I better go to sleep," I tell her. "I'm beat. Today was wild!"

"It was," she says. "And fun, too. I can't wait till we find out what the coins are worth."

"Same."

Then she says, "Grant?" and I say, "Yeah?" and she says, "Don't drink."

Those are the words that play on repeat in my head during the hardest part of the night, when I toss and turn and stare at the ceiling in the dark and think about tacos and how easy it would be to give in and go over to Brod's and do what I've done for so long. But I don't.

PART III
August

39
Nell

There's a heat wave on, which means it's even hot in the stockroom. The AC is cranked to the limit but it's barely puffing out cool air. Doris is up working the register again because Byron's on his lunch break, and we're short-staffed with Cat gone, so it's just Grant and me in the back together. The store is busier than ever after all the news coverage—people keep coming in and wanting to buy the coins, or at least see or touch them, but they're still with the appraisers. We use the opportunity to try to sell them something else, which usually works. We're unpacking as fast as we can to keep things on the shelves.

Grant's untangling a mess of cords from a laptop computer that we found in a bag I've dubbed the Nigel. When we finally get the plug into the socket, the computer powers on—but it's been wiped clean. Grant and I are debating what turn of events would have led to this, and from that we get deep into the logistics of witness protection—how do you just start responding to a new name, for instance? Don't you miss your old friends and family members, or do they get to come along with you? Is there really a town in Hawaii that has the greatest concentration of people enrolled in the Federal Witness Protection Program? Yes, says Grant, it's Puna, on the Big Island.

"How did you know that?" I ask.

"Google," he says. "Let's just say there've been some times in my life when I've wondered if what I really needed was to get away from everything and everybody I knew, too."

"But no more?" I ask.

"Not at the moment," he says, smiling.

I hear my phone from inside the locker where I've stashed it. It's Ashton's ringtone, so I can't resist pulling it back out.

I walk to the back of the inventory racks for privacy.

"Hi, baby," I answer.

"Hey, Pony," says Ashton. "I can't wait to see your face! I'm going to kiss it all over."

I close my eyes and wish him here already.

"I get into Huntsville airport at four p.m. on Friday. Can you still pick me up?"

"I'll be there! Doris and Grant are coming, too!"

"Should I be nervous? These are the people I've been hearing about all summer. The people who have replaced me in your life!" He laughs. "Or maybe I should be more nervous that I'm about to be *way* below the Mason-Dixon Line for an entire weekend."

"You are irreplaceable," I tell him. "And you're going to love them! And everybody will love you! We have a going-away party to go to Friday night. A woman we work with is leaving to get her MFA and business degree—"

"Sounds fun," he says. "But I want to spend some time with just you, too. And I can't wait to see Jack! How's my little buddy?"

"He's been talking about you nonstop since he heard you were coming." This is true, though I don't tell Ashton I only just got around to telling my family about the visit. "He wants to show you all of his new video games."

"I'm so ready," says Ashton.

Part of me is impatient to get back to the suitcase I've been unpacking, and I'm aware of slacking my responsibilities. "Hey, I'm at work. Let's talk tonight, OK?"

"You're always there!" he answers. "Do you ever get tired of it?"

"No," I tell him. "Weirdly, I really don't. It's so much fun. Especially since Doris found the bag of old coins in a suitcase. They might really be worth something!"

"Selling lacrosse sticks and bike helmets to people at the mall just doesn't compare to finding buried treasure, I guess."

"Wait till you see the stockroom. You'll understand."

"I can't wait."

"Bye, Ash."

"Bye, Pony. For now."

I walk back out to Grant. I can't hide the giant grin on my face.

"Excited, huh?" he says. He's holding a pair of rhinestone-studded jeans against his legs, as if to see if they'll fit him. They came in a rhinestone-studded duffel bag, not even kidding.

"I've been trying to name the bag these were in, but it's impossible without you," he says.

I close my eyes for a second and think. "Velma. That bag is most definitely a Velma."

"You're too good at this." He smiles and folds the jeans and puts them in the for-sale pile. "Hey," he says. "I have a question."

"Yeah?"

"There's something I've been thinking about for a while," he says. "Do you think Doris would ever go out with me?"

My grin gets even bigger than I ever thought possible.

"Don't tell her, though, OK?" he asks. "I need to think about how to approach it, and really do it right—really do *something* right, for once."

I nod. Keeping this secret from my best friend is going to be so hard, but I think it will be worth it.

40
Doris

I'm up at the register with Mr. Diamanti, the high school chorus teacher, who's buying a keyboard that came in from Los Angeles the other day. Nell posted it on the Instagram account, and the phone started ringing immediately. After we found the gold coins, the store has been one big fire emoji. Red keeps walking around saying, "It's lit!" I don't know who taught him that, but it's cringeworthy in the best way.

The keyboard has the initials SW written on it on a piece of tape, so I've been imagining the keyboard once belonged to Stevie Wonder, even though surely Stevie Wonder doesn't check his keyboard, or fly commercial, and does Stevie Wonder even live in LA? I have no idea.

Mr. Diamanti is amped about the new school year, telling me about his big plans for the fall concert. I think about music and Billy Pickens and his trombone, still in my closet. Will he ask for it back? I think about Maya, who will be home soon. According to her last postcard, she and Hannah were getting ready to go to the camp dance together, and Maya was deciding if she wanted to wear a sundress or her favorite jeans and vintage tee. I wrote back that I might be thinking about making a move, too, but I didn't say with who. Maya's got to hear about that in person. She's not going to believe it.

Something's bugging me a little, though. Grant and Nell and I bonded because we were all misfits, alone in our own ways. Come September, will that still be the case? I really hope that our friendships can continue past the store.

I think back to the balloon festival, when Grant and I were alone and he kissed my hand. He's been looking at me differently lately, like he's seeing me not just as the Number One liberal agnostic in this town, or the weird girl in the hallways at school, but as a friend. Maybe even as something more. If I do make a move, what would it even be? I need to talk to Nell about this.

Once I ring up Mr. Diamanti's purchase and send him on his way—he makes a pitch as he always does to try to get me to sing in the choir, and I politely remind him that I only sing-shout the Pixies—the store is quiet again. Byron's still on break. Then one person who definitely does not make me smile comes walking in, the doorbell tinkling gently as she enters. It's a sound that doesn't match her persona. It's not that she looks scary, exactly. She's got on a floral dress with a lace collar and ballet flats, the most delicate of Southern lady attire. But the whole feeling in the store changes as if a storm's a-coming, and I wish I weren't alone at the register, because this is Priscilla Stokes, the church youth-group director who shamed me at the water park, the woman I told off at the balloon festival.

"Hello, Doris," she says. She leans over the counter where I'm standing, so close I can smell her antiseptic perfume, and she says, "I saw on Instagram y'all had some cute new shoes that came in the other day. Are they still for sale?"

I smile and pretend that everything is peachy keen while I also marvel that even Mrs. Stokes uses Instagram. "If so, they'll be back that way," I say, pointing her in the right direction.

"Thank you," she says.

"Of course," I answer, sweeping my hand out grandly as if this is my manor, and I'm giving her consent to walk the gardens. "Let me know if you need help with anything."

Thankfully, Byron steps into the front door with a takeout bag from Ruby's, my favorite of the three barbecue joints in town. There are diehard fans of each around here, and the question of who's best is almost as controversial as who you root for in football.

"Hey, Doris, I brought you a snack," says Byron, who puts the bag next to me. It smells so good my stomach growls loudly in response. I open the bag to peer in and see three flaky golden biscuits, a tub of pulled pork, a tub of pulled chicken, a tub of potato salad, and a tub of coleslaw.

"You're my hero," I say. "This is more than a snack!"

"I thought you and Grant and Nell might be hungry," he says. "And, the truth is, Shana hooked me up now that she's one of the managers over there." He pats his stomach with satisfaction. "I'm going to get so fat, and I don't mind it a bit."

"You and Shana are both my heroes," I say, and he grins.

"I'll let her know." Byron takes a long look at Mrs. Stokes, who's now rummaging through the stack of suitcases we have against one wall.

"If you want to take your break in the back with the team and dig in, go for it," he says. "I can handle the front for a while. It's a sin not to eat those biscuits while they're still warm."

I carry the bag of food back to the stockroom. Just as I get there, out pops Nell.

"Hi!" I say. "Are y'all hungry?"

"Yes!" she says. "I was just coming up to find you and see if you wanted lunch."

"Perfect. Byron brought us a ton of food," I tell her, walking into the stockroom. "By the way, guess who's out front?"

"Not Ms. Bunce again?" asks Grant.

"No, worse. Mrs. Stokes."

"Ew," says Nell. "Why?"

"I have no idea, but we shouldn't let her affect our appetites." I pull out a stash of fragrant barbecue and start passing stuff around, along with paper plates and napkins and plastic knives and forks. My mouth is watering.

"Ruby's?" Nell asks, and I nod.

"My favorite!" she says.

"You're such a local now," I tell her.

"I've always been more of a Big Bob guy myself," says Grant as he loads his plate full of food. "But barbecue is barbecue, and barbecue is good no matter what."

Byron pokes his head in the door just as I'm biting into my biscuit. "Hey, Doris, Mrs. Stokes wants to talk to you."

"What does she want?" whispers Nell.

Byron shrugs. "No clue. I told her you were on break, but that lady is pushy. She said it was very important."

I chew slowly, wondering what I should do. I admit, I'm curious.

"We'll go with you," says Grant.

"Yeah, there's no way we're leaving you to that woman on your own," says Nell. So the three of us grudgingly step away from our feast and walk to the front of the store, where Mrs. Stokes is waiting at the cash register, a pile of merchandise in front of her.

"I was hoping you could ring me up," she says.

"Byron could have done that," I say, and she shakes her head. "I wanted it to be you."

"Why's that?" I ask.

"Well," she says, "I owe you an apology."

I'm inclined to think I've entered a parallel universe. Grant and Nell are watching, and they seem as befuddled as I am.

"I've thought long and hard about what happened at the balloon festival. I wondered why you'd say those un-Christianlike things, and I took my concerns to Pastor John. He reminded me that your aunt Stella, God rest her troubled soul, had a huge influence on you. It's hard to repair that sort of damage, so I decided not to take it personally. You simply need to be in the presence of people who know the right way forward. People who are bound for the Kingdom of Heaven, not . . . the other place."

"What I said wasn't about my aunt," I tell her. "It was about what happened on the waterslide. That boy—Teddy Scruggs— groped me. I told him to stop, and he didn't." I speak the way I wish I could have the day it happened. "And you didn't do anything about it. You took his side. Stella was the only one who defended me. Why would she be in hell for doing the right thing?"

Despite her professed desire to say she's sorry, Mrs. Stokes gets her panties in a wad fast. "You must not have told me what really happened," she says.

"I was a kid! I had just been assaulted!" I say. "You didn't seem open to listening. In fact, you'd made up your mind that what Teddy told you was the truth."

"Well," she says. "Let's not go overboard, using that word, *assault*. That boy was a member of the church. He didn't hurt you."

"*He didn't hurt me?*" I ask. She doesn't get it at all. Not one bit.

"All those priests who molested little boys were 'members of the church,' too," interjects Grant. I want to hug him for being on my side.

"Just because you're a member of a church doesn't mean you're a good person," adds Nell.

290

"And you can be a good person without ever being a member of a church," I say. "Like my aunt Stella."

"Like Doris," says Grant.

Byron's come over to see what's going on, and he's got my back, too. "It's also not real nice to go around saying people have gone to hell because they believe in a different religion than you do, or because they don't go to church," he tells her. "I may not be a Bible scholar, but I can tell you that."

Mrs. Stokes crosses her arms in annoyance and stomps one foot, like a child. "Pastor John says we should open our hearts to sinners. Conversion of nonbelievers only makes the Kingdom of Heaven greater. That's what I'm trying to do, if y'all would just let me. Why are you being so difficult?"

"So you're not here to apologize, you're here to try to convert Doris?" asks Grant.

"I'm here to try to save her," she says. "And with that windfall you've come into, perhaps you want to donate something to help others, too? Your ten-dollar bill"—she sniffs—"at the balloon festival was appreciated, but now it seems you're in the position to be a lot more generous." She's talking about the coins, and suddenly I understand her real reason for wanting to apologize, for coming in at all. "You, too, Grant, are welcome back to the fold at any time." She gazes over at Nell and gestures in a way I'm sure she thinks is generous. "The Yankee can come, too."

I try not to laugh at her sheer audacity as I ring up a new pair of ballet flats (Mrs. Stokes must have hundreds), a copy of the King James Bible, a dog collar, and a plastic chew toy shaped like a bone. "Did you get a dog?" I ask, just to change the subject.

"Yes," she says. "Animals are special, aren't they?"

"Well, dog *is* God spelled backward," offers Grant.

Instead of responding to him, Mrs. Stokes gives me the very same look she gave me back at the water park, as if she was seeing something dirty and unforgivable. "Your aunt wasn't so perfect, you know."

"What are you talking about?" interjects Nell. "Her aunt died trying to save two kids at a beach in France!"

Mrs. Stokes is bagging her own items, refusing Byron's help. She's pissed we haven't been more amenable to her attempt to smooth things over. She's probably even more pissed I haven't promised her the gold coins for the church, but they're not mine to give—not that I'd turn them over to her if they were. I can't wait for her to leave the store and take her attitude with her, but before she does, there's a final shot. "You should ask your mother about your aunt," she tells me. "You might as well know the truth. You're practically an adult now. It's high time they treated you like one."

She hustles out in a huff, and I'm left staring at my friends and wondering what Mrs. Stokes knows about Stella, and if it's something I want to find out at all.

Luckily, if there's one thing it's near impossible to ruin your appetite for, it's Ruby's.

41

Nell was right: The purple suitcase was, in its own way, a MacGuffin, though it was never owned by someone named Daphne. It was an object that had captivated Doris and Nell, and impelled them, especially Doris, to action. She wanted to find out what it was about, what its story was, and why. You can't always judge a suitcase by its cover. You have to open it up, dig around, investigate, make assumptions that may or may not be proved true. You have to trust your instincts and keep looking.

The suitcase—which bore no trace of its owner's name or the tracking tags that would have shown exactly where it had gone, and when—was quickly forgotten, a trail too cold to bother with, in favor of the bag of coins. Money is certainly a

MacGuffin, particularly to people who are less intrigued by the story and more thrilled by the idea of what a lost and found treasure might be worth, and who would lay claim to it. This monetary mystery motivated people from all over the country to follow the news closely as more information was revealed, and to make wild and speculative offers on the bag of coins, even once Red said it was not for sale.

The appraisal had come in, and the coins had their own story. They were artifacts, with a history all their own, and they were priceless. They would be donated to a museum, Red declared, so other people could see them and hear their story, too.

Maria Lopez explained it all in a segment watched immediately by townspeople and, soon after, by curious people around the world who'd heard of the discovery and wanted to know more. "The mystery has been solved!" said Maria into the camera, in a special report from news headquarters. "The gold Coronet Head twenty-dollar Double Eagles and silver Seated Liberty Half Dollars found by three Alabama teenagers while unpacking luggage at the store Unclaimed Baggage were part of a stash of shipwrecked gold that in total might be worth as much as one hundred eighty million dollars in today's currency! The boat, the SS *Republic*, sank during a hurricane off the Georgia coast in 1865, roughly six months after the Civil War ended. It was carrying Reconstruction-era coins and other precious artifacts—including pickles!" Maria stopped and gave a big wink to the camera. "No pickles were found in the suitcase."

The video of Maria talking to the three teenagers, and her follow-up once the coins were appraised and the mystery solved (insofar as it could be), went viral. The clips were seen by more people, in fact, than the amount of dollars the discovered coins were worth. But the numbers were close, and what something's worth varies, after all. It's really just a matter of who wants it the most, and what they're willing to pay.

Of course, the story went further than any newscasters or journalists or TV watchers, or even the teenagers who found the coins, would ever know—it always does. The legend of the lost coins had been handed down, generation by generation, within an old Southern family. One of their ancestors had been on the ship. He had died in a lifeboat after trying to save others, and his bones had sunk along with his gold. It was a story about courage and heroism but also a reminder of the desolation and degradation of war, how hard it is to build but how easy, and wasteful, it is to destroy.

Then the shipwreck had been discovered in 2003. The coins were no longer lore but reality. A dedicated investigator had returned them to the Scruggs family. But most of the family members didn't care about the legacy—all they wanted was what they considered their share of the gold, so they could buy fast cars or big houses or who knows what. It was a matter of bitter estrangement and infighting, and it had torn the family apart. Harvey Scruggs was ninety-five years old; he'd been the keeper of the coins since they'd been found. He hadn't seen fit to pass them on to his weak-willed son, or to his son's son, who was even worse, and certainly not to his seventeen-year-old great grandson, Teddy, who even without the coins might well bring shame to the family name. Perhaps he already had.

Harvey was sick of the family dysfunction, and he was also plain sick. He had cancer, and at his age, he wasn't a good candidate for the usual treatments. He didn't have much more time. He took this fairly well. "Heavens, I'm ninety-five," he told his doctor, who was a kind woman and a sympathetic listener. Scruggs almost considered giving the coins to her, if only he could be sure his ungrateful family wouldn't get wind of it and cause her no end of pain. "I've lived a good, long life. My wife is gone. My friends are gone. My only living family members are bent on harassing me for money. All I really want to do now is lie on the beach in Mexico, drink cold beer and eat really good guacamole, and spend a little time in peace."

The doctor nodded. "Maybe you should."

It took a while—air travel was so much more complicated than it used to be, what with the new security measures. And where did a ninety-five-year-old man even start to think about getting a fake passport, or forged travel documents? But Harvey had come up with his plan, and he'd done it. He'd flown from Huntsville to Tucson, and in Tucson he'd simply left his bag—one he thought would never be traced to an old man—at baggage claim. He'd carefully removed any identifying stickers, and he'd walked right out of the airport. He left the coins in their hiding place, a secret compartment he'd built himself in that bag, and felt a wave of serenity fall upon him. A driver met him and took him to Nogales, Arizona. He walked across the border himself, and a second driver picked him up and drove him farther south. He kept traveling, ending up in Bahía de Kino, where he ate guacamole daily and lay on the beach and occasionally visited an internet café to see if there was any news about the coins. Maybe he'd stay put; maybe he'd move on. He was playing everything by ear. But he hoped the coins would eventually be found and treated properly by someone. He felt that would restore his faith in humanity.

Meanwhile, his family could duke it out on their own. He'd left an updated will in his house and another one with his lawyer. His property would be divided among his family members when he died. But the coins, he specified, would go to whoever had found them.

Finally it happened. He saw the headline he'd been waiting for, and he breathed in deep when he saw his name wasn't mentioned at all. They had no idea. Maybe they never would. He couldn't help smiling as he watched the clip featuring pretty Maria Lopez and the teenagers who'd discovered the coins. Maria had asked the dark-haired girl what she'd do with the money, if it were hers. She'd discussed using it to pay for her college education, and maybe to start a charity in honor of her aunt, who'd died while trying to save two children from drowning. "I want to do things to connect people, like she did," the girl said. Scruggs beamed. His spoiled great-grandson would never have thought to do something like that with the money.

It all supported what the old man had by now come to believe: Sometimes you had to give something up to get what you really wanted in the first place.

42
Doris

Today is an occasion, so I put on the flowery dress my mom bought me a while back that I still haven't worn. She smiles when she sees me in it and helps cut off the tags. I haven't yet brought up what Mrs. Stokes said about Stella. Nell and Grant and even Byron all think it was just the rantings of a bitter lady. I need some time to figure out what I want to do with that information—if I should pursue it or forget it forever.

For now, I'm putting it out of my mind, because bringing Stel up to my mom has the potential to end in disaster, or at the very least, a migraine. And this day is about fun. The plan is to pick up Ashton from the airport and then the four of us will go to Cat's good-bye party at our town's best and only

Mexican restaurant, La Casita. From that, who knows? As long as we're together, it's going to be a great time.

When I pull into Nell's driveway, she runs out of her house with two giant helium balloons. One has a teddy bear on it hugging a big heart, the other says HAPPY BIRTHDAY!

"Oh my God," she says, getting into the passenger seat and holding a balloon down with each arm so they don't float up into the window as I drive. "You look so gorgeous! You should always wear dresses."

"I'd be way too cold at the store. What's with the balloons?" I ask.

"The teddy bear is for Ashton," she says. "The other's for Cat."

"I don't know how to say this but . . . you *do* know it's not her birthday?"

She's unfazed. "These were the only ones they had at Family Mart. But who doesn't like balloons? Who cares what they say?"

"Good point," I say.

Then we're at Grant's, and he's doing his lope out to the car, long legs and arms. I breathe in audibly, and Nell looks over at me and smiles.

"You like him, don't you?" she asks, and it's more of a statement than a question. "You've liked him since the balloon festival. Maybe before."

"What's the use?" I say. "It would never work."

"I wouldn't assume that," she says mysteriously. I want to know more, but he's already opening the car door and getting in the back.

"Hey, ladies," he says, leaning forward to give us a simultaneous hug. "Are we ready for a road trip?"

"Semi road trip," I say. "It's less than forty-five minutes to the airport! But I made us a mix. It's called 'Unpacking 3.0,' which includes all the best songs of 'Unpacking 2.0' and none of the songs of 'Unpacking 1.0' because I'm over that one. Plus it's got my latest favorite Harry Styles, because no mix is complete without him."

"Play it!" says Nell. "I'm so nervous. I need something to calm me down."

"What if the airplane loses Ashton's luggage and Doris is forced to find it?" asks Grant.

I forward to the song I want and press play, and "Baggage Claim" by Miranda Lambert starts. It's a little on the nose, but playlists never gain from subtlety, in my opinion. And I drive.

"Can you hold these?" Nell asks, passing the balloons back to Grant. "I need to check my phone. I'm monitoring Ashton on a flight-tracking app." As she delivers a play-by-play of his coordinates, Grant and I share a glance in the rearview mirror. He raises his eyebrows at me, and I wink back and wonder what Nell meant, exactly. I haven't dared to think too much about me and Grant, on account of Chassie, on account of everything he is and everything I am, but just like there's this question swirling in my mind about Aunt Stella, so also there's a thought, maybe even a hope, about Grant. Could we be something more than friends?

Forty-five minutes later, we're rolling through the passenger pickup at Huntsville International, and I see the suitcase first, not the guy. It's a black wheelie bag that's pretty standard until you look a little bit closer and see that it's got a huge Cubs logo on the front.

It's baseball, so. . . . "Hey, would you call that an Ashton?" I ask Nell, pointing.

"Oh my God," she yells, and I stop the car, barely, before she jumps out and runs to him. He grabs her and spins her in the air just like I've seen people do in the movies, and they kiss. I pop the trunk, and Grant gets out to help put the suitcase in it.

"Don't worry, man," Ashton says, throwing his luggage in the back.

Nell changes seats with Grant so she can sit with Ashton, and Grant is up in the passenger seat, next to me. It's like we're on the double date that Nell mentioned way back when, except my date is the most unlikely person I've ever thought about dating, and I'm sure he doesn't think about me that way. I glance at him and he's staring at me and we both blush. Does he? I look back at Nell in the rearview mirror for help, but she's occupied.

"I got you a balloon," she tells Ashton, who laughs and then reaches over and tugs her ponytail, which I happen to know she's worn on purpose today.

"I brought you a present from the girls—and something from me, too," he says. He pulls two wrapped gifts from his bag, and Nell digs in.

"Y'all, Nisha and Morgan sent a home manicure set, with really great colors!" she says. "Grant, you're going to love this dark gray matte!"

"Sweet," says Grant, and he looks over at me and smiles again, this time wiggling his fingers.

"Ashton, you didn't!" Nell's waving a book around. "It's by the author of *The Maltese Falcon*, and it's about this fabulous couple that goes around solving mysteries in 1930s New York City! How did you know I wanted to read this?" she asks, and he says, "I pay attention."

"You're adorable," she tells him.

"No, you are," he says. "Especially when you say 'y'all.'"

"OK, OK, you're both adorable," says Grant. "If I didn't like you, Nell, and therefore you, Ashton, I might say nauseatingly so."

"We haven't seen each other in months!" says Nell. "We're allowed."

"Fine, I'll just crank up the music, then," says Grant. He reaches over and turns up the volume and then, as if this is natural as anything, he puts his hand on my knee. "I'm totally into this mix," he says. I narrowly avoid hitting a parked car on the way out of the airport.

· · · · ·

Heather has gone all out decorating the private room at La Casita for the party. She's crafted a bunch of Unclaimed-themed gear, including little hanging paper suitcases and photos of the crew. There's even a piñata shaped like a garment bag. And the food is incredible: chips and salsa and guacamole, of course, plus mini quesadillas and tiny burritos and "enchiladitos" you can eat in just one bite.

"Save room, there are more courses coming out," says Heather. "Including dessert! The flan is to die for!"

Freddie is running around with another little girl, the daughter of the restaurant's owners, Hector and Julia, who have been invited, too. All the adults are clustered along the long food table—kind of the way we group around the table in the stockroom for our meetings—talking and eating and drinking. I see people noticing Ashton, who's holding Nell's hand. She starts introducing him to everyone, and there are hugs and handshakes and *Nice to finally meet you*s everywhere. Grant is standing right next to me, acting almost like Ashton is to Nell. Almost like he's my date. Minus the hand holding, that is. Or the need for introductions.

"This is amazing," I tell Heather, who comes up to say hello and give me a hug.

"Our celebrities!" she says, referring to the news segment and the coins. It's fun to have everyone notice me for something I've done, rather than for what I don't do—i.e., church. She gives Grant a sideways glance, then sneaks a quick look at me as if to ask what the deal is, but she's too cool to truly let anything on.

"You could open your own party-planning business, if you wanted to," I tell her.

Grant nods. "I especially love the garment-bag piñata."

"One party a year is enough for me," she says. "But for Cat, it's worth it!"

Cat hears her name and joins us. "The store isn't going to be the same without you," I say.

She looks happy and sad at the same time. "I'm so excited

about what's next," she says, "But I'm going to miss all of you so much." She sees Nell then, and tells her how awesome the Instagram has been in her charge. "You're really talented," she says, and Nell blushes. They start talking about brand strategy and other ways to build consumer engagement.

Ashton is standing next to Nell proudly, a grin on his face over how smart his girlfriend is. When he excuses himself to go to the bathroom, Nell turns to me, her eyes shining. "What do you think?"

"I really like him," I say. "And he really, really seems to like you. Do you still think you're in love?"

"I think I am," she whispers.

Grant and I wander to the bar, where they're making virgin daiquiris for the underage and nondrinking among us. He goes with an alcohol-free piña colada, and I get a strawberry concoction, and we raise our glasses to each other and then to Nell and Ashton, across the room, who do the same back at us. Red is about to make a toast, and more food is on the way, so we sit at the table and listen as Cat is alternately praised and lovingly roasted. When she gets up to thank everyone, she's crying tears of laughter.

"I adore all of you!" she says. "You've been my quirky, kooky family I got to choose, and, even better, got paid to work with! I will think about you every day that I'm gone. And I will be back!" she says. "I am also, of course, always available via Twitter, Facebook, and Instagram. Thanks especially to Red, the guy who gave me a chance to work with him and helped me learn more than I ever thought I could. And thanks to Nell, who is already doing an incredible job running the store Instagram in my stead." She looks at Nell and then me and Grant. "Y'all are the future!"

I'm a little weepy because this is all so sweet, and Grant pats me on the shoulder. "We really are a great family," he says. I put my hand on top of his, noticing his polish, still complete and unchipped.

"I'm so glad we finally became friends," I say.

"Me too," he agrees.

I want to say more, but I don't.

The party continues, and eventually we realize Nell and Ashton are missing. Grant and I decide to go look for them, and the very first place I check is where they are, so I guess I still haven't lost my touch (but where the heck are Red's missing keys?). My best friend and her boyfriend have found a quiet corner, and Ashton's got his arms around Nell, and they're making out the way I saw Chassie and Mac Ebling making out, but there's something different here. With Chassie, it seemed like she had something to prove, like she was doing it to show everyone else. With Nell and Ashton, well, it just seems like they're in love.

Grant and I back away, not wanting to interrupt. And that's when something happens that changes everything. There's a harsh voice from behind.

"Get your hands off her," this guy says. "You Oreo." He sounds vaguely familiar, but I can't place him. We turn around, and he's tall and white and wearing nondescript clothes—jeans and work boots and a plain gray T-shirt. He's got a bandana tied over his face. I get a really bad feeling.

"Oreo?" asks Grant. "What are you talking about?"

Nell and Ashton have stopped making out and are looking at the guy.

"He means 'black on the outside and white on the inside,'" says Ashton. "That's a pretty racist thing to say, dude."

"You shouldn't be in here kissing white girls," says the guy, and Nell draws a sharp intake of breath. "You shouldn't be kissing white girls anywhere."

"Leave us alone," she says. "We're none of your business."

"It's my business when cute blondes are fucking black guys in my fucking town," the guy says. "Why don't you go back to where you came from?"

"Um, like, Chicago?" Ashton asks.

"Fuck you," says the guy. He reaches to grab Nell and pull her away from Ashton, and that's when things really go crazy. Grant, who's standing behind me in the doorway, clears his throat in a way I've never heard before, releasing what almost seems like a growl. Ashton tries to pull Nell behind him to protect her, but the guy is grabbing at her, too, yanking the skirt of her dress. There's a tearing sound as the cloth rips, leaving a gaping hole at the waist. I go into some sort of fugue state, in which I run at the racist guy with all the strength I have. It's not particularly effective, but then, neither was escaping from Teddy Scruggs, which is what this is reminding me all too much of.

"Don't touch her!" yells Ashton, who draws back to hit the guy as the guy shoves me aside. I fall to the floor and then Grant and the guy and Ashton are this writhing mass of testosterone and fear and rage. I wriggle away from them and join Nell in the corner.

"Are you OK?" I ask, and she nods breathlessly.

"Are you?"

"I think so?"

But there's no time to talk, or even to check if the pain in my shoulder is just a bad bruise or something worse. Grant and Ashton are hitting the guy, but the guy is big and strong, and he's fighting dirty. I can't shake the feeling that I know him from somewhere. I don't forget a face, but his is mostly hidden. Then I hear something crunch in this ugly way, like bones are breaking.

"Stop!" Nell is yelling.

"Help!" I shout.

All of a sudden Grant has this guy up against the wall, and he's spitting in his face. "Don't you dare bring your racist shit here and try to hurt my friends," he's saying. His mouth is bleeding, and his right eye is already swollen up tight. Ashton's arm is turned back funny and he's cradling it and emitting little groans. Nell's screaming for help, and I'm crying, and all of a sudden, Grant says, "You know what? You're not even worth it," and drops the guy and walks out of the room. Which is when Hector and Red and Byron rush in to see what all the commotion is about.

"Grab him!" we shout, but the guy punches Red in the stomach.

"Oof!" he yells, hunching over in pain.

Hector tries to pull the bandana off the guy's face, but the guy knocks Hector away and holds his makeshift mask even closer, leaning into that football position, like you're ready to bust through the defense. Byron tries to tackle him, but he maneuvers past and is out the door, leaving Byron on the floor. We all look at each other, stunned, until we can speak again.

43
Grant

I'm standing in the sun outside the restaurant, just breathing.
I feel blood trickling down my face, and my right eye isn't
quite working. My head is pounding—there's what feels like
an actual drumbeat in my ear. This is exactly the sort of situation that would once drive me to drink. I steady myself by looking at my fingers, and I realize that my left thumbnail has gotten
chipped in the fray. I reach into my pocket where I carry Fireworks to make sure the bottle's not broken—there's something
that stings in that region of my leg. I pull out the polish and am
holding the bottle in my hand, relieved that it hasn't shattered,
at least, when the racist guy bolts out of the restaurant like he's
running from the law. He sees me, and before I can do a thing,

he's smacking the polish out of my hand. We watch it arc beautifully like a football across a field before it busts into a thousand tiny pieces on the concrete parking lot.

"Loser," he says. "Pussy. Drunk. I'm glad you finally found the pathetic freaks you should be hanging out with. Stick with them and leave my sister alone." This is particularly ironic given that he crashed *our* party, but then bullies aren't really known for their cohesive dialogue.

He punches me in the face again, and I fall to the ground.

I have a feeling then, like a hot-air balloon that has come untethered and is floating, maybe peacefully at first, but just you wait till the wind picks up—there's no telling what will happen. To my credit, I don't even look at the guy. I don't pick up my head as I hear him run away. His boots crunch the gravel beneath his feet, all those tiny rocks and stones that are digging into my face. I already know who he is. I know where he lives. I don't scream at him or tell him he's a shitbag to the millionth degree. I don't vow revenge. I just lie there, and as soon as he's gone, I get up, brush myself off, and start walking as fast as I can, trying to ignore the pain. I don't have a car, but one of the benefits of a small town is you can get anywhere by foot if you've got the time. And I've got all the time in the world.

44
Nell

Doris and Red and Byron and I run outside, but it's too late; the guy's gone, and Grant's nowhere to be seen, either. Heather stays inside to tend to Ashton, who we think has a broken arm. Hector is getting Doris a bag of frozen peas to put on her shoulder. We've called the cops and an ambulance. All the Unclaimed party guests are offering help and hugs and condolences. Byron and Red are beating themselves up that they couldn't stop the guy.

"He surprised us all," Doris says. "I don't know who he was. But there was something familiar about his voice, and the parts of him I could see."

"What a coward," says Hector. "Covering his face like that!"

"Why would someone do that, just start attacking a group of people?" asks Red. "How did the fight start?"

"He was saying racist things about Ashton," Doris explains, and Byron and Red give each other a look and shake their heads.

I walk to a corner of the parking lot to call my mom. She answers on the first ring. "Hi, honey!" she says. "How's it going? Are you having fun?"

I thought I was holding it together, but at the sound of her voice, I start crying.

"What happened? Are you OK? Is Ashton with you? Are you still at the airport?"

Slowly, I tell her everything. That Ashton and I were the target of this unidentified racist at the restaurant. That he's been beaten up pretty badly, but we're taking care of him. That the cops have arrived and are making a report. That Grant's gone, too, and that we're terribly worried. That I now have a giant hole in my favorite dress. But, yes, Doris is with me. I'm OK. We're OK.

"Stay where you are," she tells me. "I'll come and get you. We'll figure this out."

"The ambulance is coming," I say.

"I'm on my way," she says.

. . . . .

Ashton's on a stretcher outside the ambulance, being prepped for his trip to the hospital. He's in a lot of pain—the EMT says his arm is most definitely broken. His eyes are closed and he's quiet.

"I'm so sorry," I tell him. He opens his eyes and looks at me, confusion mixing with everything else that hurts.

"Nell, sorry doesn't fix anything." He grabs my hand with his good arm and holds it tight. "Sorry just makes *you* feel better."

I open my mouth and close it. I don't know what to say.

"Don't be sorry. Do something," he tells me. "Make sure the cops get that asshole. And all of the other assholes like him."

He closes his eyes again and lets go of my hand as they lift him into the back of the ambulance.

"Is he going to be OK?" I whisper to the EMT.

"Is anyone, really?" she answers, which doesn't help at all. "Yes," she finally says quietly. "Your boyfriend will be OK. Which is more than I can say for the world we currently live in."

"We'll be right behind you," I tell Ashton as they pull the ambulance door closed, but he doesn't respond.

In the car, my mom is ranting about how there are still all too many pockets of the South that are hopelessly behind, and she never should have agreed to Ashton's visit, we never should have moved here, she regrets everything, look at poor Ashton, look at what's happened.

"Mother," I say, and in a rush, my sadness has turned into anger, and it's directed at my mom: "Why didn't you just come out and say that, then?" A terrible thought occurs to me. "Oh my God," I say. "The move wasn't to break us up, was it?"

"No!" she says. "This job really is a once-in-a-lifetime opportunity. Remind me to tell you about the upcoming rocket launch." She gives me a little half smile, but I look at her stoically. It's time for the whole story. No sugarcoating it this time.

She looks at me with glossy eyes. "The truth is, I was always worried about something like this," she admits. "Even when we lived up North. That's why I was so hesitant about you two getting serious. People can be so cruel, and sometimes there's no time to try to convince them anything other than what they're dead set on believing. I worried about your safety, yours and his. . . . Oh, I feel so terrible," she says. "What will I tell his parents?"

"The truth, I guess," I say. "That something awful happened because there are some really shitty people in this world, but we're taking care of him and he's going to be OK."

Doris clears her throat in the backseat, which I take as a sign of support. My mom keeps going.

"It's hard," she says. "I know what the right thing is, but I can't help worrying. I know it's ridiculous, but sometimes I wish I could just lock you away and keep you safe from anyone who wants to hurt you." We're waiting at a stoplight, and she turns to look at Doris. "I want to keep all of you kids safe. You and Nell and Jack and Ashton and Grant. There's too much ugly stuff out there!"

"Mom, you can't shield us from what's going to happen in the world," I tell her. "There are bad people, no matter where we go. But most people aren't bad. Most people are pretty good, actually." I think of Grant, who stood up for Ashton and fought back—and of Red, and Byron, and Hector. I think of Doris, sitting quietly behind me in the car, listening and ready to help me do whatever is next.

"And the more people of different races and religions and whatever else who fall in love, the better," I say. As it comes out of me, I know it's true, and I feel stronger for saying it. "That guy isn't going to keep us from being together. No racist is. If Ashton and I aren't going to be together, that's up to us, not anyone else."

Doris pipes up from the back: "Mrs. Wachowski, if what I've seen is any indication, I'd say Ashton and Nell are going to be together, possibly for a very long time."

I hope she's right.

"Do you love him?" asks my mom.

"I really think I do," I say.

"Then let's get you to the hospital so you can see him," my mom tells me, putting her foot on the gas pedal and driving faster than I've ever seen her go.

45
Doris

It's late by the time we leave the hospital. Ashton's arm has been set, and he's been given painkillers that make him sleepy and a little loopy. He keeps touching Nell's hair and saying "Pony" in this little-boy voice. Nell won't leave his side. He doesn't have to stay the night, and we're all happy about that. It was a clean break, and the doctor says it should heal well. His parents and Nell's mom have had a long talk, and he's going to stay for the rest of his trip, though he'll probably spend the next day and a half pretty woozy and in bed. A nurse helps him into the backseat of the car. Nell puts her arms around him to keep him from jouncing too much, but I suspect it's really because she just wants to be close to him.

I sit up front. A doctor checked out my shoulder, too, and pronounced my injury merely a deep bruise. He told me to keep icing it. "You kids got off lucky," he said, shaking his head at some of the stuff he's seen. He didn't expound, which I was glad about.

"Would you like to spend the night?" Nell's mom asks me. "I can drop you off at your house if you need to get home. But I'm sure Nell would love to have you keep her company tonight."

"Yes, please. Stay," says Nell from the backseat.

"Pony," murmurs Ashton.

My car is still parked at La Casita. I don't feel like going back there yet, especially not alone and after dark. And if I go home, I'll be too worried about Grant to sleep, and have no one to talk to.

"I'd love to sleep over," I tell Mrs. Wachowski. "Let me just check in with my parents."

I'd called my mom from the hospital to tell her what had happened, and I can tell she's been impatiently awaiting another update. She picks up on the first ring.

"Hi, sweetie, how are you? How is your friend doing?" she says. "I've been praying for y'all."

Prayer may not be my method of bringing peace and hope to myself and others, but in this moment, I appreciate her effort— I know it's her way of saying she cares.

"Thanks," I say. "They set his arm and now we're going back to the Wachowskis'. Is it OK if I spend the night? I'd like to be there for Nell. Then she can take me to get my car in the morning. It's still parked at the restaurant."

"OK, but be back for lunch, please. I want to see you, and I've got an afternoon catering job."

"Will do," I say.

"I love you, honey. I'm so glad you're safe."

"I love you, too, Mom."

After we get back to Nell's and help Ashton inside and tuck him into her bed—he smiles groggily at both of us and whispers, "Nice to meet you, Doris," before turning to Nell and saying, "Good night, Pony"—we head out to the playhouse to talk.

The new plan is for us to stay out there, since Ashton's in Nell's room. So we bring sheets and blankets to put on top of the air mattress and set everything up for a sleepover. We curl up and talk about what happened to Ashton for a long time, and about what it means to do something about it. I'm still racking my brain trying to figure out who the guy is, and Nell is outlining her best revenge schemes. Then we try to figure out what we should do about Grant. All our calls are going straight to voice mail. I don't even know if he has his phone. I don't know where he is, or how hurt he might be. I think for a split second that maybe the person my mom should have been praying for is him.

"I'm scared he's drinking," I confess to Nell.

"Me too," she says. "Did you see the look in his eyes when he held that guy against the wall? I've never seen him like that before. It was so intense."

"I'm going to call his mom," I say. "I think it's time we told her everything."

"Are you sure? What if he hates us?"

"I think we have to." I've been pondering this all evening. "If something bad happened to him, I'd never forgive myself."

"You're right," Nell tells me, and she and I call Grant's mom on speakerphone. Even though it's super late at this point, Mrs. Collins, like my own mom, picks up on the first ring. There's panic in her voice, this time not even concealed.

"Doris, I'm so glad you called. Have you seen Grant?"

"Not since this afternoon," I explain. And then we tell her everything.

46
Grant

Muscle memory is a weird thing. After I do what I have to do at the police station, the next thing you know, I'm on autopilot. I go where I've always gone before. The place I can count on in a crisis. Or the place I used to be able to count on.

There's Brod on the couch, a bong in front of him and a six-pack of icy cold Bud, condensation dripping onto Brod's mom's coffee table. In Brod's dad's La-Z-Boy, there's a guy I've never seen before, older—maybe in his thirties—with a perma-scowl on his pinched face.

"Hey, bud," says Brod, lifting an arm in the air as if to high-five me, but not getting up from the couch. "You know Mercer," he says. She giggles and pops a fresh beer open. "You're a wreck," she tells me. "Did you fall on your face again?" Her giggle isn't nice.

"And this is Dave," says Brod.

Dave lifts his eyebrows at me and looks even meaner. "You the big football star?" he asks. "'Cause you don't look like it. You look like you got your ass whupped."

"No," I say. "I'm not the big football star."

"Yeah, you are." He squints at me like I'm trying to play a joke and he's not having it, not at all. "You Grant Collins? Why you gonna lie?"

"I'm not lying," I say. "Yes. I'm Grant Collins. I'm not a football star."

"I've seen you play," he says.

"I'm not playing anymore." I reach for my own beer, which I open and chug, mostly so I don't have to talk to him. He keeps a beady eye on me, gesturing at Brod to pass him the whiskey, which Brod silently does.

"If you ain't playing, you ain't a star," he finally says, drinking a huge swig straight from the bottle. He hands it to me, and I take it, but I don't want to put my mouth right where his has been, so I put the bottle gently on the table next to Brod. Mercer watches us, her eyes going back and forth between me, Brod, and Dave. I feel sick to my stomach.

"You too good for us?" Dave asks.

"Chill, dude," Brod says in his placating way. "We're all friends here."

"I don't want to chill," says Dave, who's apparently about to get way less chill. "I want this piece of shit who comes here and drinks all your beer and takes whatever he wants because he thinks he's some superstar football player to settle up what he owes."

Mercer giggles in a freaked-out kind of way.

"I don't think I'm some superstar football player," I answer. "I just told you I wasn't. What's your problem, man?" I reach for another beer because, what the hell, this stranger is not going to tell me what to do, and I chug that one down as they watch me.

"My problem is that you're a user." Dave stands and points at me. "You're a user and a loser. Hey, do me a favor, buddy?"

"What?" I say, and regret it immediately.

"Ask your girlfriend whose dick she likes better, mine or yours."

You know what's funny? I can tell from the way Mercer sucks in through her teeth that she thinks he's talking about her. But she's not my girlfriend. She never was. And Chassie's not my girlfriend, either, not anymore. No, now when I hear "girlfriend," I think of the person whose face I've been watching all summer. Her dark hair and eyes. How she tells it like it is. How she'll fight for people who are weaker or who need help. How she never took my shit, but also was there for me when I needed her, even when she didn't know if she could trust me. It's Doris. The person I'm least likely to ever be with romantically. And the person I want to be with the most.

"Or are you too busy hanging out with those nerd bitches to have a girlfriend anymore? I hope you're at least doing them both," says Dave, sneering at me. "The whole damn town is laughing at you."

"How do you even know Nell and Doris?" I ask.

"Chassie told everyone," he says. "She says you're dating that lib-tard snowflake who doesn't believe in God. Or are you dating them both, her and her Yankee friend? Are they lesbos, like that other girl she's friends with?" He makes this grotesque face.

Then I'm punching him, and he's punching me, and Brod is trying to separate us, and Mercer is saying, "Oh my God," over and over again.

I vaguely remember running out of Brod's apartment, through the back door, and I definitely remember grabbing a liter of Jim Beam that was there on his kitchen counter, and I remember running some more out into the night, drinking and running and running and drinking, grass squishing under my feet, cicadas calling each other around me, wondering who was invading their private nighttime space, and then stopping when my sides hurt so bad I couldn't run anymore, and touching my face and looking at my hand and seeing blood. And I remember finding a door, and opening it and going inside, and falling onto something surprisingly soft, and that, I guess, is when everything went black.

I wake up.

There's a drumbeat in my head like the entire high school marching band is outside. The fog clears a little, and I start to panic because I realize I'm in Nell's playhouse, of all places. I'm on an air mattress. Around me there are blankets tangled up like a tornado has made its way through here and piles of books lying around, mysteries and some dog-eared paperbacks and *The Maltese Falcon*, which I remember Nell mentioning.

MacGuffins, what's a MacGuffin, again? I wonder if football is my MacGuffin. Or maybe it's my albatross. It's something bad. My fingers have been making a pillow for my head, and I raise myself and look at them, and see that all the fighting has left my nail polish a mess, black flecks on my fingers. And that's when I remember. I put my head down again, and I close my eyes.

There's a scraping noise, and the door to the playhouse is being opened, and I try to gather myself, shielding my aching eyes from the sunshine streaming in. There she is, as if I've conjured her. Doris is standing in front of a backdrop of morning light, and she looks like someone sent from heaven or somewhere even better. Maybe I've got a concussion. But she looks . . . beautiful, her dark hair tousled from sleep, her expression confused but also expectant, as if it's not even unusual that she might find me here. As if she's sort of happy to see me.

"Grant," she says, light and a little nervous and filled with so much want it almost embarrasses me, "we've been trying to find you all night." I stare at her and she starts talking fast, the way people do when they're trying to fill an awkward silence. "Nell and I were sleeping out here, but, well, she went inside to see how Ashton was in the middle of the night, and I woke up and didn't want to be alone, and I ended up sleeping on the couch inside. I just came out here to get my phone. And . . . what *happened to you*? Did you get our messages?"

"I don't know," I say slowly. It's not entirely a lie. I don't know where *my* phone is, either. Consider that just another casualty of the last twenty-four hours.

She comes in and closes the door and kneels down next to me. She touches my face, and I wince. I haven't seen myself, but I must be covered in cuts and bruises, even more than I was when she saw me last. I lean into her touch, and even though it hurts more, it's a good kind of hurt. I feel her hands, and I see her soft mouth, real and right in front of me, and I kiss her.

47
Doris

This was not, I assure you, how it was supposed to go. This was not the plan. But when I'm lying in the pink playhouse with Grant's arms wrapped around me, I can almost believe it's the right thing. I snuggle in closer to him, breathing in the boy smell of his neck and feeling so safe. So the opposite of how I felt the day before.

That's when the door to the playhouse swings open and I see Nell's brother.

"Not now, Jack!" I say. Behind Jack is someone who gasps, the way that people gasp in soap operas when they find out so-and-so has been having a secret affair with so-and-so, and all the so-and-sos are also first cousins, or maybe brother and sister.

Except it's just Nell, and she loves love, and she's been wanting this to happen for most of the summer. She's not mad. She's excited.

"Oh," she says, pushing her brother away from the door. "Oh. Doris! Grant! Are you OK? Should I leave you alone? Oh my God, is this finally happening? Are you guys . . . are y'all . . . together?

"Holy shit," she says, finally really seeing Grant. "You look worse than Ashton."

"He was here when I came back out to find my phone this morning," I say. "He must have come inside in the middle of the night and fallen asleep. He . . . surprised me. And then . . ."

I trail off, because there's little room to hide the fact that I was making out with Grant Collins, who passed out drunk in the playhouse after God only knows what he did last night after the fight at La Casita. From the looks of it, ran amok through town getting into more fights and drinking his face off. His swollen eye is turning black, and there's blood spattered across his white T-shirt, which is ripped at the neck and hanging off one shoulder.

He smells like a distillery, and I let him kiss me anyway. I kissed him back.

I'd do it again.

"Hey, what's going on?" says Jack, who's back in the doorway. "What are you guys doing? I wanna see. Hey, Grant, wanna play video games?"

Grant has lifted himself upright and all of a sudden looks

327

yellowish-green. "I . . . I gotta go," he mutters, and stumbles toward the door. I stand up to go after him, try to hold his hand, but he jerks away.

"I . . . can't," he says. "Right now."

"Let me help you," I tell him.

"Don't leave," says Nell. "We can have breakfast. Me and Ashton and you and Doris! My dad will make pancakes. You should eat something. And then you can tell us what happened to you. Are you OK? You don't seem OK."

Grant ignores us. He's hobbling out of the playhouse, limping on one foot, and then he breaks into a weaving, wobbly run. Nell and I watch him disappear into the neighbor's backyard. He was here, and now he's gone.

"Why'd he leave?" asks Jack.

"Maybe he just needed to clear his head for a second," says Nell, and I almost cry because there's so much hope in her voice, but I'm scared that what Grant told me at the balloon festival is true: Wanting doesn't change things. You can want and want and want, but that doesn't bring your aunt back, that doesn't prevent a racist from hurting your best friend's boyfriend, that doesn't get you the guy you want, even if you've spent most of your life telling yourself you don't want him— only to realize one day how very much you do.

I try to turn my mouth up in a smile, to give Nell back a little of the hope she's trying to give me, but nothing seems to be working the way it's supposed to.

. . . . .

When people are scared or alone or threatened or sad or even bored, usually the place they most want to go is home. That's what Jack did. That's what I did, after the waterslide incident. But home isn't always a house, or even the place you grew up in. It's where you feel most yourself, most right in your own body. Is it any surprise that that place, for me, is Unclaimed?

The summer before, I'd spent so much time in the store by myself after hours. I'd stay late and organize things just to be by myself, and it was nice, a home away from home. This summer, surrounded by my two new friends, it was even better. At least that's how it seemed. But maybe I was wrong. Maybe being alone is better than being hurt.

It's still so early in the morning the store hasn't opened yet, and I'm the only one there. It's so quiet! I open the door and lock it behind me and listen to the low hum of the fluorescent lights coming on. Then I walk slowly from the front of the store to the back, pausing by racks of clothes and goods. I reach out and touch some of the things I remember unpacking, like they're old friends. The fur coat with the raccoon-tail collar (that coat is not a friend to raccoons!), the four-book collection of A History of the English-Speaking Peoples, a sequined ball gown that appears to be made by Versace but is probably a knockoff because the *a* on the tag looks like an *i*, the pile of stuffed animals with the furry owl, the weird dog that kind of looks like a bear, and the manatee. Wait, who put the manatee out here? Like a toddler, I think, *The manatee is mine.* I grab him and carry him back to the safety of the stockroom.

My phone beeps. Nell.

Hey, u there? Worried about u. Pls write back

I text her fast.

Don't worry. I'm OK. I'll b in touch soon. Is Ashton OK?

Her answer comes immediately.

Yeah. Still sleeping. Call if u need me, K?

♡, I write back. **Same.**

I look again at my incoming messages. My mom wants to know if I'm still at Nell's and if I'm OK; I text back and say I'm at the store for a little bit and will be home soon.

There's nothing from Grant. I didn't really expect anything. I turn my ringer off and slip my phone into my bag. I need time to think.

I head to the stockroom. I walk through the stacked shelves, looking at all the old familiar items that have been there so long, and the new ones, and the boxes of stuff we have yet to unpack. Another shipment just came in. There's no end to what people can lose.

I pick up the Magic 8 Ball and I ask it the question I've been wondering ever since Mrs. Stokes told me there was something I should know about Aunt Stella, and maybe even from before that. There were clues about Stella's life beyond our town. I knew she had adventures, she traveled, she had a million boyfriends—but she'd always remind me never to get stuck on one. I'd ask questions, and she'd say she'd tell me everything when I was old enough. I'm old enough now, but she's not here.

I think some more. Maybe the real question is DO I REALLY WANT TO FIND OUT THE TRUTH? I think of the line from that '90s movie, *A Few Good Men*. Can I *handle* the truth? I'm not sure. I can never hear her side of the story, so why, like Nell would say, open up this can of worms, anyway? What if it ruins my belief in Stella—and in some ways, my belief in myself? What if the truth is about . . . me?

I shake the 8 Ball and look down at it. *Ask again later* is what it says. Stupid toy. I set it back on the shelf, and that's when I notice that right next to it, waiting for who knows how long, are Red's master keys. The ones we've been looking for all summer. I put them in my pocket and shake my head.

"Universe," I say, "clearly, you are trying to tell me something. But what?"

I pace back and forth for a while, and then I sit down at the table where we used to eat our doughnuts and drink our coffee when life seemed so much simpler. I grab the manatee—he feels like a final reminder of that more innocent time—and I hug him to my chest, hard, squeezing him tightly, clinging to him like he's an inflatable life raft. Which is when his stuffed-animal guts make a strange noise, like paper crinkling, the kind of noise a stuffed animal generally does not make.

There's a zipper at the back of the manatee's neck that I've never noticed before. But now I unzip it. I reach inside and feel around, grab ahold of something that's not just the usual plush stuffing. It's something smooth, something paper. It's a note, wrinkled and yellowing, and the writing is smudged and messy, but the name is unmistakable.

If found, please return to 555 Pomegranate Street. He is my best friend. I love him.

Chassie Dunkirk, age 8
P.S. You can keep the flashlight. This is only my third favorite.

Here's the thing about the truth, I realize. It's always there, waiting. It might be hidden away, somewhere you least expect it, ready to pop out at the worst—or best—possible time. It might be stored away in a secret compartment, which you've got to figure out how to open. It might be covered up by whatever people keep shouting is the truth instead, grown so faint you can barely hear it whispering. But wherever it is, sooner or later, it's there, and it's going to be found. So you might as well go after it.

48
Grant

I climb gingerly up the tree outside my bedroom window, still half drunk. I can barely hang on, and I think about just giving up and dropping, but the idea of my mom finding me on the ground below and having to deal with whatever remains sobers me up a little, and I persist. I reach the top and open the window to my room and there, sitting on my bed, is Mom.

"Grant!" she says, and of course she's been crying—I've been gone all night, and now here I am, bruised and beaten and smelling like hell—but there's also something new in her tone, something steely and resolved. She helps me in through the window, and then she stares at me for a long time, like she's finally really seeing me, not just the football Grant or the son-you-want Grant but the real Grant, the messed-up, scuffed-up, drinking-problem Grant who needs to be faced head-on and dealt with because he's not going to just get better on his own, no matter how he tries. The Grant who needs help.

"I've been waiting for you," she tells me. "I want you to take a shower, put on clean clothes"—she points to the folded-up T-shirt and jeans on my bed—"and then you're coming with me. Dr. Laura will be at her office in fifteen minutes. I've also packed you a bag."

There's a suitcase next to my bed, and it strikes me that I've been unpacking mystery bags like these all summer and now here's one that's been put together just for me, its contents also a mystery. I'm going on a trip. I can only hope that my baggage and I both make it to our destination and back again.

"OK?" asks my mom.

"OK," I say.

Dr. Laura's office is dark when we arrive. It's still pretty early, which means, luckily, there aren't many nosy drivers on the road to catch us traveling at top speed to my therapist's office first thing in the morning. Then she pulls up next to us, and she and my mom help me out of the car and into her office. I sit down in my usual chair, and I don't swivel it one bit this time as I tell them both everything. How my head always hurts. How I am always so, so thirsty. About the balloon festival and how I blacked out there. How the nail polish trick worked, and then it didn't. What happened at La Casita, and then afterward. How this is something more than just Grant Collins not feeling like himself.

"I had another blackout," I say.

Dr. Laura scribbles something in the notebook that's always just within her reach but far enough away that I can never see what she's writing. "Can you tell me the specifics?" she asks.

I nod. I'll tell her everything, except for the part about Doris. I don't want to pull her into this mess. "There's dull pain. That stops, and it's dark for a while. I feel and see nothing. Every once in a while, I wake up. Then I see things from my own perspective again, but blurry, wobbly. Like I've been drugged or I'm really, really drunk. Wandering around at a party. Getting in a fight. Chassie screaming at me. A bed. The grass of the football field. Feeling cold. Feeling alone. Feeling so much shame. There are these blips of reality, and then it's black again, and I'm awake, but all I want to do is go back to sleep because everyone finally sees me for what I am."

"What are you, Grant?"

"Well. I think, or I'm pretty sure, I'm some kind of alcoholic. Like, if I had a beer in front of me, I would probably drink it, and I would want another. It would be very hard for me to stop. You know how I told you it was peer pressure and I'm not drinking and things are great?"

She nods and frowns. "You're *not* great?"

"I'm not great. I haven't been great."

"So these blackouts aren't isolated events."

I lean forward, and it's almost with a kind of relish, the thrill of telling the truth and there being no question indeed about who Grant Collins really is, that I say this: "Dr. Laura, if we look at the past few years, the 'isolated events' might actually be the times I've been sober."

She doesn't even blink, scribbling again in her notebook. "How many times would you say that these came after football games, after being hit in the head or falling to the ground?"

I provide the greatest hits reel of Grant Collins's messed-up behaviors, bookended by a greatest hits reel of my football plays (and injuries), and she keeps writing, occasionally looking up solemnly and posing another question, prompting but never condemning me. I tell her about all the nights at Brod's. I tell her about the games. I tell her about Chassie's arm. I even tell her about tacos.

Dr. Laura does a really weird, unexpected thing. She gets up out of her chair, and she comes toward me, and she hugs me. I sit there, stunned. My mom hugs me, too.

"You are so strong," Dr. Laura says. "And there are so many people rooting for you. We're going to help you. You've done a very brave thing by telling us this."

My mom nods. "You are going to get better."

I don't feel particularly brave or even very confident I'm going to get better, but I nod and offer them a small smile. In the car, Mom is uncharacteristically quiet, fumbling for her keys in her handbag as we sit in the parking lot. I'm wondering if she's about to start lecturing me. The silence is making me nervous, so when she starts the car I reach to turn on the radio to fill the void. She puts her hand over mine and turns the car off again.

"Grant," she says, and I wait.

"I love you," she says, her voice cracking.

I know I'm supposed to say it back, but my voice doesn't seem to be working, so I just look at her and hope that I really can figure out a way to be the Grant Collins she, and everybody else, deserves. She starts the car again, and we drive.

49
Nell

The drive to the airport with Ashton is a lot different from the semi road trip Grant and Doris and I made to pick him up. There's no playlist. It's just the two of us, and he's got his arm in a sling and a cast on that arm, which, kind of ironically, used to be Chassie's look. The closer we get to the airport, the more of a sinking feeling I have in my stomach. I don't want him to go. But he's been given the all-clear to travel, and I'm sure he's ready to get back home, and out of the South.

I miss the support of my friends, but it's good we're alone, because we haven't had much time to just be together and talk about everything that's happened.

The thing we're not talking about is whether he'll be able to play baseball again. We're just going to have to wait and see, say the doctors. But he's young and in good shape, and there's a physical therapist in Chicago who works with Major League Baseball players who he's already got an appointment with. If I had a Magic 8 Ball, I hope it would say *Outlook good*.

"This sure wasn't how I thought this trip would go," I say.

"Me either," he says. "It sucks."

"It does."

He's not done, though. "It really sucks that this is the world we live in. It sucks to be seen as a color, or a race, or a fucking *cookie*, before you're seen as a person, if you're even seen as a person at all. It sucks that this guy might have ruined my chances to play baseball in college. And it sucks that that's something you'll never truly understand, even if you want to."

"I do want to," I say, at the same time that I know he's right. I think about what my mom said, how she was scared for me, but also about how I'm protected because of what I look like. I think about how people are still dressing up like they fought in the Civil War, more than 150 years after the Civil War has ended, and how that feels to me, but how it feels even worse to Ashton. I think about what happened to Doris on the waterslide, and how she was treated afterward. It's not fair, that's what I feel like screaming. None of this is fair.

"I've been so worried that once the painkillers wore off and you had time to think about everything you'd hate me. That you'd regret coming," I admit. "That you'd never want to come here, or see me, again. And that you'd probably be right to think that."

"No," he says. "Pony, here's the thing: It's not about you. This is my body, my arm, my life. You're going to have to let me process this, and not make it your thing, you know?"

I stare at the road, feeling tears well up in my eyes. "I'm sorr—"

"Don't say it!" he turns to look at me. "And no crying, OK? I don't think I can handle that right now. Plus, you're driving."

"OK," I tell him, wiping my eyes. "Ash. I'm here for you, whatever you need me to do."

He reaches over and takes my hand. "Listening is good. Not apologizing, not asking me how you should be or what you should do, but just really listening."

"OK," I say. "I can do that."

"And there's another thing." He smiles. "I think it's your turn to come see me next."

"Really?" I ask. "You want me to?"

"I hate what happened here, but I'm not sorry I came to visit you. There was no way I was spending the whole summer without you. If I hadn't been able to afford a plane ticket, I would have taken the freakin' bus down here. And I feel like I know you even better now, even though it's only been three days together here, and we had three months back in Illinois."

"I guess there's something about going to a hospital together that will do that to you," I say.

"More like sleeping in your room," he says. "I mean, I always knew you were kind of a nerd—" He's grinning now.

"You did!?" I hit him—gently—on his good arm. "Well, you knew about the detective fiction at least. I can't wait to start *The Thin Man*."

"Hey, be careful!" he says, play-yelping. "Anyway, now that I've seen all your crime novels—"

"*Detective fiction*," I correct him.

"Now that I've seen all of those lined up next to your books about coding and *How to Become an Internet Entrepreneur*—"

"Cat gave me that!" I say.

"Well, let's just say I'm even more impressed. Dating a really hot girl who's good at field hockey is one thing. Dating a future internet billionaire who loves books is even better."

"Shhh." I poke him in the stomach, and he starts giggling.

"Ow, don't make me laugh! It hurts too bad." He gets serious. "Hey, what's going to happen with Grant? I still want to thank him for reporting that guy to the cops."

We found that out yesterday, when a policeman stopped by the house to tell us Grant had been by on the night of the incident at La Casita, all bruised up. He'd told them Deagan Dunkirk had perpetrated a hate crime in the restaurant, attempting to hide his identity by wearing a bandana on his face.

"How did you recognize him?" they'd asked Grant.

"He told me to stay away from his sister," Grant had apparently said. "Which points to a certain older brother in town who has a pretty good reason for beating the crap out of me. But his only reason for going after Ashton was because he's not white. I think that makes it a hate crime, doesn't it?"

"We'll look into it," the policemen had told him, and then tried to persuade Grant to go to the hospital to get checked out, but he'd refused. Later, they'd picked up Deagan. Once they found the bandana in his pickup truck, he'd admitted everything.

"Grant's not returning any of our calls," I tell Ashton. "And his mom won't respond, either. We're pretty worried."

"You'll hear from him," Ashton says. "A guy like Grant isn't going to ghost. You girls are too important to him."

"Doris denies it, but I'm pretty sure Grant's in love with her. Even after all this. Especially after all this."

"He is," says Ashton. "I'd recognize that look anywhere."

50
Doris

Chassie's house is picture-perfect from the outside. It's trim and bright and shiny, with a pretty blue door. Unlike the neighbor's parched brown August grass, Chassie's is a lush green. I know for a fact that it's maintained by Grant's stepdad's lawn service. I've waited until Sunday to make the trip, figuring they'll all be at church and I can just sneak in and leave the manatee, doing this one good deed for someone just because. I knock and knock, and no one answers. I grab the doorknob and turn. I'm not surprised to find it unlocked. What startles me is that the inside of the house is as different from its outside as you can imagine. It's a wreck, with piles of clothes and magazines and video games and random stuff everywhere.

The last time I was at Chassie's house was for a birthday party when I was seven years old. It wasn't a mess inside then; it was neat and clean and full of flowers. It was before the invitations got exclusive, before alcohol was flowing. It was before her mother died, before anyone really knew she was sick. I can remember how pretty she was, Mrs. Dunkirk—like Chassie but different. She had this long dark hair that she'd let all of the girls and some of the boys (those who expressed an interest, and she didn't judge) take turns braiding.

"My mom is part Cherokee," Chassie had bragged back then, before she knew that some people in our town didn't think that was something to be proud of. I remember eating cake, and playing with everyone, and watching Chassie open her presents and feeling embarrassed when she saw my gift and made a face and said, "Oh, it's just books!" I remember her mom telling her that wasn't a kind thing to say, and holding me on her lap and rocking me when I cried because I was ashamed. She told me our hair looked alike. She smelled fresh, like lemons and lilacs. I close my eyes for a second, remembering.

"What do you want?" I hear, and my eyes snap back open.

Chassie is standing in front of me, her mouth turned down in a frown. "This is breaking and entering! That's not going to look great on your college applications." Then her eyes drop to the stuffed animal in my hands. "Oh my God!" she says. "How did you find him?" She reaches out for the manatee, and I put him in her arms. She buries her face in the top of his fuzzy head. The eyes that look out at me are eight-year-old Chassie once again. "Bernard! I never thought I'd see him again!"

I feel a lot of things, but what comes out of my mouth is "Bernard? You named your favorite stuffed animal *Bernard*?"

I see a legitimate smile. "I was kind of a dork, I guess. Plus, that was the name of . . ." Her eyes narrow then. "Where did you get him? I lost him when I was a tiny kid. Around the time my mom . . ."

I pull out the note and show it to her. "I found him at Unclaimed. He was shipped to us in a Hello Kitty wheelie bag, with nothing else in it but a flashlight."

"That was my suitcase!" says Chassie. "But how did you find it now? It went missing years ago. The airline could never recover it. They 'compensated us for our loss,' whatever that means, and washed their hands of it."

"I don't really know," I say. "I guess it got lost at the Huntsville airport somehow. The box it was in came to us this summer. It was full of bags that had left their original destinations eight years ago."

"I thought he was gone forever," she says.

And then Chassie Dunkirk asks me to come inside.

"Have a seat," she says, gesturing to a cozy-looking floral couch and moving a pile of laundry from it to the table to give me space. She takes the chair across from me and gives me kind of a sheepish look. "I haven't been really on top of keeping the house clean, with my arm situation."

"It's OK," I say.

"This was a really nice thing to do." She has the manatee—er, Bernard—in her lap, her hand on the top of his head. "Why would you do that when I've only been shitty, or worse, to you?"

"I'm trying to be a connector," I say. "Like my aunt—like Stella was."

"Did Grant put you up to it?"

I shake my head.

"Hmm," says Chassie, and we just stare at each other for a long time. "I was so jealous of you," she finally says.

"You were?" I ask. "Why in the world would you be jealous of *me*?"

"Well, Grant always liked you, back when we were kids. And then, because of my mom. After you came to that birthday party, I remember her talking about you. She kept saying how sweet and smart and pretty you were. It made me so mad! And then she got sick."

"That must have been really hard," I say.

"We were flying back and forth from here to Dallas all the time. She had this rare blood disease, and there are, like, three doctors in the country who've studied it, and one of them was there. On one of those trips I saw the manatee in the gift shop. I wanted him so badly. I love manatees. They wouldn't hurt a fly. They get maimed by speedboats because they swim so slowly. They're even vegetarians! I started going into the gift shop every day to see the manatee, and finally, when things were looking pretty bad with my mom, my dad bought him for me. I named him Bernard, after her favorite nurse, and I'd fly back and forth with him in my suitcase. Deagan told me it was dark in there and he was probably scared, so I started packing a flashlight with him, too. I wrote the note, just in case. And then one day the suitcase just wasn't there. My dad called and called.

We filed all the claims. No one could find it. When Mom died, we kind of gave up. She was gone, and so was he. There was no bringing anything back at that point."

"You lost Bernard."

"I lost everything." She looks at me, and her eyes are wet. "Can I keep him?"

"He's yours," I say. "He always has been. I don't take things that belong to other people."

She wipes her eyes and keeps watching me. "Are you with Grant?" she asks. "I thought you were dating."

"No," I say. There's an ache in me as I say it. I haven't gotten a single text from Grant since he left me standing in the playhouse. But here I am in front of Chassie, and there are some things I want to say. "I'm not with Teddy Scruggs, either. I don't share a mat with anybody these days."

"What are you talking about?" she asks. "What do you mean, share a mat?"

"Remember the waterslide?" I say, and she still looks confused. "With youth group. You told me Teddy Scruggs liked me. You set me up to get humiliated. Worse. You and Grant and Teddy all laughed at me, and Mrs. Stokes chastised me for not being a good Christian."

"Oh," says Chassie. Her mouth goes open and then goes closed and then goes open again, and I'm pretty sure she's picturing the scene at the water park that day. "I haven't . . ." She looks down at her lap and then back at me. "I was going through a lot then. My mom had died. I was jealous. I . . . Look, sometimes I'm just mean."

"Does being mean make you feel any better?" I ask. I'm genuinely curious.

She hangs her head, looks at her arm, frowns. "Maybe for a second. But mostly not. I felt bad after the waterslide incident."

"It would have meant something for you to say you were sorry," I tell her.

"I should tell you, Grant never laughed at you. He was angry at me and Teddy for doing what we did."

This makes my heart yearn even more for Grant, but I'm certainly not going to tell Chassie that.

"You should know another thing," she says. "Grant wasn't running away from the scene of the accident. He was running to get help for me. He was so drunk he doesn't remember. I mean, he did a really awful thing, drinking and driving with me in the car. I might never be able to be on the top of a cheerleading pyramid again. But he would never willingly hurt me. He's not like that."

"You should have said something earlier!" I say. "He thinks he's a monster."

"I probably should have," she admits. "But I didn't. You have to understand—I was so, so mad. The coach and everybody made me promise I wouldn't talk about it. They said it was for the good of the team, the school. Grant's our chance to win the championship, blah, blah, blah. But I was the one who got hurt!"

"That was really unfair," I say. "I'm sorry. I know what that feels like, boys being protected when girls aren't."

"That's why I didn't say anything. Plus I didn't feel like

helping him out with his new girlfriend, you know?" She looks at me, and her smile is as close to real as I've seen it.

"I promise, I'm not."

"I don't know about that."

"Look, we don't have to be friends," I say, as I get up to leave. "But we can at least acknowledge that we're both human beings living in this town."

"OK," she says.

"We've both lost someone," I say. "That if nothing else should make us decent to each other."

"I'm sorry about your friend's boyfriend," she says. "Deagan . . . he shouldn't have done that. He might have cause to beat up Grant, but what he did to the other boy, well, that's just hateful. And I'm not OK with it. I told him so."

"Good," I say.

"He might spend some time in jail," she says. "I should be at church praying for him, but you know what? I just don't feel like it right now."

"I wouldn't, either," I say. I'm right at the door when I think of something else. "I really liked your mom," I say, and she looks teary again.

"I liked your aunt Stella, too," says Chassie. "She was cool." She clutches the manatee, and I catch a glimpse of the eight-year-old little girl who wanted a stuffed animal, got it, and then lost it and everything else.

51
Grant

My eyes snap open, and I look around. For a minute, yet again, I don't know where I am. But I'm not in the playhouse this time. I'm alone in a boxy, quiet room with walls painted a mellow blue. There's a whole host of machines around me and an IV in my arm and a medicinal smell in the air, so I make the brilliant deduction that I'm in some kind of hospital. There's no clock around to tell me what time it is, which is disconcerting. I yell, "Hello! Hello?" a couple of times before a woman pops her head into my room.

"What's all the noise about, honey?" she says. She's wearing a white coat, and her name tag says DR. SIMPKINS. Then I remember.

The car ride with Mom. I was so worn out and hungover and weak, I could hardly stay awake. Her voice hummed in the background. This place was highly recommended, and she'd been researching it for a while now, she told me, ever since she found that I'd been Googling "signs of alcoholism" on our home computer. Doris and Nell finally calling to tell her everything was the last straw. A bed was open. They took our insurance. Dr. Laura agreed it was the right thing to do. I just had to sign the papers; Mom would cosign. I'd agree to stay for thirty days, and after that, we'd see where we were. This was the best thing I could do for myself, for everyone. And here I was. The IV was to rehydrate me. The machines were to check my vital signs. And the doctors were to help me get better, which started with me telling them the truth.

"My head is killing me," I say. Dr. Simpkins looks mildly sympathetic.

"A hangover will do that to you. You're lucky it's not worse. I'll ring the nurse for some Advil," she says. "And you should drink." She gestures to the plastic cup on my bedside table. I shudder at the word, and she clarifies: "Our finest H_2O, just for you."

I take a small sip and then another, awakening my thirst, and then I pour the water into my mouth like I'm my own parched desert, downing the contents of the cup. She claps as I set the empty glass down. "I like a man who finishes what he starts."

Dr. Simpkins is writing things down on a clipboard and poking around at the various machines I'm attached to. "I want to get you in the MRI machine this week," she says. "We need to figure out what all these blackouts mean. I suspect you have sustained a number of concussions through football that have gone untreated, and the drinking has exacerbated the problem, causing fainting, headaches, and loss of memory, among other things."

"Is my mom still here?" I ask. "Where am I, again, exactly?" Maybe I don't remember everything. I don't know where exactly in Alabama I am. Or if I'm even still in Alabama.

"She left yesterday." She purses her lips. "You're smack-dab in the middle of the state, about three hours from home. Don't worry, you're in good hands. We're one of the best facilities in Alabama, and I don't say that just because I work here."

I look down at my hands and see the last remains of the Fireworks polish on my thumbnails. There's a tiny chip on each, hanging on for dear life.

· · · · ·

A bit later, a perky woman comes in to go over my schedule. They really pack the activities in around here; I guess it's part of the don't-get-bored, don't-get-tempted program. Which I suppose I'm grateful for because I don't have much to do, otherwise. The only personal items I have with me are the T-shirts and jeans and shorts and hoodies my mom packed. They won't even let me have a razor, and my wallet and my ID are locked away in a safety deposit box, waiting for me when I'm ready to leave.

After breakfast, the lady explains, there's an individual session in the morning with a therapist, followed by a group session with a bunch of other people of all ages. Later there's lunch, more sessions, depending on the various challenges we're facing, outdoor activities and exercise, meditation and journaling, and then dinner and TV time. There are a couple free periods in that, too, time for letter writing and phone calls and reading. It all sounds exhausting, or maybe that's the hangover talking.

Once I get unhooked from my machines and am given the OK to walk around by Dr. Simpkins, it's time for a group therapy session with Dr. Keebler, an appropriately elfin guy with a twirly mustache. I head to a room with a bunch of folding chairs in a circle and listen to everyone introduce themselves and talk about why they're here. Natalie is a mom of two who got hooked on prescription drugs after a surgery; she tells us how much she misses her kids and wants to get better for them. Tim says he was a functioning alcoholic for years, holding down a job and lying to his family, but in the last six months he lost his job and just pretended to go to work every day—he'd instead park in a nearby Walmart parking lot and drink from a stash he kept in his trunk. He got busted by a family friend who was shopping for new patio furniture. Eva is this girl in her early twenties who escaped an abusive boyfriend who introduced her to cocaine and then heroin; she tells us all to suck it up, everybody's got problems, it's what you do with them that matters. BJ is also in his twenties, and he's trying to get off opioids, and I think he has a crush on Eva. And Pam is a grandma in her sixties who had a bunch-of-bottles-of-wine-a-day habit. (She won't say how many.) Her kids did an intervention, and now she's here.

"I'm Grant Collins. I'm the former captain of the football

team. I used to be one of the most promising young players in Alabama, but I guess I'm mostly just an alcoholic," I tell them. It doesn't feel great. But it feels better than I thought it would.

"Hi, Grant," they say.

In a way, it reminds me of the way I used to talk with Doris and Nell. I haven't reached out to them yet. For one, my cell phone was never recovered after that last night I had in town. I'm guessing it's somewhere in one of the backyards between my house and Brod's, which means it's a goner at this point. But there is an old-school phone vestibule we can use for fifteen minutes at a time during our free periods. So the real reason I haven't called Doris or Nell is that I'm not sure what to say. I left everything in such a mess, kissing Doris and then bolting because I got so freaked out and scared. All I could think about was how I ran from Chassie after I hurt her. I can't hurt someone like that again—but maybe I already did.

I have talked to some folks from home. Mom and Brian called to tell me they'll be here on the next visiting weekend. Dr. Laura called to say she was proud of me for doing what I did, and that she wanted to schedule some talks with the counselors here so they could all be "on the same page." Even Coach called to say I should "get better soon" so I can play in the fall.

There's another call I need to make. He answers on the fifth ring, right when I'm about to hang up.

"Hello?" he says, sounding breathless.

"Dad," I say.

"Grant," he says. "I'm so glad you called."

Old habits die hard, I guess, because the only thing I can think to say is, "Are you driving?"

"I'm in the car, but I just pulled over so we can talk properly," he says. "I should have stopped to listen to you a long time ago."

It's not perfect, our phone call. Dad doesn't get mad, but he doesn't let me off the hook, either. He tells me I can't shut him out. He wants to know everything the doctors have said, and he tells me that he and Mom have been talking already, and they're going to keep talking, to figure this out. But when I tell him I feel like he left me behind a long time ago, that I didn't think he was interested in my problems, he tells me he wants to make up for that. By the time we hang up, we have plans for another phone call. Maybe more.

"Will you think about coming out here for a visit when you can?" he says. "It would be really good to see you, son."

I don't tell him yes or no. Just that I'll think about it. This time, I really will.

$$\cdots\cdots$$

A few days later, I'm sitting over my lunch of stewed chicken and green peas (get me some of Nell's mom's potato salad, stat) when Eva comes over and whispers in my ear, "Your girlfriend's on the line, lover boy."

I chew and swallow. "Who is it?"

"Don't you know your own girlfriend? Or do you have

too many to count? Grant, you're such a player!" She loves to tease me.

"I don't have a girlfriend," I say.

"You're not supposed to keep a lady waiting! Go get the phone!" she tells me, and punches me in the arm.

I head to the phone vestibule, and I look at the clock as I pick up the handset of the landline.

"Hello?" I say, not sure of who's going to answer, but hoping.

"Hi," says the voice.

"Hi," I say, and my heart soars like I've retrieved a lost thing I never thought I'd see again. "I'm really glad you called."

"A lot has happened," Doris says. I close my eyes and see her face as she talks. "Your mom finally got in touch and told me everything."

God bless my mom. Usually I'd be mad at her for butting in, but I guess she found a way to explain to Doris what was going on with me when I couldn't. That I didn't just ghost. That I've been wanting to talk to her every day. Not that my mom would know that. Oh well, I've got Doris on the phone now. I guess it's time to spill.

"A lot has happened," I echo. "I miss you. And the store. And everything. Doris, I have to tell you something. I'm sorry I ran away that morning. I was drunk, and I was scared. But I think I'm starting to get better. Rehab is helping. And I hope . . . when I'm really, truly better . . . maybe we can go on an actual date?"

She's so quiet, I'm almost afraid she's hung up on me.

Then she laughs. "Yes, obviously, you fool," she finally says. "I've been waiting for you to ask that for half the summer. So has Nell. She's going to be thrilled. But you have to get better first. I was Googling before I called you, and it's not good to start a relationship when you're this early in recovery."

"My doctors would love you," I say. "Wait, you researched starting a relationship with me?"

"Don't get a big head; information is power!" she tells me. "By the way, there's something important you should know. You didn't run away from Chassie after the accident. You ran to get help."

"Are you kidding me?" I breathe in and then out, processing this. My whole body releases a tension I didn't even know I was holding.

"She didn't say anything because she was angry. I almost can't blame her, after the vow of secrecy the coach made her take. She finally told me the truth when I found the note in her manatee at the store and brought it to her."

"That was *Chassie's* manatee? There was a note? I have a lot to catch up on."

"Let's start here. You're not a bad person. You're a pretty good person, actually."

"I think I might be on my way to understanding that," I say. "And another thing, too. Doris, I was wrong about what I said at the balloon festival. Wanting does change things. What people want matters."

She laughs. "Wanting matters. Even when you don't get what

you want, it still matters. I wasn't sure about that for a little bit, but I know it now."

"I want you to get what you want," I say.

"Get better soon, then," she tells me. "I want you back."

I press the phone up against my ear and imagine I'm holding her the way I did that morning in the playhouse.

52
Doris

I've often thought that if finding things is my true talent, the one thing I have to do is keep looking. That's the only way to locate what really, truly matters.

But what if something's been in front of me the whole time, staring me in the face, and I never acknowledged it? I don't need the Magic 8 Ball to tell me it's time. I have to ask my parents about Aunt Stella. Nell offers to come over the way I did when she talked to her parents about Ashton. But this is something I have to do on my own.

I find my mom sitting on the couch, leafing through a magazine. I steel myself. Whatever the answer will be to the question

I'm about to ask, the truth is the only place where any of us can start. It's a beginning, not an end.

"Mom," I say.

"Hi, honey," she says, still entranced by how celebrities are just like us.

"Mom. Did Aunt Stella have a secret?"

She jerks her head up then, and looks around as if someone can save her. But it's just her and me in the room. Dad's at the gym. The TV's not even on. No distractions.

"What do you mean?" she asks.

I explain what happened with Mrs. Stokes at the store. "Why would she tell me to ask you about my aunt, that it was time I knew the truth? What did she mean?"

Her face blanches. My mom has a terrible poker face. Not that she's ever played poker.

I keep flashing back to the moment at the water park, and what happened afterward. The muffled tears. How Stella said authority figures aren't always right, and that she would tell me everything when I was old enough. I have this wild idea: "Was Stella . . . my mom?"

"What?" my mom says. "No. That is not true."

I can't quite let it go. "Isn't that exactly what you would say if you didn't want me to know?" I ask.

"Doris. Wait here!" instructs my mom, who jumps up and runs to the other room. She comes back with my baby book, which she opens to the first page. There's my birth certificate. "Here's my name, and your father's, right here," she says, pointing. She turns the page. "And here's a picture of me, pregnant with you, about to pop. We didn't know it then, but it turned out, you were the only baby I could have," she says. She gazes at me. "We were so lucky to get you."

She looks down again. "And here's one with me and Stella that same day. You'll notice she's not nine going on eleven months pregnant." She stares at the photo, and I follow her eyes, admiring my aunt's slim, erect posture and my mom's big smile. I notice again how much the two sisters looked alike, the same dark hair and eyes, the heart-shaped faces, just like mine.

"Oh," I say, relieved. I don't know if could forgive Stella for keeping *that* secret.

"You were practically twins," I say, touching the picture.

"I always thought it was an irony, how much we resembled each other on the outside and yet how different we were," my mom says. "She was nineteen years old there. I was the ripe old age of twenty-five. I always thought I knew better than my baby sister." She frowns. "Even when I didn't."

"Then what was Mrs. Stokes talking about? What was it I should know about Stella that would prove she's not as great as I think she is?"

My mom sighs. "Priscilla. She should keep her mouth shut and her nose out of other people's business," she says. "That woman really *is* a hypocrite." She pats the couch next to her, and I move closer.

"What is it, Mom?"

"Priscilla's right about one thing. Your father and I should have let Stella tell you a long time ago. It never should have been such a secret at all. When I think about how she had to go through all of that as a girl just a little bit older than you . . ."

"Mom. Say it. You're freaking me out."

She looks at me, her eyes teary. "Two years before that picture was taken—before you were born—Stella got pregnant. She had a baby of her own, a boy. Our parents persuaded her to give him up for adoption, and to never speak of him again. In the brief time she had with him, she called him Oliver."

53
Nell

It's the last week in August, and Doris and I have a plan, but first, I need to make a trip. I take Jack to the big Target in the next town over and let him roam the aisles, pointing out every video game he really, really needs. (I'll buy him one, I really will, after I find what I've come for.)

There it is in the cups and plates section: a mason jar, the kind Stella used to drink out of, the kind that Doris drew in her illustration of her aunt. I grab two, one for me, and one for my friend. Then I add a third to my basket. Afterward I let Jack pick two games, and we pay and head home so I can put our plan into action.

Next I pack a bag for the water park. I put in the mason jars and three cans of actual Diet Coke (not RC!), Stella's drink of choice. You're not really supposed to bring glass, or beverages of your own, into the water park, but I cover everything with towels and figure what security doesn't know won't hurt them. This is a special occasion. I add the book of Mary Oliver poetry that Doris let me borrow, a special page dog-eared. I put on my swimsuit, and then I pick up my phone.

Ready? I text.

I'm leaving now, writes Doris. **C u in 15 at the front?**

Yep! I say, and add a smiley face emoji.

· · · · ·

She's standing there waiting for me when I arrive, and this time she slips the paper wristband on *my* arm. "My treat," she tells me. "For helping me with all this. And—for being you."

I smile. "What do you want to do first?" I ask her. "Wave pool or waterslide?"

"Let's hit the waves first," she suggests. We head over to the pool where, just a few months ago, she met Jack for the first time; soon after that she found him. It's an overcast, cooler-than-usual Monday at the end of the summer—Red has given us the day off—and we're the only people in the pool. We bob up and down along with the waves as she updates me about everything she's found out, everything that was too much to text about, that she needed to tell me in person.

"So, here's the deep, dark Dailey family secret," she begins, her dark hair clinging to her shoulders in the blue water. "You know Aunt Stella lifeguarded here the summers she was in high school. The summer after her junior year, she met this boy— man, really. He was in town for the summer, running space camp at the Space and Rocket Center. They fell in love. She got pregnant."

"Ohhhhhhh," I say, paddling water. "WOW."

"My ultra-conservative grandparents swiftly packed Stel off to this facility for 'girls in a family way' down in Mobile, and that's where her baby was born. She gave him up and came back home and everyone pretended like nothing happened. My grandparents decided this was the least shameful option for everyone."

"I can't believe she went along with it. That doesn't sound like Stella."

"She was so young, just a year older than us," says Doris. "They made her think she had no other choice. It's kind of like Grant not talking about what really happened so he could still play football. She thought her life as she knew it would be over, so she went along with what the authority figures told her. But it totally changed her. After that is when she started getting into Buddhism and thinking organized religion wasn't all it was cracked up to be, and really speaking her mind. I remember her telling me how hard it is to be brave, but that it gets a little easier as you go. That makes so much sense now. So does my mom's irrational fear that I'll get knocked up."

"This is so sad," I say. "Imagine having your baby taken away from you. Imagine not having a choice, and then not even being able to talk about it. How do you get over that?"

"I think that's why she traveled so much, lived in so many different places. She couldn't just stay put here and pretend like everything was A-OK. She had to get out. And she liked helping people. That made her feel better."

"Poor Stella," I say. "So what does your mom say about all this now?"

"I actually think she regrets it. Maybe she's got some Stella in her, too."

"What about your dad?"

"He's not exactly Mr. Chatty about these things. But he took me aside to say that he always thought Aunt Stella got a raw deal. They'd agreed Stel would tell me the truth on my sixteenth birthday. I would be old enough to know then. But when she died, they thought it was too painful to bring up the subject. Why not just let me believe what I'd always believed?"

"Because it wasn't the truth? Hey, do you know who the father is?"

Doris looks at me. "Well, this is where Mrs. Stokes comes in. This is the extra-dramatic part of the drama, as if it could get more dramatic."

"Stella slept with Mrs. Stokes's *boyfriend*?"

"No, but Mrs. Stokes was making a play for this guy and tried to seduce him that same summer, at the water park! Apparently he was a tremendous hottie."

"Ew, Stokes. Go, Stella!" I punch the air. "Where is he now?"

"No one knows that, either. He could be anywhere. He never even knew Stel was pregnant."

"What about the baby?" I ask.

"My mom tried to find Oliver after Stel died, but all she got were dead ends. It was a closed adoption. There's no way to track him down."

"There's always a way," I say.

She looks over at me and grins. "Well, I *have* been thinking about a few courses of action. And, you know, you're pretty good with the internet. . . ."

"My skills are there for you, whatever you need. As if *you* need help finding anyone. Hey, are you ready for the waterslide?"

"I've never been more ready."

We get out of the wave pool, grabbing our towels at the edge and rubbing ourselves with them briskly. "It's almost fall-ish today," says Doris. "Pretty soon it's going to be jeans and hoodies weather!"

"Not that it wasn't all summer, at least at Unclaimed. Does Red heat the place in the winter?"

"Does that mean you're going to keep working there once we're back in school?" Doris asks, grinning.

"How could I give it up?" We pass the ice cream stand. "Remember how you found Jack this summer?" I ask. "I'll never forget walking up here and seeing you and Dad with him swinging between you."

"You know what I was remembering?" Doris says. "The Planned Parenthood balloon, and what Alanna said about having real conversations to help people who need it. Health class with Coach Deez-Nuts leaves a lot to be desired. And a lot of parents are probably like mine—they don't even want to think their kids are having sex, or they're afraid talking about it will promote it. But if you don't talk about it, well, then it might be too late. What if I could help create something to give girls—and boys—the information they need to make the best possible choices for themselves?"

"Hey, if you start something like that, you could name it after Stella," I say. "Stella's Room, maybe. Do you still have Alanna's card?"

"Yes! I know exactly where it is."

"Of course you do."

. . . . .

We link arms and walk with our towels wrapped around us to the waterslide, and before we go down together, we pour a mason jar of Diet Coke for each of us. We toast and we read Stella's favorite poem, "Wild Geese." We leave Stella's Diet Coke waiting next to the book of poetry on a picnic table right near where Mrs. Stokes chastised Doris so many years ago. ("It's a small town. No one's going to steal a book of *poetry*," Doris says.) Then we go up to the top of the waterslide, and we get on a single mat together—maybe we look like we're not to be trifled with, or they've just given up at the end of the season, because the lifeguard nods us on through—and we spiral down to the bottom, plunging into the water and shrieking with joy.

"I miss you, Stella," says Doris into the sky.

"I wish I could have known you, Stella," I say.

Doris opens her arms and turns to me, and I wrap her in a hug. We're crying and laughing at the same time, our tears mixing with the chlorine of the pool. I can't help thinking about Grant, the missing part of this circle, but I know we'll see him again. You've got to hang on to the people you love, in whatever way you can.

54
Grant

I remember thinking once that Grant Collins—the me that appeared to the world—might look like a brand-new, expensive suitcase, but inside, I felt like a battered piece of luggage about to explode on the conveyor belt, revealing all of my ragged boxer briefs to the world. Now, though, I feel like my insides are getting a lot closer to matching my outsides.

Doris and Nell came to visit me last weekend. They brought me a present—the purple suitcase we all still call the Daphne, even though we're pretty sure it was never owned by someone named Daphne at all. It holds a lot. Secrets, money, and more. The stuff that makes up a life.

I put a bunch of folded-up shirts in the suitcase, and then

add all the things people have given me while I've been here. Byron sent me his lucky elephant necklace with a note explaining that he used to drink too much, too, way back when, but he's been off the stuff for years now, in part thanks to the necklace, which acted as a reminder to help him stay clean. "I hope it helps you like it helped me," he wrote. Pam made me a cross-stitch that says HANG IN THERE, with a picture of a kitten dangling from a tree. There's a rock from the garden outside that Eva gave me; she said she likes to hold a smooth, cold stone in the palm of her hand whenever she thinks about using. It makes her feel strong.

Speaking of friends, there's a collage of our favorite store Instagram pics, complete with hashtags only we would understand, from Nell, plus a letter from Doris I'll never share the contents of—that goes in the suitcase's secret compartment. There's also a drawing she made me that arrived the other day. This one chronicles the things we've lost and the things we've found this summer. At the top there's a picture of me running like I would with a football under my arm, except instead of the football I'm clutching the purple suitcase I'm now packing to go spend some time with my dad before I eventually make my way back home. I can't stay away from the twins, or Mom and Brian, or, for that matter, school, for too long. And while Doris and I have promised to FaceTime daily until I'm back, there's no substitute for in-person, which is something Nell knows all too well. (Her parents are letting her fly up to visit Ashton for a long weekend in the fall.)

Will I ever play football again? I'm not worrying about that for now. I just want to make sure that what I'm doing is right for me, the Grant I want to be. That means regular calls with all the doctors in my life, and outpatient visits to a substance abuse counseling service that Dr. Laura has recommended. There's no quick fix, I've been warned. Finding your truth takes time, but as long as you keep going, there's a good chance you'll get there.

I stare at the drawing, running my fingers over it. My nails sport a new color of polish that Nell sent me: a dark, dark purple called True Grit that looks black in certain lights.

Doris has outdone herself. There's the water park, with a picture of the three of us hugging Jack. There's Chassie and Mac Ebling standing nearby. Chassie's got her arm in a sling, and I feel a pang about how her injury was my fault, but I do what we've been learning to do in therapy and accept that I've made mistakes but that I can change, that just because I did something bad doesn't mean I'm worthless. At least I know now that I ran for help. I'm never going to be perfect, but the Grant who tries to do the right thing and admits when he's wrong is the Grant I want to be.

There's a box of Krispy Kreme, with our three favorite doughnuts—classic, chocolate iced, and a lemon-filled for me. A scene from the balloon festival, with the Planned Parenthood balloon extricated from the tree and floating above, and the old Civil War balloonist on the ground pointing at it in bafflement. There's Stella looking beatific and holding an infant, the baby she had to give up. There's Mrs. Stokes alone in her white tent, praying while the rest of us dance in the field. There's Deagan being cuffed by the cops, his bandana on the ground next to him. There's a bag of gold coins and a crowd of people staring at it in wonder. There's Ashton, standing next to his Cubs suitcase, waiting for Nell to jump into his arms. There's an airport, where things come in and things go out and sometimes things go missing and stay too long. And, of course, there's Unclaimed Baggage, where three friends found what they needed the most—each other.

DORIS'S PLAYLIST
UNPACKING 3.0

1 hr., 9 mins.
Mary J. Blige—"Suitcase"
The White Stripes—"I'm Bound to Pack It Up"
John Denver—"Leaving on a Jet Plane"
Alicia Keys—"Samsonite Man"
EELS—"Packing Blankets"
Aretha Franklin—"Packing Up, Getting Ready to Go"
David Gray—"Sail Away"
Jenny Lewis and the Watson Twins—"Handle with Care"
The Beatles—"Across the Universe"
Bright Eyes—"Another Travelin' Song"
Pixies—"Where Is My Mind?"
Iggy Pop—"The Passenger"
Erykah Badu—"Bag Lady"
Miranda Lambert—"Baggage Claim"
Simon & Garfunkel—"Homeward Bound"
Harry Styles—"Two Ghosts"
Crosby, Stills & Nash—"Just a Song Before I Go"
Leonard Cohen—"Going Home"

ACKNOWLEDGMENTS

While this book isn't based on a true story, I had the experience of moving from Downers Grove, Illinois, to Decatur, Alabama, midway through fifth grade. I spent my first few years in the South feeling like a total weirdo, struggling to understand traditions and behaviors that felt utterly strange to my Yankee-transplant self. *Why are adult women called "Miss" and their first name? Why did my teacher call it "The War of Northern Aggression"? Who were you supposed to root for, Auburn or Alabama? Why did I say "roof" wrong?*

These questions seemed both hugely important and also somehow impossible to navigate.

By seventh grade, though, I'd met someone who would

become my best friend. And by ninth grade, I was really starting to find my place, or at least to adapt to it. Those of us who've moved frequently become very good at camouflage, and I'd made eight different moves by the time I was eight, on account of my dad's job. My family left the South after I graduated from high school, which meant more changes, and even more adaptation. You might say I'm a writer because of it.

Now, I've lived in New York City for almost twenty years, and I'm keenly aware that my time in Alabama has shaped me in ways I'm still learning about. I'm the Southerner without an accent, the Northerner with roots extending far below the Mason–Dixon Line. A part of my heart lives in Decatur, and it always will.

Each place I lived taught me a little more about myself, and eventually, I got better at moving. That doesn't eradicate the pain of losing and having to start over—having to find people to love again. It's always hard, but it's harder when you're a teenager. Still, I think it makes you strong. I don't have just one hometown; I have several. And while I'm a little bit like Nell, I'm also like Doris, and Grant, too.

Decatur is not the town in *Unclaimed Baggage*—it's a whole lot bigger, for one, and far more diverse—nor are any of the characters in the book modeled after people I knew when I was there. There are some similarities, however. Decatur does have a pretty awesome water park with a wave pool they claim is America's first, as well as an annual balloon festival. (It takes place Memorial Day weekend, and it's worth a visit if you're ever in the area! I don't know that a Planned Parenthood balloon ever existed, either at the Decatur festival or any festival, though I like the idea.) There *was* an outpost of the real Unclaimed Baggage store near the dollar movie theater and the Little Caesars Pizza. The city still has really great barbecue, especially Big Bob Gibson's. (Some people really like Whitt's, too.) The nearest Krispy Kreme back then was in Huntsville, Alabama—home of the U.S. Space & Rocket Center and the Marshall Space Flight Center. We'd drive there every once in a while to pick up fresh doughnuts to sell for charity. Usually I'd end up keeping at least a box for myself. They really do melt in your mouth.

Doyle Owens's story is real. But I have taken liberties with just about everything else with regard to his great invention. The Decatur Unclaimed has since closed, although the one in Scottsboro continues to do brisk business. (They have a fantastic Instagram account.) I'm certain the way the business functions in my mind is different from its workings in real life; the tales of found luggage in these pages come strictly from my imagination. But I have all the respect in the world (and a little bit of envy) for the people who work at the in-real-life store. They have the incredible experience of discovering lost things regularly.

So many thanks to Ryan Harbage at the Fischer-Harbage Agency, my perceptive agent who always has my back. This book wouldn't be what it is without my editor, Joy Peskin, who knows the value of a well-placed smiley face and is one of the best humans I've ever had the pleasure of working with. Molly Ellis, Mary Van Akin, Nicholas Henderson, and the team at Macmillan Children's, I'm so lucky to have you.

Paige Clancy, meeting you in seventh grade changed my life. JP & CP, Anne, Lori, Eleanor, Pam, LT, Kristi, Julie G., Patty (and Alana), all you Decatur High peeps: I'm so glad I moved to Alabama, because it meant I got to become friends with you. Doris, Mike, and Raj: I left you behind in Illinois, but that doesn't mean I don't think about you. George Gonzalez, wherever did you go? Are you in witness protection?

To all of my friends in New York City and beyond who listen and talk me down from various ledges on an ongoing basis: Thank you, always. Bob and Jane Stine, I'm grateful for all the real talk about publishing, and the lobster Cobb salads at the Redeye. Bij: You are such a good editor.

A huge thanks is due to those who read versions of the book and gave me their thoughts, especially Carolyn Murnick, Glynnis MacNicol, Mary Traina, Kate McKean, and Mary Kate Flannery; MJ Franklin, who made me cry with his wise and thoughtful notes; and Maureen O'Connor, who read an early version of this book and kept me going with her critique, then read a second version and helped me make it better. Jenny Fan, you were so patient and generous in talking to me as I worked out characters. Jo Piazza, thank you for reading while you were tending to a newborn! Soo Youn, that walk we had in Greenport really helped. Daisy and Quinn, y'all are the best at ideas; thanks for humoring me.

A shout-out to my therapist, who introduced me to Mary

Oliver. Sari Botton, I adore you and Kingston Writers' Studio, where much of this book was written. Sara Eckel, I can't thank you enough for hosting me last year and for being you. Rumaan Alam, you were there on Twitter when I thought I couldn't finish my revision; now I know I can do it. Colin Dickey and Nicole Antebi, it was lovely to spend time with the sweet, soft, and furry Alistair in your creative lair. He was a tremendous help! V— you're the best. So are you, Eric Reid. Leila Sales, Katherine Howe, Jenny Han, Mary O'Connell, Adele Griffin, Melissa Walker, Tahereh Mafi, Jeffery Self, Richard Lawson, Meg Wolitzer, Jen Smith, Kat Brzozowski, and so many others— thanks for the YA support. Martin Wilson, I'm so excited you're my newest Alabama friend.

A special thanks to Michael A. Steele, PhD, Professor of Biology and H. Fenner Chair of Research Biology at Wilkes University, from whom I learned some fascinating things about squirrel behavior (red and gray!), as well as Lucia F. Jacobs and Emily R. Liman for their 1990 research paper, "Grey squirrels remember the locations of buried nuts," for the Princeton University Department of Biology.

Love as ever to my family; I wouldn't be who I am without you. To future young adult reader Vivienne: I can't wait to discover everything with you.

Ezra, I'm glad I found you.